D0807964

WINDS OF HEAVEN

BY
KATE SWEENEY

WINDS OF HEAVEN
© 2009 BY KATE SWEENEY

All rights reserved. No part of this book may be reproduced in printed or electronic form without permission. Please do not participate in or encourage piracy of copyrighted materials in violation of the author's rights. Purchase only authorized editions.

ISBN 10: 1-935216-06-6
ISBN 13: 978-1-935216-06-3

First Printing: 2009

This Trade Paperback Is Published By
Intaglio Publications
Walker, LA USA
WWW.INTAGLIOPUB.COM

This is a work of fiction. Names, characters, places, and incidents are the product of the author's imagination or are used fictitiously, and any resemblance to actual persons, living or dead, businesses, companies, events, or locales is entirely coincidental.

CREDITS
EXECUTIVE EDITOR: TARA YOUNG
COVER DESIGN BY SHERI

By Kate Sweeney

The Kate Ryan Series

She Waits
A Nice Clean Murder
The Trouble with Murder
Who'll be Dead for Christmas

Residual Moon
The O'Malley Legacy
Away from the Dawn
Survive the Dawn

Dedication

To my niece and godchild, Hannah Rose, who was the inspiration for Skye in *Winds of Heaven*.

Hannah is now a beautiful young woman and teacher, but I will always think of Hannie as the feisty little kid with a wonderful sarcastic sense of humor—I have no idea where she got that...

Acknowledgments

As always, thanks to, Denise, for her insight and thoughtfulness. To Jule and Tena, for taking the time to beta. And finally, to my editor, Tara Young. Thanks to all.

Chapter 1

The dark, sterile corridor greeted Liz when the elevator doors opened. How many times in the past three months had she walked these halls? She passed the nurses' station; the familiar faces greeted her with a sad smile. Liz had gotten to know all the nurses in the past few months. She smiled in kind as she made her way to the room for the last time. She swallowed the wave of nausea, and as she reached for the door, it opened and Elaine stepped out. Elaine Hanson was the head nurse on the oncology floor. She took a special interest in Liz, and Liz welcomed it; it had been a rough three months.

Elaine was an older woman, perhaps in her late fifties. She absently pushed a lock of graying dark hair off her forehead, then placed her hands on Liz's shoulders. "You okay, honey?"

Liz nodded through the tears that suddenly sprang to her eyes. "I just wanted to be here when—"

Elaine pulled her into her arms. "You had no way of knowing Julie would go so quickly. It's a blessing, Liz."

Liz backed up and took a deep breath, wiping the tears from her cheeks. "I know."

"I'll be right here. She's in peace." Elaine opened the door to allow Liz to go first.

Again, Liz nodded; the numb detached feeling settled within her when she entered the room, which was dark, except for the small light over the bed that cast a soft illumination. Liz cocked her head as she approached the bed. Julie looked so peaceful, as if she were just sleeping. However, as she neared, Julie's pale, cold appearance told her differently. She looked down at the lifeless form, which a short while ago was her partner in this life. Lightly placing one hand on her unborn child, Liz caressed the cold cheek of her companion.

"You'll never get to see her, and for that I am sorry, Julie," Liz whispered with tears streaming down her cheeks. "You're not in pain anymore."

Liz stared off into space, and for a brief moment, remembered a time when there wasn't any pain, only laughter.

"What should we do today?" Liz asked as she cleared the morning dishes.

Julie struck a thoughtful pose as she opened the dishwasher. "Hmm. I don't know. It's a beautiful autumn day. I think we need a pumpkin."

Liz shook her head and turned around. "We have one, you dope. And if you were home more often, you'd have seen it on the porch."

"We have one? When did we get it?"

Liz wiped her hand on the towel and leaned against the counter. "*We* did not. Skye and I went last Saturday when you were in San Diego." She tried to keep the sarcasm out of her voice, but it was becoming a losing battle.

Julie seemed to sense the sarcasm. "Honey, it's my job."

"I know. I know. You're a pilot. I understand, but you could have taken the shorter runs—"

"For less money," Julie interjected with a frown.

"Which I have never cared about," Liz countered evenly. She then took a deep breath.

"Look, this is the first time I've been home in weeks. Let's not argue over this again." Julie walked over to her and put her arms around her waist, pulling her close. "Let's not go out," she whispered against her lips.

Liz sighed and returned the kiss as she wrapped her arms around her shoulders. "You always get out of an argument with sex." She sagged against the counter.

Julie smiled as she slowly unzipped Liz's jeans. "I do not," she grumbled playfully. "I just love the feel of you." She slipped her hand inside. "Skye's taking a nap, right?"

Liz closed her eyes and nodded as Julie pushed her jeans down her hips. She gasped when she felt her lover's warm fingers dance through her.

Liz smiled sadly now as she remembered those happy memories that were all too infrequent. Julie was constantly working during their five-year relationship. She gave no time to see Skye growing and now...Liz placed her hand on her stomach and sighed.

"Goodbye, Julie," she whispered. She bent down, kissed the cold cheek, and walked out of the hospital room.

Once outside, she put a hand to her mouth and let out a heart-wrenching sob. Elaine was at her side, guiding her to the waiting room. "You sit for a minute."

"Thank you. You know, I've been preparing for this for six months. Julie and I got everything in order. But somehow..." She stopped and put a shaky hand to her forehead.

"You've been so strong through this whole ordeal, Liz," Elaine said, trying to comfort her.

"I have to be. Poor little Skye doesn't know what's happening. She's so young. I told her God was lonely and needed Julie more than we did. She doesn't get it, and I'm almost glad she doesn't. Julie's job took her away a good deal of the time, and as much as I hated it, it probably made it easier on Skye." Liz let out a heavy sigh before continuing. "I would have never agreed to this baby if I knew how sick Julie was. We just wanted a child of our own. Was that selfish?" She looked up at Elaine with pleading eyes.

"No, you two loved each other. Skye is a beautiful happy little girl. And this one," she patted Liz's stomach, "will be just as happy. It's because of you and Julie. However, I have to be honest, it's mostly you."

"I know. Julie wanted children but didn't want the responsibility. I remember begging her to switch shifts with the airlines just so she could be home more." She sighed and put her head back.

Julie's six-month battle with cancer took its toll; her death was almost a relief. Liz felt guilty thinking that, but she couldn't help it. When they found out Julie had bone cancer, it spread quickly. She was in so much pain that it was unbearable to watch. "She isn't in pain anymore."

Both women sat for a moment in silence. The elevator doors opened, breaking Liz from her reverie. A young woman walked out, holding a blond curly-headed girl, who was squawking up a storm. The minute she saw Liz, she reached for her.

The woman set her down, and Skye rambled over to her, giggling all the way.

Liz laughed and threw her arms around Syke as the child tried to climb on her lap. "No. Here, sweetie, sit next to Mommy." Liz looked up and smiled. "Did my little girl behave, Joanne?"

"Of course, as usual," Joanne said. She locked gazes with Liz, who smiled sadly and shook her head. Tears sprang into Joanne's eyes; she quickly wiped them away.

"Thanks for taking care of Skye, Joanne."

"It was no problem. We had fun," Joanne said, regaining her composure. She ruffled Skye's hair. "Didn't we, kiddo?"

Skye nodded. Liz put her arm around her daughter. "Did you, sweet pea?" Liz asked as she pushed her auburn hair away from her face.

Little blue eyes looked up, and the girl grinned. "Mmm-hmm. I have ice cweem."

"And did you say thank you?" Liz asked and Skye nodded.

Liz stood with a groan and took Skye's hand in hers and whispered, "C'mon, Skye, let's go home."

"Mama. Uppie, peas."

Liz lifted her and held her on her hip. "Pretty soon, Mommy won't be able to lift you like this," she said and kissed her head.

They all walked to the elevator in silence. Now what will happen? Liz thought. Their money depleted, she'd have to give up her part-time job when she had the baby. All at once, she hated Julie, hated her for dying, hated her for not being there as she should and taking care of the family she wanted. Liz took a deep quivering breath and held on to Skye.

"You call me whenever you like." Elaine kissed Liz on the cheek. "Let me know of the funeral arrangements and if I can do anything." She laughed as Skye turned her cheek, as well; Elaine kissed her, then looked into the blue eyes. "You take care of Mama."

"'Kay."

"Thanks for everything, Elaine," Liz said, desperately trying not to cry.

Skye frowned as she looked at Liz. "Don't ki, Mama."

Liz sniffed and laughed. "I'm not crying, sweet pea. Let's go home. How about hot dogs for dinner?"

Skye's eyes widened as she nodded. "And ice cweem."

The next morning, Liz sat at the kitchen table feeding Skye. "Open wide for Mommy," Liz said, and like a little bird, Skye opened her mouth and waited. "Here it comes." Liz laughed and made a smooth landing of oatmeal in the little one's mouth.

"More." Skye playfully banged her spoon on the table.

Liz laughed and played airplane again. "Now, sweetie, you try," Liz encouraged.

Skye happily took the spoon. With fierce concentration, Skye took to her task.

Twenty minutes later, Liz had cleaned the floor and the table and got the oatmeal out of Skye's hair. "You're getting the hang of it, sweet pea. Just like the potty. Good girl," her mother exclaimed as she pulled her daughter out of the booster seat.

Skye raced to her toy box. After tossing a few unnecessary items aside, she found the book. She promptly sat down in the middle of the room.

"Play nice now, Skye," Liz whispered and kissed her head.

Liz looked at the desk, noticing all the unpaid bills. Not wanting to delve into them at the moment, she glanced at a picture of her and Julie, holding each other and laughing. As she looked closer, she noticed for the first time that she was not smiling. She looked pensive; only Julie was laughing.

"Where were we and why wasn't I smiling, Skye?" she asked her daughter, who laughed and struggled to her feet, then dropped to a thud on her bottom. "Whoopsie-daisy."

Skye laughed and clapped her hands. "Mama funny."

Liz laughed with her daughter as she gently rubbed her stomach. The baby was moving as if wanting to be in on the family joke. Then inexplicably, Liz started to cry. She put her hands to her face and sat at the desk.

Skye frowned as she watched. "Mama cryin'." Her bottom lip quivered.

Liz quickly wiped her tears and laughed. "No, Mommy's not crying." She looked around. "What in the hell…heck am I going to do?"

When the phone rang, Liz groaned and stretched her back as she bent down to pick up the phone. "Hello?"

"Ms. Elizabeth Kennedy?" a man's voice asked.

"Speaking."

"I'm John Harris, Ms. Bridges's lawyer. I'm sorry to disturb you at this time, but there are matters that need your attention. At your convenience, would you stop by my office? It's regarding Julie's will."

"Will? I had no idea she had a will." Liz frowned deeply. Why hadn't Julie told her of a will? They never discussed it, she thought. She nearly missed Mr. Harris's next words.

"Yes, her will and another matter, but I would like to see you in person."

"That's fine, Mr. Harris." Liz jotted down the address. She tossed the pen on the end table, along with the phone. "Wonderful. Another bill."

The following days were a blur to Liz; she thanked God for Elaine and Joanne. The memorial was mercifully over. Liz just couldn't cry anymore. She was grateful Joanne watched Skye back at the apartment. The few mourners had left the gravesite, which left Liz standing there alone. A surreal feeling engulfed her as if any moment Julie would walk up and laugh at the joke she pulled. That would be just like Julie, Liz thought as she absently ran her hand over her stomach. She felt the baby move and smiled at the thought of life growing inside her. In the next instant, she thought of how she was going to provide for her family now.

As she walked away from the grave, she hoped whatever was in the will could answer that. Deep inside, she knew she hoped for too much.

Liz sat in the lawyer's waiting room, feeling bloated and hot. It was August and she was five months pregnant. She thanked God she took care of herself and didn't gain too much weight. Still, she felt like the Hindenburg on its maiden voyage as she looked around the office. She wanted a chocolate ice cream cone badly.

"Ms. Kennedy?"

Liz looked up to see the smiling face of Mr. Harris as he beckoned her in. She rose slowly.

"May I help you?"

She waved her hand as she walked into his office. "Nope, I got it, thanks," she said with a sigh as she sat back in the offered chair.

"Well. Let's get right down to it." He opened the file.

As he read the preliminaries of Julie's will, Liz listened, and once again, an irritated feeling swept through her. She didn't know Julie had taken the time to make a will; they had never discussed it.

"I am sorry, Ms. Kennedy. Julie had no life insurance to speak of. Her medical insurance through the airline paid for the hospital and doctors. However..." His voice trailed off.

"I know, Mr. Harris. Julie thought she'd live forever." Suddenly, Liz was angry with Julie. No life insurance, no provisions for Skye or the baby.

"I took the liberty and found that if you wish to continue with your daughter's health insurance, you can convert the policy into a private policy. Unfortunately, that would be—"

"Vulgarly expensive," Liz said irritably. "However, I really have no choice."

"I will look into the matter for you," Mr. Harris said.

Liz nodded. "Thank you."

"Well then, to continue. Any money is in a joint account, as you well know. So there will be no problem for you to access those funds."

"There isn't much money left, Mr. Harris," Liz said. "After we decided to have a child, it took most of our savings. I'm only working part time, which I can continue until the baby is born. I'll use whatever is left to pay any outstanding bills." Inwardly, she became angry with herself. Was she selfish for wanting another child? She and Julie had such plans. Now she felt guilty for all the times she was angry over Julie being gone so much of the time. She was only trying to provide for her and Skye. All at once, she felt alone and terrified of the future.

"Ms. Kennedy?" Mr. Harris asked, bringing her back to reality.

"I'm sorry. What were you saying?"

"A letter. This was left for you. I have another I am to give to a Ms. Casey Bennett."

Liz's eyes widened. "Casey Bennett? Julie left that woman something?" she asked angrily.

Mr. Harris was shocked at her reaction. "That letter is sealed, and as Julie's lawyer, naturally, I cannot tell you. Please, read your letter."

Liz took the letter and angrily opened it.

Hey, darling,

We both know what the deal is if you're reading this. I'm sorry for all this. Now look, I want you to do me a favor. I'm contacting Casey Bennett. Don't go getting angry.

You know I love you, but Casey is a solid woman and she will help you have the baby. I know she will come through for me. She's got a good heart. I know she's been a thorn in your side, but that was my fault. At first, it was hard for me to let her go, but I loved you.

I know I wasn't the best partner. We started a good family and I wasn't around a lot. I am sorry about that. You were just so good at being a mom. And me, well, I tried my best.

Now you let her help take care of you, Skye, and the little one on the way, just until you can get on your feet again...

I'm so sorry I'm not there... So sorry I wasn't there... But I did love you...

Julie

Liz sighed and closed the letter, choking back the tears that stuck in her throat. With trembling hands, she folded the letter in half, then in half again. A desperate lonely feeling tore through her as she took a deep quivering breath.

She felt Mr. Harris watching her carefully. "Do you know Casey Bennett?"

Liz heard the kindness in his voice, but she ignored it and grunted. "Casey Bennett is a former lover of Julie's, with whom Julie broke up five years ago because Casey Bennett is an arrogant, egotistical playgirl who didn't want to settle down," she said through clenched teeth. While in the throes of passion, the fact that Julie had called out Casey's name on more than one occasion did little to abate her anger. "No." She sighed heavily. "I never met the woman."

Mr. Harris smiled weakly and nervously stretched his neck. Liz looked at him. "Are you married, Mr. Harris?"

"Yes, and I have three children."

Liz nodded. "Then you've been through the insanity of pregnancy."

He said with a laugh, "Yes. When my wife was pregnant, she had the same look. I recall staying out of the kitchen when she had a knife in her hand."

They were both silent for a moment until Mr. Harris continued. "I'm afraid you may have to meet this Casey Bennett. This is a legal correspondence, and I'm bound to deliver it to her attorney and have her read it. Whatever happens from there is up to—"

"Casey Bennett," Liz said with a low growl. "Now I really need some ice cream."

"Julie thought she'd be a good solid woman to assist you," he offered.

Liz raised a dubious eyebrow and said nothing.

Chapter 2

"Oh, Casey. God, what you do to me." Suzette moaned. She lay naked on the pillows in front of the huge fireplace. She sighed and looked down at Casey kissing her breast, her long lanky leg gently rubbing against her. "My God, you're the best lover I've ever had," she whispered with a deep moan.

Casey lifted her head, her green cat eyes dancing. She purred against Suzette's breast, sending the woman gasping and clutching Casey's salt and pepper short hair.

"I take that as a compliment since I believe you've been with half the North Shore of Chicago," Casey mumbled.

Suzette laughed and tugged Casey's hair. "I'm serious. You're so amazing."

"My mama said anything worth doing is worth doing well. And, my darling Suzette, you are worth doing well." Casey moaned against her breast, her teeth gently nipping at her hardened nipple. She picked up the ice-cold martini shaker and poured the contents into the long-stemmed glass. As she put it down, she traced the icy metal against the side of Suzette's breast.

Suzette arched her back. "Casey," she exclaimed.

"Yes?" Casey offered her the martini.

They both drank in silence for a moment, then Casey took an olive out of the glass and sensually placed it in Suzette's navel. She laughed as Casey murmured against her ear, "I'll get to that later."

Casey then showed the lovely Suzette just how amazing she could be...

They lay entwined in front of the fire. Casey lay across Suzette's body, both breathing heavily. "Did I eat that olive?"

Suzette laughed. "Yes, you did and everything else in sight."

Casey raised her head and looked up, her green eyes smiling. "I was hungry."

"You should get back to your work. I'm afraid I interrupted." Suzette sighed as she ran her fingernails up and down Casey's strong back.

"A most wonderful interruption. I needed a break. I couldn't sit at that piano another minute." She kissed her shoulder. She let out a deep groan when the phone rang. "Ugh..." Casey growled and did not move.

"Get it. It might be your producer," Suzette said, gently urging Casey.

"Shit." Casey rolled over on her back and picked up the phone. "This better be good," she said into the phone while she stared at the ceiling.

"Casey? Roger. You had better get back to Chicago. I have a registered letter here from an attorney in Albuquerque. Who do you know in New Mexico?"

Casey frowned when she heard her lawyer's worried tone; she continued to gaze at the log-beamed ceiling. "No one. I don't think so, anyway." She laughed and looked down to see Suzette moving between her legs. Casey held her breath as Suzette parted her legs and kissed her inner thigh. She ran her fingers through Suzette's blond hair.

"R-Roger, I'll be in t-tomorrow m-morning..." She sighed and dropped the phone.

"Who was on the phone earlier?" Suzette asked sometime later. She snuggled against Casey, who was staring at the fire; she absently stroked Suzette's shoulder.

"My lawyer, Roger. Someone in..." She stopped and struck a thoughtful pose. "I can't remember the name of the place.

Anyway, he got some letter. He sounded worried." She stopped and yawned. "But Roger always worries."

Suzette pouted. "This means we have to leave?"

Casey laughed. "Don't act like it bothers you. I know how you just love the outdoors."

Suzette looked up with a lazy smile. "I am a city girl. I love Chicago."

Playfully bucking Suzette off, Casey grunted and stood. She offered her hand. "You love to spend money." She hauled Suzette to her feet and pulled her close.

"Don't get all country on me, Ms. Bennett. You love the limelight of the city, as well. You can't stay out of Chicago for long." She reached in and cupped Casey's breast. "I'd like to take credit for that.'"

"As well you should," Casey whispered, then laughed and pulled away. "I need to get organized. We have to leave in the morning." She slapped her bottom and padded down the hall to the bedroom.

It was a long drive back from Wisconsin. Well, long for Casey. Suzette snored all the way to Chicago. She pulled into the underground garage of Suzette's apartment building. "Rise and shine, Sleeping Beauty."

Suzette groaned and stretched. "Are we back already?"

"Yes, darling. Thanks for keeping me company." Casey slipped her seat belt off. Suzette put her head back and closed her eyes. "C'mon, Suzette, I have an appointment with Roger." She popped the trunk and took out two pieces of luggage. Shaking her head, she walked them to the elevator. Two pieces of luggage for three days, she thought.

Suzette lazily met Casey at the elevator. "I assume you can handle two suitcases alone," Casey said as the elevator door opened. She kissed Suzette and patted her cheek. "See you at rehearsal. Study your music. I'd like to hear a little feeling in those chords."

"Don't be a dud, Case," Suzette said as she hauled the luggage with her and pushed the button. "I had a great time. See you later." She waved and blew a kiss as the door closed.

Casey stood there for a moment looking at the elevator door; she smiled ruefully. "I love you, too." She shook her head and walked away.

After dropping Suzette off at her elegant high-rise, Casey drove the busy downtown streets of Chicago—something she loathed doing. Ever since she made enough money composing music for the movies and television, she moved out of her high-rise and into a comfortable log home in upper Wisconsin, her beloved adopted state. Situated on a small lake, it was a world apart from her bustling hometown.

Casey smiled as she remembered her childhood in this city. Her mother was always there, encouraging Casey with her love of music and piano. She laughed openly when she remembered the day she told her mother and her grandmother she was gay.

She was nineteen and just entered college on a music scholarship...

Casey sat at the piano in the den. She ran her fingers through her long black hair and cracked her knuckles.

"Arrrgg," her grandmother called out. "Don't do that. Eleanor, tell her to stop that."

Casey heard her mother laugh; she did it again. Sometimes she just loved to tease her grandmother. She then opened the sheet music and started playing, feeling alive as her fingers touched the black and white keys. With smiling eyes, she played the music she composed. As she played, she looked up to see her mother smiling though the tears that welled in her green eyes.

Her grandmother sniffed loudly and drank her tea. "How in the world are you going to get to Carnegie Hall if you don't play the classics?" she asked gruffly.

Casey grinned as she played. "Want me to stop?"

"No, you might as well finish," her grandmother said, then winked at Casey's mother.

Casey stopped and frowned deeply.

"What's the matter, Case?" Eleanor walked over to the piano.

"I can't find an end for it," Casey said.

Their eyes met; her mother cocked her head and smiled. "It sounds very romantic."

"I guess so."

"For anyone in particular?"

Casey shrugged. "Maybe."

With that, her grandmother quickly walked over. "Who? Don't tell me. The Gentry boy, what's his name," she said eagerly.

Casey's mother never took her eyes off her. "It's not him. Is it, sweetie?"

She felt the tears welling in her eyes; they mirrored her mother's. "No, Mom. It ain't the Gentry boy."

"Who then?" her grandmother asked happily. Casey knew she had visions of a grand wedding at St. Patrick's Cathedral; she will be so disappointed, Casey thought.

"I don't think you want to know," Casey said, breaking eye contact with her mother as she looked down at the keys and fondly ran her fingers over them.

Her mother put her hand under Casey's chin. Casey turned toward her mother's smiling face, filled with curiosity. "I do."

"Well, so do I," her grandmother said, not wanting to be left out.

Casey took a deep breath and glanced at her grandmother's eager face before saying, "Nancy Folberg."

Her mother blinked and for a moment looked stunned; a curious smile then found its way to her lips. She swallowed and hesitated as if trying to register this information.

Casey waited, her heart beating in her chest. She looked at her grandmother, who was completely confused.

"Nancy?" she asked. "But she's a woman. I don't under—"

Casey's mother held up her hand. "Mother, please."

"I'm sorry, Mom." Suddenly, Casey felt ashamed.

"Well, I should think so—"

"Mother," Eleanor said in a warning voice. She regarded Casey with such love in her eyes that Casey nearly started crying. "Is this someone special? I've met Nancy. She's a nice girl."

"Oh, my God," her grandmother exclaimed and collapsed into the nearest chair. "Eleanor Casey-Bennett, I cannot believe your daughter is telling you this and you..."

Casey and her mother paid no attention. "Yes, she is, Mom," Casey said. "I—I don't know why or how, but all I know is she makes me feel the same way you said you felt about Dad."

Her mother nodded as she grinned. "Then she is special, and I'm happy for you, Case. We'll talk about this later. You finish that song for her."

Casey frowned. "I'm not sure it's for her, but for someone..." Her voice trailed off.

Eleanor walked behind her and gathered her long black hair in her hands and ran her fingers through it. Casey closed her eyes as her mother absently braided her hair. She knew this wasn't easy for her mother. She didn't want to hurt her, but she knew the truth had to be told.

"I love you, Case." She kissed the top of her head. She then walked up to her mother. "We need to talk, Mother."

The elder woman stood and Casey smiled. "I love you, Gram."

She narrowed her eyes at Casey. "You're like your mother with those charming green eyes," she said, then grudgingly smiled. "I suppose I can see what the ladies are after." She then stood tall and cleared her throat. "And why not? You have Casey blood flowing in your veins, as well." She walked up and cupped Casey's face. "I suppose the wedding at St. Patrick's is out?"

"Until they change the laws, I'm afraid so," Casey said. She then held onto her grandmother's hand. "But if the time comes, a-and I meet someone, you'll be there, wherever it is?"

Tears sprang into the old woman's eyes. "I don't pretend to understand this or agree with it." She then nodded. "But try keeping me away."

Casey smiled now and wiped the tear that found its way down her cheek. Her mother was gone, but that day would never fade from her memory. And speaking of memories, Nancy Folberg was a distant memory now, though she was Casey's first encounter. Casey had many loves since, but no one touched her heart enough to finish her song.

She concentrated on her music career and now, at forty years old, Casey could choose her own work and only come to Chicago when it was time for the studio work. That usually took a couple of weeks, so she stayed at her Lake Point Tower high-rise then. The rest of the time, she was lost in the woods. She could be making a boatload if she lived in Los Angeles or New York, but she'd rather have peace of mind and a small bank account than the hectic rat race of Hollywood. Her grandmother was pleased with that decision. Since Casey's mother passed away, her grandmother stepped in and took care of Casey. Not that Casey Bennett needed to be taken care of. Her grandmother, Meredith Casey, was bound and determined to see her only granddaughter healthy and happy. Wealth was secondary. And if being gay made Casey happy, her grandmother grudgingly agreed.

Casey grinned now at the thought of the elder Casey taking an interest in her life. She picked up her cell phone and dialed the familiar number. "Gram? Hey."

"Who is this?"

Casey laughed. "It's your favorite granddaughter."

"Hmm. I only have one, you're lucky. How are you? You're still alive, that's good."

Casey winced when she heard the scolding voice. "I'm fine. Sorry, Gram. How about dinner?"

"You're paying?"

"Of course."

"Then yes, I'd love to have dinner with you. You pick the place, make it expensive."

Casey laughed. "I will. How about Mickey's on Halsted?"

She waited patiently for an answer.

"I am not spending an evening in that rat-hole tavern of your ill-spent youth. For the life of me, I will never understand you going to that place and playing that piano for the neighborhood. And not even getting paid for it—"

"I remember you and Grandpa going in there from time to time."

"Don't be insolent. And for that, you'll take me to Charlie Trotter's—"

Casey groaned. "Oh, Gram. We have to get all dressed up."

"It wouldn't hurt you to wear a dress every now and then, Casey Bennett. For no other reason than to remind yourself you are a woman."

"I know I'm a woman, Gram. Ask Suzette."

There was a deafening silence.

"You love to torment me with your lesbianism, don't you? And while we're on the topic, if you insist on this lifestyle, can you please find a nice woman? One with an IQ above that of a turnip?"

"Now, Gram. Suzette plays the cello."

"So? She's an idiot savant."

Casey rolled her eyes as she pulled into the underground parking. "I'm at Roger's office."

"What have you done?"

"Nothing. I'll pick you up at seven. I love you."

"Hmm. You're still not getting my money. I love you, too, dear."

Casey laughed and closed the phone. In the back of her mind, she wondered if she were in trouble; it was the guilt-ridden Irish in her. She stepped out of the elevator as it reached the eighth floor.

"Casey Bennett to see Roger the Dodger," she said with a wink. The young secretary blushed and laughed along.

"Must you flirt with my secretary?" Roger's voice called out of the office.

Casey laughed and walked in. "No, but sometimes it's necessary." She sat and stretched her long denim-clad legs out in front of her. She absently twirled her sunglasses as she brushed a thick lock of hair off her forehead.

"Well? Is somebody suing me, Roger?"

"You sound serious." He then mumbled, "If Casey Bennett could be serious."

"I heard that." She wagged a finger in his direction. "You sound like my grandmother."

"Meredith is well, I hope." Roger opened the manila envelope. "And I have no idea if someone is suing you. You must have a guilty conscience." He ignored Casey's laughter. "The letter of introduction states you're part of someone's will. One Julie Bridges." He looked up over his glasses.

Casey stopped twirling her glasses and frowned deeply. She sat forward and took the offered letter.

"I take it you knew her?"

"Knew her? Yes. I knew her," Casey said slowly as she swallowed with difficulty, her heart pounding in her ears. She gingerly opened the letter.

Dear Case,

It's been five years, hasn't it? Sorry to be writing you like this, but there isn't any other way.

Long story short? I found out I have bone cancer, and by the time you're reading this, well... It sounds like something out of the movies you write the music for.

Anyway, I have a big problem. The last time I talked to you, I told you about this wonderful woman I met and fell in love with, remember? Liz Kennedy. Well, she fell for me, go figure. We started a family; you know how much I wanted one.

You know, you were right all those years ago. I wasn't ready for a family. You told me I was in love with the idea of a family but could never face the responsibility. You were right.

Liz wanted a family, as well, she's a great mom. We've got one daughter, Skye, a great little girl, though she doesn't know me very well. I'm still working for the airline and gone a good deal of the time. For that, I will always be sorry. I missed the time with Skye. Now I'll miss everything.

I've screwed up with this. Liz tried so hard to plan a life for us and I just didn't see anything coming. I'm afraid I left the poor woman with a child and one on the way. She's due in December.

Please, please help her. She knows about you. She just needs someone to help her until the baby comes and she can get back on her feet.

I figure you're about the only one I have left that I haven't pissed off. Even Liz was going to leave me a few times.

You loved me once. I know I'm pulling out all the stops and I

have no right to ask, and you have no obligation to me. But I'm begging you to watch out for them. I've got no one else, Casey.
   Julie

   Casey sat there stunned. Roger came around and sat on the edge of the desk. "Casey, as your lawyer, may I?" he asked gently, and Casey, as if in a trance, handed him the letter.
   Roger read it, then read it again. He looked up at Casey, who was staring at the ground scowling.
   "Well," he folded the letter, "what are you going to do?"
   Casey shot an angry look at her lawyer and friend. "Do?" she bellowed and stood, pacing back and forth. "Nothing. Julie left me five years ago because she wanted kids. Well, you read the letter…and I was right. She fucked up and now has a woman with one kid and another due to pop any day. Fuck!"
   Roger winced but let her go on her tirade. "Casey," he started. She glared at him. Roger took a deep breath and let it out slowly. "I haven't seen you this irate since, well, the incident at Orchestra Hall comes to mind. The poor violinist cried for a week," he said and smiled slightly. "That wasn't a nice thing to do to poor Donald."
   For an instant, Casey relaxed and smiled slightly. She did indeed make the poor guy cry. He was a lousy violinist. In the next instant, she was angry again. "Fuck!" she said angrily. "And now, she goes and dies," she cried out and sat down, burying her face in her hands.
   "She obviously knew she could turn to you."
   Casey snorted. "Well, she was wrong. What do I know about kids? Look at my life," she said slowly, trying to explain.
   Roger laughed at her sarcasm.
   "I'm single. I like being single. Yes, I'm gay and I like the freedom of a physical relationship that does not demand the second date involve a U-Haul. I live in the woods on a lake. And do you know why I live in the woods on a lake?"
   "Not to steal a title from the movie, but to be… Far from the Madding Crowd," Roger answered obediently.
   "Yes. That's right."

"She's pregnant with nowhere to go."

Casey stood and frowned in confusion. "How the hell do you know she has nowhere to go?"

He walked around, took out the letter of introduction, and handed it to her. Casey read it aloud. "Dear Mr. Blah—that's you. I'm Mr. Harris—that's him..." She scanned the letter, then came to it. She read it and her shoulders slumped. "Fuck. No money, no place...Fuck me." She flopped down into the chair. "No."

"Casey," Roger insisted. "She's almost in her third trimester."

"Then when she graduates, I'll throw her a party."

"That means she's due to give birth in December," he said dryly.

Casey blinked. "Oh," she said stupidly and threw her hands up. "There, you see? I don't know nothin' about birthin' no babies," she exclaimed dramatically.

Roger said nothing but gave her the fatherly glare Casey just loved to get. She saw the look and sat back down.

"Casey Eleanor Bennett."

"Here it comes."

"I've known you since you were, well, a young woman. All your life, you've been able to live as you please. You're confident, out of the closet, and you don't care who knows it. You're talented and beautiful—"

"I like it so far, but I'm afraid the other shoe is about to fall and kick me right in the ass on the way down," she grumbled and rubbed her temples.

"I've seen you do great things with your music. Seen you help all those kids when you didn't think anyone knew. But you can be the most arrogant, obnoxious, self-indulgent, wayward snot I've ever met," he said firmly. Casey raised an eyebrow as he continued, "You need this woman. You need her badly because one of these days, Casey Bennett, you're going to wake up alone and lonely. You're halfway there now."

"I'm only forty," she said in a logical voice.

"I give up." He tossed down his pen. "If you can't see the importance of this..."

Casey grimaced and took a deep breath. "Fine, give me her number—"

"I-I already called her attorney last night. He put her on the morning bus. She'll arrive at the Greyhound station in Rhinelander in two days. I offered her the plane fare, but it seems Ms. Kennedy is a proud woman. This will be difficult for her, as well, Casey." He gave her a sick grin.

She glared at him and loomed over his desk.

"Now, Casey. You're doing a great thing here. Y-you know it," he said and leaned back. "Don't let that legendary temper get the better of you."

Casey sported a feral grin. "Yes, and I don't regret throwing that musician's music stand out the window. The musician was lucky he didn't follow it."

Roger smiled weakly and quickly hid behind the protection of his glasses.

Casey stopped and took a deep angry breath. She then put on her sunglasses and stretched her neck from side to side.

Roger heard the vertebrae crack in alignment and winced slightly. "Y-you could use a rubdown," he offered, smiling, and Casey glared at him. "If you need anything, call me or Trish. She's had both my kids." He waved off Casey's odd glance. "You know what I mean."

"Good day, Roger. I will definitely keep in touch," she said through clenched teeth and stormed out of his office, leaving the door open.

His secretary poked her head in.

"Betty? I need a drink."

Casey swam lap after lap in the pool at her gym. *Fuck me. Kids? A mother? What in the hell am I supposed to do about this?* she thought.

Twenty minutes later, she stopped, out of breath. She stood in the shallow water, ripped off her goggles, and angrily threw them across the pool. Heads turned, and people watched as she easily hoisted herself out of the pool and picked up her towel.

Even the sauna didn't help. Casey sat there naked, a sheet

partially covering her long tanned body. She took a deep breath as she remembered Julie Bridges.

They were together for almost four years. Casey was happy and content. Julie worked for the airlines and was gone a good deal of the time. That was probably why Casey was happy and content. However, she loved Julie more than she ever loved anyone, and that was saying something for Casey Bennett.

Then Julie dropped the bomb about kids. Casey tried to understand. However, it just wasn't for her. A child should have a mother and a father or at least a married couple, gay or straight. Julie wanted it and left Casey because of it. That was five years earlier. Since then, Casey went back to her old ways of casual partners, satisfying sex, and nothing long term.

Well, I'll help this Liz Kennedy and her family. I'll let her stay at the cabin and I'll stay in the city, she thought. "Shit. I hate the city."

She then thought perhaps this Liz might like the apartment. No. A little kid on the tenth floor? Hell, that just begged for a 911 call. She could just see the little rug rat hanging from the balcony.

"Shit," she cursed rudely and headed for the shower.

Chapter 3

Meredith Casey looked in the mirror and touched the silver hair at her temples. "Not bad for a seventy-nine-year-old," she whispered to her reflection and continued, "and having a daughter at eighteen and a granddaughter at thirty-nine." She glanced at the clock on the mantel. It was precisely 7:15. She sipped her martini and shook her head. "Idiot child. If she calls me with some lamebrain excuse…" When the doorbell rang, she called out, "It's open."

Casey walked in sporting a deep frown. "You have to lock your door, Gram. Good grief."

"I live in a good neighborhood. Besides, I have a pistol." She laughed and noticed her granddaughter did not join her. Casey walked into the living room and flounced on the couch. "What's the matter?" she asked. "You did do something wrong, didn't you?"

"No, I did not do anything wrong." Casey eyed the martini. "Did you make enough for two?"

"I made enough for four," she said. "And by the looks of you, you need them."

Casey walked over to the bar and poured the martini into the stemmed glass, adding several olives. Meredith said nothing as she watched her granddaughter sit once again on the couch. Casey took a long sip and let out a deep sigh.

"I think we'll stay in for dinner," Meredith said evenly. "You don't look like you're in the mood for Charlie Trotter's." She kicked off her shoes. "Come with me." She picked up her glass and started down the hall. "Bring the pitcher," she called over her shoulder.

"You don't have to make dinner, Gram." Casey dutifully followed down the hall with the martini shaker in hand.

"I'm not. You are." Meredith sat at the kitchen table. "Maria just went shopping. The fridge is stocked. Have at it." She raised her stemmed glass, then took a sip.

"Gram, I don't cook."

"Still? How on earth are you going to get someone if you can't boil water? Sit down." She watched Casey as she sat at the kitchen table, sipping her martini. Meredith stuck her head in the refrigerator. "What do you have a taste for?"

"How about a thick steak?"

"Something light and Italian. Now tell me what's wrong."

Casey groaned as Meredith gathered the fixings for an antipasto salad. "I got a call from Roger."

"I gathered that, what for?" She placed the meats and olives on the table, along with the cheese and tomatoes. "Cut the cheese."

"Very funny," Casey mumbled and took the offered knife. "It seems my past is coming back to haunt me."

"How so?" Meredith asked. "Don't tell me you got someone pregnant." She smiled sweetly and batted her eyelashes.

Casey glared at her. "Can we cut the Marx Brothers routine for a minute? It seems an ex-lover of mine has passed away."

"Oh, sweetie. I'm sorry." Meredith turned around and placed the olive oil on the table along with the loaf of crusty bread.

"It's okay. I haven't seen Julie in five years. We, well, we weren't a good match. She wanted kids."

"And you didn't?" her grandmother asked. "I thought you liked children."

"I do. It's just that Julie wasn't equipped to handle the responsibility. And at the time, neither was I. So it was a deal breaker for her. I couldn't see bringing a child into this world under the conditions Julie and I found ourselves in."

Meredith arranged the plate and drizzled the oil. "Which were?"

Casey took another sip of her martini and contemplated the question. Meredith waited while she sliced the thick bread.

"I was back and forth from Chicago to LA. Julie was a pilot, or co-pilot, at the time and flying all over the place. She was living in Colorado, but I'd fly and meet her on layovers wherever she was. We had a very Bohemian lifestyle."

Meredith nodded in understanding. Casey glanced up, looking apologetic. "I know you don't approve of my lifestyle, and I'm not apologizing for it."

"Casey, I told you many years ago when we sat in the living room with your mother, I don't pretend to understand your being gay, but through the years, seeing you grow into a mature, caring, and talented woman, I'm hard pressed to find a reason to argue against it." She arranged a small plate and handed it to Casey. "And as for living a Bohemian lifestyle, let me fill you in on something. Your grandfather and I were not always old and stodgy."

Casey had a mouthful and looked up. "What do you mean?"

Meredith smirked and sat back with her martini. She popped an olive in her mouth and grinned. "We too were quite the Bohemians when we were young."

Cocking her head, Casey playfully glared at her grandmother. "C'mon. Give."

Meredith laughed. "I met your grandfather when I was sixteen. He was nineteen and in college."

Casey's eyes bugged out of her head. Meredith nodded. "Yep. I fell in love with that nitwit George Casey and never looked back. I finished high school and married him when I was seventeen. Had your mother a year later. We traveled all over the country with his small band. You know your grandfather was a musician, played the clarinet." She sighed and munched on the cheese. "That's what got me, damn it."

"What?"

"The clarinet. The minute he started, I was hooked. He played that thing like a lover, and he would serenade me until I was weak in the knees." She laughed and ate another olive. "He was a devil."

Casey laughed along. "I only remember him as a music

teacher. Why didn't you tell me this? And why did you always want me to go to a fancy college?"

"I suppose I wanted more for you than I had and your mother had. You had such a talent. We saw that when you were so young."

Casey reached over and took her hand. "I have what I want, Gram. I'm happy and content. And I haven't sold my soul for the dollar." She sat back and frowned. "I thought I was happy with Julie. But when she threw the curve at me about having kids, I-I don't know. Warning bells went off and I needed to make a decision."

They sat in silence for a moment or two before Meredith spoke. "What does Roger have to do with this?"

Casey, broken from her reverie, looked up and blinked. "She had bone cancer and died a couple weeks ago. She left behind a family, who has little money, and she asked for my help."

"Wow."

"Yeah, wow."

Meredith appraised her only granddaughter. "How big of a family?"

"One kid and one on the way, it seems." Casey refilled her martini glass and plopped several olives in to emphasize.

"What are you going to do?"

Casey took a deep breath before answering. "I'm going to let this Liz Kennedy stay at my cabin. She's going through some trimester thing, and she's due in December."

Meredith frowned, then laughed. "Trimester thing?"

Casey turned bright red and ran her fingers through her hair. "So you see how stupid this is? What the shit do I know about kids?"

"First off," her grandmother said. "You'll have to stop swearing. When do Liz Kennedy and her family get to Wisconsin?"

"I'm leaving in a couple days. She'll be there by late afternoon."

"So she's agreeable to this, to travel being pregnant and with a small child?"

"Well, she's probably used to being taken care of. And if

she thinks I'm gonna wait on her hand and foot because she got herself pregnant, she's mistaken."

Meredith raised her eyebrow at the outburst. Casey sat back and folded her arms across her chest in a childlike manner. "Don't judge too quickly, Casey. You don't know the whole situation."

Casey grunted. "I know the situation, Gram. It's the one I avoided. Two irresponsible women having babies. Only one of them dies, leaving behind a mess for someone else to clean up."

"That sounded very cruel, Casey Bennett."

"Probably. But very true."

Meredith heard the bitterness in Casey's voice. She wondered what this Liz Kennedy was really like. Whatever she was like, she had to be an improvement over the cellist.

Chapter 4

"Are you sure you want to do this, Liz?" Elaine asked. She sat on the couch and accepted the glass of wine Liz offered.

"I have to, Elaine. Joanne said she had a friend who could rent this place furnished. I'm hoping once the baby is born and I can get back on my feet and get a job, I can come back here." Liz looked around the apartment and sighed. "Though Julie was gone most of the time, there are memories here." However, the stream of endless nights, lying alone in bed, flashed through her mind.

"Won't you let me help you?" Elaine said. "I can help with—"

Liz shook her head. "No, please. You're so busy at the hospital and you have your own family and bills to pay. You're doing enough just to take the few things and store them for me." She sat down with a tired sigh and patted Elaine's knee. "I've thought this through so much since meeting with Julie's lawyer, I can't think anymore. I have no job, and I have no money really to pay for this apartment. Skye needs stability, and before you know it, this little one will be here." She ran her hand over her belly.

"I do see your point. And if this woman knew Julie, perhaps it will work out. It's awfully generous of her to help."

"I feel like a charity case. Thank God, Julie's lawyer has a nephew who bought the car. I needed that extra cash."

Elaine raised her glass. "Well, sweetie. If you ever need anything, you know I'm here for you." Elaine raised her glass. "Here's to Wisconsin and a new beginning."

Liz smiled and offered her iced tea glass. "Let's hope so."

As they got off the bus in Wisconsin, Liz held on to Skye's hand. She groaned as her back ached horribly.

The hot August sun beat down on her daughter's head. "Mama, I hot," Skye complained as she rubbed her eyes.

"I know, sweetie. Somebody will be meeting us," she said and patted her head.

The driver helped unload her few bags and walked with her into the terminal. He set the bags down and Liz felt horrible. She opened her purse and held the ten-dollar bill in her hand. Having nothing smaller, she just couldn't give all of it to him.

"Don't worry about it, ma'am," he said with a wink and tipped his hat, then walked away.

She eased herself onto the bench, and Skye crawled up next to her. "I tired," she grumbled, her cheeks flushed from the heat.

"Ms. Kennedy?" a woman's voice called out.

Liz looked up to see an absolutely stunning woman standing in front of her. Tall, tanned, and scowling. This must be Casey Bennett, she thought.

"Yes. Ms. Bennett?"

Casey nodded. "I...Let me help you. We can get out of this infernal heat," she said and looked down at Skye. Liz hid her grin as Casey Bennett smirked when Skye looked up.

"Hi," Skye said with a giggle.

Liz looked away, trying not to laugh as Casey frowned.

"Hello," she said gruffly and picked up the bags.

Liz was amazed as she picked up all three, including the diaper bag. "I can take one," Liz offered.

Casey looked at her stomach. "I...You probably shouldn't be carrying anything." This came out as a question and Liz raised an eyebrow at the confused look on Casey Bennett's face. She nearly missed the next comment. "Or riding a bus. Why didn't you take the plane tickets?" Casey asked, scowling. She turned and started out the terminal.

"Mama say no!" Skye put her hands on her hips.

Liz's eyes widened in horror as she looked down at Skye,

who looked very much like Shirley Temple.

Casey raised an eyebrow and gave Liz a smug grin. Liz turned bright red remembering how adamant she was about taking money unnecessarily from this woman. It was hard enough to leave New Mexico.

"Well, whatever Mama says," Casey grumbled and headed out the door.

Liz sneered and held on to her daughter. She proudly tried to keep up with the long strides, but after two or three, she gave up and followed.

"You don't have a car seat?" Liz asked.

Casey packed the trunk of her shiny Lexus and slammed it. "Nope. Sorry. It's a short ride."

"You'll get a ticket," Liz warned.

Casey rolled her eyes as she slipped on her sunglasses.

She got a ticket. The patrolman took off his sunglasses and looked into the car. "Sorry, but it's the law."

Casey glared at him. "I'm well aware of the law, Officer. As I explained, I didn't have enough time to get one."

"Well, purchase one. If you want to contest the ticket, the court date's on the back."

Casey, avoiding Liz's grin, looked at the ticket. "Two hundred and fifty bucks? Are you guys insane?"

"Too much for a child's life?" he asked and smirked.

Casey opened her mouth but closed it and put on her glasses.

"You two have a nice day," he said and walked away.

The remainder of the ride was quiet—too quiet.

"Mama, I sick," Skye said.

Casey looked over. "Not in my new Lexus, kid," Casey grumbled and stepped on the gas.

"Ms. Bennett, do you want another ticket?" she asked anxiously.

Casey pulled down the access road that led to her cabin. Being deep in the woods, the weather cooled off considerably.

Liz was exhausted and Skye was sound asleep in her lap, resting on her stomach. Liz then saw the lake come into view and smiled.

She felt Casey's gaze on her and continued to look at the lake. She nervously tucked the wayward strand of auburn hair behind her ear. "This is yours?" Liz asked as the log cabin came into view.

Casey grunted her acknowledgment. "I'll get your luggage, looks like Shortround is pooped."

Liz glared at her assessment of Skye but said nothing.

As Casey opened the trunk, Liz groaned and couldn't move. "Ms. Bennett?"

Casey came around and opened the passenger door. Liz looked up into the green eyes. "Please, can you take her? I can't get out with her on my stomach."

Casey frowned and took a step back looking as though she had no clue which end to take. "She's not a hand grenade," Liz offered. Good grief, she thought. Julie wanted to have children with this woman?

Casey grunted and took Skye, who immediately latched onto Casey's neck, laying her hot head against her shoulder. Casey swallowed and looked as if she were holding a time bomb. Liz struggled and Casey offered her hand. "Thanks, I'm beginning to feel like a turtle on its back."

Liz actually saw a smile as Casey gently assisted her. Once again, Liz was amazed at her strength; she groaned and stretched, then reached for her daughter. "Thanks. Let me take her."

As she pulled Skye away, Skye whimpered in her sleep and clung to Casey's neck tighter. "Well, Ms. Bennett, you've got a friend," Liz said, and Casey grunted again.

"I'll come back for the luggage." Casey then picked up the diaper bag and walked around the front of the cabin.

"This is spectacular," Liz said.

"I like it." Casey opened the front door, awkwardly juggling Skye, who was still clinging to her neck.

Liz walked in and gazed around in awe. The room was huge and open. A fireplace took up most of one wall, and a black grand piano sat near it. A comfortable couch placed in front of the fireplace and a couple of overstuffed chairs rounded out the area.

The dining room was behind the living room. No walls separated the living room from the dining room or kitchen; only a counter separated the kitchen from the other two. It was spacious and airy. The cathedral-beamed ceiling made the log cabin seem larger than it was.

"I-I only have one bedroom. The other has my work in it. The loft isn't set up with beds yet. So you and Shortround can have the bedroom. I made room for your clothes. You can use the smaller dresser in the room. I-I think there should be enough drawer space for you. "

"No. Please—"

"Ms. Kennedy, don't argue. You're going to have a baby and you need a comfortable place to sleep. This couch is fine for me."

With that, Skye woke up, belched, and promptly vomited on Casey's shirt. Casey held the child away from her.

"Mama, I sick," Skye whimpered and started crying.

Casey thrust the bundle of joy at Liz and said angrily, "Here… Mama."

Liz bit her bottom lip as she tried desperately not to laugh while taking Skye.

"The bathroom is at the end of the hall." Casey pulled her shirt out of her jeans and headed for the kitchen, mumbling all the way.

"Skye, baby, that was not a very good first impression." Liz sighed and picked up the diaper bag and headed down the hall.

After getting Skye settled down for a nap, Liz lined pillows all around the child so she wouldn't fall off Casey's huge bed; that's all she needed. Liz then raised an eyebrow. That is one big bed, she thought as she looked around Casey Bennett's bedroom.

Tastefully done in a somewhat rustic, Southwestern motif, the soft mauve and earth tones accentuated the pine logs. The room smelled of pine and a hint of perfume. Liz closed her eyes and took a gentle whiff and smiled.

"Everything okay?"

Liz jumped to find Casey standing there, still wiping off her shirt. "I-I'm sorry."

Casey shook her head. "Don't worry about it. Interesting fragrance." She walked by Liz and opened a dresser drawer. She then stripped off her shirt right in front of her, and Liz blinked but did not turn away.

Casey stood there for a moment in a white sports bra, rummaging for a clean T-shirt. She slipped it on over her head. "She can yak on this one all she wants. It's an ex's..." Casey smirked and walked out.

Liz stood there dumbfounded as Casey Bennett had felt no compunction about taking off her clothes in front of her. Maybe because I'm pregnant, she thinks I don't... Liz took a deep breath. Thinking of Casey Bennett's fit figure, she looked down at her stomach, just able to see her feet.

"Attractive," she grumbled. She took her cell phone out of her purse and dialed Elaine's number. With all this, she had forgotten to call her. She smiled when she heard the familiar voice.

"Well, you're alive."

Liz laughed. "Yes, we're safe and sound."

"So," Elaine said. "What's she like?"

"Too early to tell. She's doing a kind thing, although I'm sure she'd rather not. And who could blame her?"

"Hmm. True." There was silence for a moment. "So, what does she look like?"

Liz heard the curiosity in Elaine's voice and grinned. "She's very attractive. Tall, dark, green eyes. And she's arrogant. How's that?"

Elaine laughed. "Oh, hell, they're calling me. We've got patients up the you know what today. Look, you take care of yourself and give Skye a kiss. Keep in touch, Liz. I love you."

"I love you too, Elaine. Bye," Liz said and closed the phone. All at once she missed New Mexico. Oh well, she thought and walked out of the bedroom, stealing one last glance at Skye as she slept.

"I'm out here," Casey called out.

Liz noticed Casey had made some iced tea. "I thought we'd sit outside. It's a little cooler."

"Thank you."

They sat on the deck, not saying much. Finally, Liz glanced at Casey, who was staring out at the lake. "I-I do appreciate your helping us. It's just that, well, we didn't—"

"Ms. Kennedy, I knew Julie, so you don't have to explain."

Liz heard the sarcasm in her voice and bristled. "Just what does that mean?"

Casey searched Liz's face; her gaze traveled down her body. Again, Liz felt a wave of indignance sweep through her as Casey shrugged. "Nothing, just that I knew Julie for four years."

"Look. I know you and Julie had a relationship before me. I'm well aware of it. However, Ms. Bennett, if this arrangement is going to work, I think it best we leave the past exactly where it belongs." Liz set her glass down. "In the past."

"I couldn't agree more, Ms. Kennedy. I agreed to help you and your family until the baby is born and—"

"If you think for one minute this is easy for me or that I want to be in this situation, you are mistaken."

Casey took a deep breath and let it out slowly. "I don't want to get into an argument with you, especially in your condition. Let's skip it, shall we?" She took a long drink and turned toward the lake.

"A very good idea." Liz damned the tears that rose in her throat. Her hormones were all over the place, something she hated. When she realized the tears were about to overtake her, she abruptly turned and stumbled over the rocking chair.

Casey was at her side. "Are you okay?"

Liz felt her strong hand under her forearm to steady her. "I'm fine," she said, wiping the tears off her cheek.

"Did you hurt yourself?"

"No, I did not hurt myself." Liz wrenched her arm away. The last thing she wanted was to lose control in front of this woman.

"Okay, okay." Casey stepped back awkwardly.

"I think I'll go lie down with Skye. I'm rather tired," Liz said, sounding every bit of it.

"F-fine. Okay."

Liz looked up and saw the confused posture. "I'm sorry, it's a hormone thing."

Casey smiled weakly. "Look. Why don't you go in and take a nap? Later I'll, well, I don't know what I've got in there for dinner," she said and stood. "I don't usually cook for myself."

Liz nodded and started for the screen door. Casey reached in and opened it; for a moment, they stood close, then Casey quickly stepped back, looking at her stomach.

"Don't worry, Ms. Bennett, I'm not going to explode," she said and walked in. "Yet," she threatened over her shoulder.

Liz lay on the bed next to Skye and listened to the sound of the piano coming from the living room. She is good, Liz thought, then snorted. Go figure; she's a smirking, arrogant playgirl who plays a beautiful piano. She listened and fell sound asleep, feeling safe and content for the first time in years.

She woke with a start, and for an instant, she was disoriented. Skye was still fast asleep on her stomach. Gaining her bearings, she remembered where she was and why she was here. As she lay in bed, Liz took in the surroundings of Casey Bennett's bedroom. The clock on the mantel looked like an antique; she doubted if Casey was an antique collector.

She did notice how the fireplace gave the room a rustic, romantic feel. Romantic, she thought with a smirk. I will just bet she has a steady stream of women in and out of this bedroom. She carefully slipped Skye off her stomach and covered her with the light quilt, then eased off the bed and crept out of the room.

Casey was sitting at the piano, a pencil behind her ear as she plunked out a few chords.

"Hi," Liz said.

Casey growled and waved.

"Good grief," Liz mumbled and walked into the kitchen; she was starving. "Mind if I look—"

"No. Do whatever," Casey said dismissively.

Liz rolled her eyes and opened the refrigerator. "Good Lord," she exclaimed. She picked up several containers of old Chinese food and winced, then picked up a little jar. "Caviar?" She shook her head. The food consisted of a pizza box, several bottles of beer, and a carton of orange juice that looked liked it had been there since the Reagan administration.

Then she heard a grumble and the slam of the piano top. She jumped and looked out into the living room to see the retreating figure of the angry pianist flying out the front door.

Liz bit her lip anxiously and walked out onto the deck. "I-I'm sorry if I disrupted you."

Casey was standing there leaning against the railing staring out at the lake. "It's not you," she said with a heavy sigh. "I've got a deadline, and I'm just not clicking, that's all."

"What do you usually do to click?"

Casey turned to her, her green eyes narrowed into a wicked grin. "I have sex. That usually works."

"Sorry if I'm crimping your style."

Casey raised an eyebrow. "Don't worry. You're not."

Liz felt her anger rising and Casey laughed, which did nothing to abate her anger. "Look," Casey started, "I don't have much in the way of food."

"Yes, I noticed."

"I can go into town and pick up a few things for the next couple days. You look all done in, and I'm sure Shortround is still pooped," she offered with a shrug.

Instinctively, Liz put a hand to her hair, suddenly feeling tired and bloated. She looked up at Casey, who fidgeted in the awkward silence. She was sure Ms. Bennett was not used to this at all—neither was she. "I could make a list. I'm afraid I need a few things for Skye."

"Sure, make your list." Casey walked into the house.

Liz jotted down a few items and turned to Casey, who picked up the keys. "Oh...Skye's toilet trained, but at night she still needs the occasional Huggie." She stopped and looked up into the green eyes. "You do know what Huggies are, don't you?"

"Yes, I know what Huggies are, for chrissakes," Casey countered and snatched the list out of her hand. She slipped on her sunglasses and headed out the back door.

"For three-year-olds..." Liz called and waved.

"Toilet trained! Huggies," Casey repeated angrily as she

parked the Lexus at the small grocery store in Rhinelander.

She took a cart, and as she walked down the aisle, she stopped and glanced around. "What the hell am I doing?" She took out her cell phone and dialed the number. "Gram?" she said in a gruff voice.

"Hmm, you sound frazzled. How's the domestic life so far?"

"This is the stupidest thing I've ever done."

"Ah, ah, remember Suzette. What's Liz Kennedy like?"

"I dunno. She's…" Casey stopped and thought of the long auburn hair, the blue eyes that shimmered when she was trying not to cry. "Pregnant."

She heard her grandmother laugh. "You be nice to that woman. She has a lot to deal with."

"Her?" Casey voice screeched as she perused the list. "What about me?"

"What about you? Are you five months pregnant with a three-year-old and no money?"

Casey took the phone away from her ear and looked to the heavens.

"Where are you?"

"I-I'm at the grocery store in town." She winced when she heard the peal of laughter.

"Don't tell me," her grandmother said. "She gave you a list."

"Gram," Casey warned as she guided the wobbling cart down the quiet aisle.

"So why are you calling me, dear?"

"I…what the hell is a Huggie?" Casey blurted out. Again the laughter.

"It's a diaper, you fool. Good heavens, you're a woman." Casey stopped and closed her eyes. Meredith Casey cleared her throat. "Go down the aisle with the toilet paper and all that."

Casey steered the cart and found them. "Okay. Got 'em."

"Anything else… Mom?"

Casey took the phone away from her ear and almost threw it across the store and remembered it was her phone. She took a deep breath. "No. Thanks. Goodbye, Grandmother."

"I think I want to meet this woman and—"

"No," Casey said. "I'll call you later. You know I love you."

Neither spoke for a long moment. "Of course I know. I love you, too. Where did that come from? Ms. Kennedy or the little one? What's her name, by the way?"

"Skye," Casey said with a chuckle and juggled the phone while she picked up the next item on the list. "She's kinda feisty."

"Hmm."

Casey felt her face getting hot. "What does that mean?"

"Oh, nothing, nothing. You go and finish grocery shopping. I'm sure laundry awaits."

"Very funny," Casey said. "Bye, Gram."

"Goodbye and good luck, dear."

She was too busy reading the last item on the list to hear her grandmother's laughter as she hung up. "Chocolate fudge swirl and whipped cream," she repeated. Then it dawned on her, and she laughed in spite of herself. Cravings... She picked up two.

Liz was throwing away all the old junk in the fridge when Casey came in the back door struggling with the bags.

"Did I have that much on the list?"

Casey gave her an incredulous look. "Did you have...?" She stopped as she set the bags down. "Yes."

Liz handed her several folded bills. "I-I'd like to help pay."

Casey looked from the money to the proud blue eyes. She gently pushed the money back to her. "I'll take care of this round. We'll talk later about the future." By the look on Liz's face, Casey wasn't sure if she was going to argue or start crying again.

"Thank you," Liz said.

The awkward silence between them, which was getting all to frequent, was mercifully interrupted by a small voice.

"Mama, uppie."

Casey looked down at the girl standing there, her arms outstretched.

Liz bent down and groaned as she lifted her. "Hi, sweet pea," she said with a kiss on the cheek.

Casey watched the exchange for a moment, then concentrated on the groceries. Casey felt Skye watching her with great interest and became extremely self-conscious under her scrutiny. So much so that she dropped an egg on the floor.

"Damn it!" Casey cursed and grabbed a napkin.

"Damment!" Skye repeated.

Completely caught off-guard, Casey looked up and let out a hearty laugh.

Liz was less than thrilled. "Ms. Bennett, please."

Skye laughed watching Casey, who was still laughing.

"Damment," Skye repeated and clapped as she watched Casey, who now roared with laughter.

Casey sobered after seeing the blue-eyed glare from the mother; she looked down at similar laughing blue eyes. "Okay, Shortround, no."

Skye stopped laughing but reached for Casey—Casey recoiled.

"Uppie," Skye said.

Liz gave her a smug grin and made the introductions. "Skye. This is Casey."

Casey gave Skye a weak smile. What in the hell is going on? she thought.

"Cafey. Uppie…peas," Skye begged.

"Oh, all right. C'mon," she grumbled and took the girl, who immediately hugged her around the neck. She turned bright red and avoided Liz's smile.

Casey sat at the kitchen table bouncing Skye on her knee as she watched Liz prepare dinner.

"Why kids?" Casey asked out of the blue.

Liz gave her a curious look, then smiled and shrugged. "I love children. Just because I'm gay doesn't change my love for them."

"Yes, but look at what's happened."

"What? My partner died. It's the same as if a husband died or a wife. Love is love, Casey, uh, Ms. Bennett."

"You can call me Casey." Still Casey thought it was irresponsible of this woman and Julie.

"If you keep bouncing her, she's going to throw up again," Liz warned as she chopped the tomatoes.

Casey lifted Skye over her head and looked up. "Nah, Shortround wouldn't do that twice..." she started and stopped as the belch came.

Liz winced and took Skye as Casey angrily headed toward the bedroom. "I'll run out of T-shirts at this rate."

Dinner was an adventure. After making the statement, "How hard can it be?" Casey tried her hand at helping the little humanoid, and the spaghetti wound up on the floor, in her water glass, and all over Casey's wristwatch. In the meantime, her dinner was untouched; so much for her ego.

"Please, I can't watch anymore." Liz took the spoon from Casey, who sat back and watched this pregnant woman not only feed her daughter, but manage to eat her own meal and keep the table and the surrounding area spaghetti-free.

Casey was grudgingly impressed. She watched Liz while she laughed and fed her daughter. "How old are you if you don't mind?" She sipped her wine.

"Twenty-nine. How old are you?"

"Forty. Did you work in New Mexico?" She continued eating. The pasta was delicious as was the salad and garlic bread. I guess some people do eat at home, she thought.

"No. Well, that's not exactly true. I worked part time. It paid well enough for me to contribute. A neighbor watched Skye in the afternoon..." Liz's voice trailed off. All at once, she looked exhausted. Then she jumped and held her stomach.

Casey bolted up and in one stride was next to her. "This can't be it. You're not due till December," she said in a panic.

Liz grimaced and waited for the pang to subside. "She's just a little active, that's all. Casey, please relax. We've got another four months."

Casey's heart was somewhere on the floor. She would never last four months.

After dinner, Casey watched Liz as she cleared the table. "Let me do that," she said, taking the dish out of Liz's hand. "Why, um, why don't you go sit down?"

"If you're sure," Liz said, relinquishing the fork and knife.

"I can wash a dish, for chrissakes," Casey said and walked to the sink.

"I didn't mean…"

Casey heard her sigh heavily as she left the kitchen. Damn it, she thought. This is not going to work. She looked around for the dish soap, which was nowhere to be found. She then opened the cabinet and there it was. Casey grimaced when she realized it hadn't been used yet. All at once, she felt inadequate in her own home. "This will not work," she whispered.

When she finished, she put the coffee on, grateful Liz put it on the list; she put the last of the pots and pans away. She felt a tug on her shorts and looked down to see Skye standing there. "Uppie…" she said and reached way up.

"Look, Shortround, I can't be picking you up all the time," she said in a gruff voice.

"Uppie…peas!" Skye begged.

"Will you scram?" she asked. "Hey, you're a pest." She then dropped the pot on the floor. "Damn it."

"Casey!" Liz's voice called out.

Casey winced and looked down while Skye giggled. "See what ya did? Now bugger off."

Liz looked up when Casey walked into the living room. "Don't you have any control over this dwarf?"

Attached to her leg was Skye, her arms and legs wrapped around tightly as she giggled and held on for dear life. Casey dragged her burden into the living room.

"She is not a dwarf, and if you had any sensitivity, you would understand that perhaps she misses Julie. Or maybe, and for the life of me I do not know why, she likes you." Liz winced again.

Casey got nervous and started to walk over, then picked up Skye like a sack of potatoes and held her around the waist, tucked under her arm. Skye laughed as her arms and legs flopped about as Casey quickly went to Liz.

"Okay, that's two. Is that normal?" She knelt down, depositing Skye on the floor.

Liz nodded emphatically. "Yes, really. She's just active,

probably all the yelling."

"I-I wasn't yelling," Casey countered with a frown.

"No. I was. I'm sorry. I'm just irritable," she said through clenched teeth.

"Mama mad," Skye said, looking up at Casey.

"No, sweet pea. Mommy's not angry." Liz sighed tiredly.

Casey leaned back, then it struck her. "How about some of that ice cream you had me buy?"

Liz's eyes lit up and she nodded happily. Casey turned and walked into the kitchen. "I help Cafey," her shadow said, waddling behind.

The three of them sat on the front porch eating ice cream. Casey realized that she had never really liked ice cream. What a ridiculous thing to think of. She was missing what Liz was saying.

"Sorry. What?" Casey asked as she looked up. Liz Kennedy was a very attractive young woman. Her blue eyes sparkled against the glow of the citronella candle on the table as she fed Skye ice cream out of her bowl.

Casey shook her head in wonderment as she looked around. Citronella, instead of a roaring fire; ice cream instead of a martini. Liz Kennedy instead of…

"I asked if you were involved with anyone," Liz repeated absently as she laughed at her daughter.

"Oh. No, I'm—"

"Single? I got the impression from Julie you were good with the ladies," Liz said and turned red.

Casey's green eyes danced wickedly. "She was right. I am, and I enjoy the company of a couple women. I enjoy my freedom," she added, and for the first time in her life, she felt like she was defending herself. She did not like that feeling at all. Her grandmother's smirking face flashed through her mind.

"Hmm." Liz grunted as she fed Skye.

"What's that supposed to mean?" Casey was getting irritated as she took a spoonful of ice cream.

"You just haven't met the right one yet."

"Christ, now you sound like my grandmother," she countered sarcastically, "and Roger." She saw the questioning look on Liz's face. "My lawyer and sometime friend."

"I see. He likes to act as your conscience?"

"Yes, it's quite annoying."

Liz smiled and looked at the near full moon rising over the tree line. "I see why you like it up here." She sighed pensively as she and Skye rocked on the porch swing.

Skye then struggled off the swing and waddled up to Casey, who was leaning against the porch railing. She looked down and frowned. "What? Uppie again?" she asked gruffly and Skye wrinkled her nose.

"'Gen...'" She reached up her hands.

In one effortless movement, Casey grumbled and lifted her into her arms. Skye wrapped her arms around her neck and laid her head on her shoulder, playing with her necklace.

Liz grinned while Casey continued frowning but said nothing. "She likes you. I guess you do have a way with the ladies, Ms. Bennett." She let out a groan, struggling again to get up. Casey reached over, offered her hand, and helped her to her feet.

"In about three months, it's not going to be that easy," Liz said with a groan. "C'mon, Skye. Time for beddy-bye."

Skye clung to Casey's neck and Casey pushed the child back. "Go on now, Shortround, listen to your mom," she found herself saying.

"Say night-night to Casey, sweet pea," Liz whispered as she took the child.

"Ni-ni," Skye said, reaching back to kiss Casey on the cheek.

Even in the darkness, Liz saw the color rise in Casey's face.

"G'night, Shortround," she said awkwardly and grinned as the girl waved.

Liz walked in; she turned and smiled, "I think I may join her. Ni-ni, Cafey."

Casey grinned sarcastically. "You're hysterical. Good night." She watched Liz disappear into the cabin. Skye waved once more and Casey raised her hand, then quickly scratched her head.

Nature called for poor Liz. She struggled getting out of bed and made her way to the bathroom. "She's sleeping right on my bladder." Liz yawned loudly.

As she walked back, she thought she would check on the other child in the living room.

Casey lay on the couch, her feet over the end. "God, she's tall," Liz whispered as she picked up the sheet that had fallen on the floor and lightly covered her. She watched Casey as she slept and resisted the urge to brush the thick lock of hair off her brow.

Casey Bennett was doing a kind thing—probably out of guilt. Liz suspected her lawyer probably had a good deal to do with it. Well, for whatever reason, Liz was grateful. Once she had the baby, she would regroup, get a job and a babysitter, and get her life and her family going.

All at once, Julie's face flashed through her mind. Julie may not have been very good at responsibility, but she was very good at taking care of her in the bedroom. However, Julie had a hard time with intimacy, which had nothing to do with their sex life. It was the closeness that Liz always wanted but never truly got from Julie. She longed for someone to hold her in the quiet of night not saying much, just listening to another heartbeat.

Liz took a deep breath. And sometimes, she just plain missed sex. Then she looked down at the slumbering playgirl.

I'm not that desperate.

Chapter 5

Something was poking her face. Casey grumbled in her sleep and swatted with her hand. Then she heard a giggle and her eyes flew open. There stood a mass of blond curls framing a cute sleepy face.

"I hungy," the girl whispered, nose to nose.

"Go back to bed," Casey countered in the same voice.

Skye frowned and pulled her arm. "Peas," she pleaded and tugged.

Casey growled and lifted the child onto her stomach. "Please doesn't always work, Shortround," Casey tried to explain. Skye yawned, then rubbed her eyes.

"See, you're still pooped. Go back to bed," she urged and the girl fell on top of her chest. "No. C'mon, Shortround," she said and looked down. Skye had her thumb in her mouth and her eyes closed.

"Shit," Casey grumbled and yawned. She reached up and gently pulled the thumb out. Casey knew nothing about being a mother, but thumb-sucking she knew.

Instinctively, she gently shifted the little pain in the ass to the inside of the couch. That is all I need, she thought—a trip to the emergency room.

Liz woke in a panic. She looked over and Skye was gone. She struggled into her robe, ran down the hall, and stopped short. She was shocked, but she smiled.

Stretched out on the couch was Casey's long frame and Skye nestled against her chest, Casey's arm protectively around her. Both children were sound asleep, and Liz tried not to think of how natural this sight was. Casey was breathing deeply with a slight smile on her face. Or did Liz hope it was a smile?

Well, as least she could take a shower in peace...and alone. While she loved her daughter, she loved any minute she could have to herself. She quickly grabbed her robe and headed for the shower.

"Ooh, I love this." She sighed as the warm water soothed her body. Liz instinctively looked down, fully expecting to see Skye standing in the shower with her.

While she washed her hair, she laughed, remembering Skye's innocent anatomy questions during their communal showering. Liz obediently answered all questions from the three-year-old regarding breasts, and Skye was satisfied when Liz told her that her tummy was big because that's where her new brother or sister was growing. However, she was dumbfounded when Skye asked about her "fur" between her legs. Liz tried to explain the concept of pubic hair and adolescence all the while the water was getting cold. She remembered the look of confusion on her daughter's face. "Mama, it fur," Skye had insisted.

Liz relented, "You're right, sweet pea."

"Oh, my little Skye." Liz now laughed heartily as she rinsed her hair.

She stood in the shower for a moment or two longer, reveling in the peace and quiet. She shut off the warm spray and heard the knock at the door.

"Mama, potty."

Liz laughed and slipped into her robe and opened the door. There stood Skye, legs crossed and sleepy. "Good morning, sweet pea. You're such a good girl. Did—"

Skye waddled past her and lifted the seat.

Casey smelled coffee. She smiled in her sleep, then felt the poking again. She opened one eye to see the sleepy mass of curls pulling at her eyelid.

"Geh up," the midget insisted.

"Did you go potty?" Casey mumbled.

"Hmm. Geh up," Skye insisted.

"No, you get up," Casey countered, then tickled Skye, who giggled and let out that contagious childlike laugh that came from pure innocence. Casey laughed along.

She looked up to see Liz standing there, hands on her hips and smirking. "Good morning, Cafey," she said dryly.

Casey cleared her throat and sat up. Skye was still giggling as she climbed on her back. "Get this off me, will you?" she complained, and as she stood, Skye clung to her neck and wrapped her feet around her waist as much as she could.

"I feel like Quasimodo. Shit."

"Thit," Skye repeated, and Liz glared at Casey, who turned red.

Liz pulled Skye off Casey's back and headed for the kitchen. "Breakfast will be ready in a few minutes."

Casey frowned deeply, again feeling awkward in her own home.

Liz saw the look on her face and came back. "I-I'm sorry. I just thought I'd make breakfast for us. Skye has to eat."

Casey ran her hand through her hair and waved her off. "I'm just not used to having anyone here that's less than five feet tall," she said honestly. Liz blushed and hid her grin.

They both looked at each other for a moment; the banging of silverware broke the silence.

"Shortround sounds like she's hungry," Casey said.

Liz didn't know if she was joking or making fun as she watched her walk down the hall. She turned back into the kitchen. "Hungry, sweetie? How about some eggs?"

Casey stepped into the shower and let out a loud yelp. There was no hot water. It was the quickest shower she had ever taken. As she ran the towel over her body, an image of Liz doing the same earlier was overpowering. She shook her head, trying to erase the picture of Liz.

"Good grief, Bennett, the woman is pregnant," Casey scolded

herself as she dried off.

Liz and Skye looked up when Casey came into the kitchen wearing a long terrycloth robe.

"I'm going for a swim. I'll be right back."

"I fim," Skye said quickly and tried to get down. Liz reached over and put her back in her seat. "Mama, I fim..." The girl struggled against her mother, who glanced up at Casey.

Casey bit her lip in an effort, Liz was sure, not to laugh. "She's a feisty little critter."

Liz tried to control her and Casey walked up to Skye and looked down. Skye peered way up.

"Tell ya what, Shortround. You eat breakfast, then I'll take you swimming, deal?" She stuck out her hand. Skye giggled and Casey took her little hand and shook. "Deal?" she asked again.

"Dea..." Skye giggled as Casey shook.

"But you have to eat all your breakfast," Casey said firmly as she shook the hand vigorously and let go.

Casey glanced down at Liz, who saw the smug look of superiority. Without a word, but still a smirk, Casey walked out.

Liz glared at the tall retreating figure and back at her daughter. Liz gave a stern look into the innocent blue eyes.

"Mama angwee?"

Liz then laughed and kissed her daughter. "No. Mommy's not angry. Cafey just has a way with women. The arrogant... Probably thinks she's up for Mother of the Year," she grumbled as she fed her daughter.

Liz sat on the deck and watched. "Oh, Cafey..." she offered smugly as Skye dashed out of Casey's grasp and headed for the beach.

"Hey!" Casey yelled as Skye giggled and once again ran around her.

It was a sight: The tall lanky woman chasing a—what had Casey called her? Ah, yes, a dwarf. The dwarf was winning.

"Please don't kill my daughter, Ms. Bennett," Liz called from the porch as she sipped her iced tea in the shade.

Casey glared up at her and quickly looked back. Skye was

headed right for the water, laughing. Casey made a dash for her and in two long strides, she scooped her up, holding her by the back of her swimsuit.

Arms and legs dangling, the little sack of potatoes cried angrily, "I fim..."

From the porch, Liz saw Casey's devilish grin. "Don't you dare, Casey Bennett."

Casey let out a dejected groan and walked into the water, holding Skye.

For the next hour, they played and laughed on the beach. Casey put Skye on a rubber raft and pulled her around in the shallow water. Of course, Skye climbed off and Casey struggled to keep the laughing child from drowning.

"Cafey," Skye said, pointing in the water.

In the shallow water, a school of fish gathered by a boulder. "Fith."

Casey laughed. "Yep, little fish. When they grow up to be big ones, I'll show you how to catch them."

"I want fith." Skye put her hand in the water and splashed, laughing as the fish swam in all directions.

Liz watched as Skye and Casey headed up the beach; playtime was over. It was then Liz noticed how attractive Casey Bennett was. All legs, Liz mused. Casey had a fit figure. She wore a modest one-piece bathing suit that Liz instinctively knew she wore for her and Skye's benefit. "Probably swims naked with the ladies. All the single un-pregnant ones," she added gloomily.

Skye was full of sand, as was Casey. "Your daughter knows no fear," she said as she walked up on the deck with Skye behind her. Casey grabbed a towel. "I have sand in places I didn't know I had places."

Skye ran to her mother. "Mama, I fim. I see fith," she cried out.

Liz wrapped a towel around her, giving her a big hug. "I saw you. I'm so proud of you, you did great, sweet pea," she said affectionately. "Do you like the fish?"

Skye nodded emphatically. Casey watched as Liz laughed and whispered something in Skye's ear. Skye nodded and waddled up to Casey.

"Yes?" Casey asked, grinning.

"Thank you, Cafey," the girl whispered.

Casey turned bright red, completely unaccustomed to this. She coughed and avoided Liz. "You're welcome, Shortround."

Skye reached for Casey, who bent down to her. The little snot kissed her right on the lips, her hands patted her cheeks.

Later in the evening, with Skye in bed, Liz and Casey sat out on the deck in the warm summer night.

"I've got to go to Chicago for a few days. I have the last of the compositions done and I'll be in the studio. I hope I won't be gone for too long. I've asked Marge to stop by. She lives a quarter mile or so around the lake. Just in case. I'll be at my apartment. The number is by the phone, as well as my cell phone, in case you need anything. Y-you can call anytime," she finished awkwardly.

Liz smiled as she watched her. "Thank you. I don't want to disrupt your life any more than I already have. I truly appreciate all you've done so far," she said in a quiet voice.

"Well, I know I was aggravated and surly. I apologize. I'm not used to, well, I've been on my own and…" She stopped, knowing she sounded like an idiot.

"I know. This is a change for both of us, Casey. I didn't want to leave New Mexico. I didn't want to admit I couldn't do this on my own. However, I have Skye, and in three months or so… Well, sometimes pride takes a backseat. I just want to do the best for us," she said and gently ran her hand over her stomach.

Casey gave her a curious look. "What does it feel like?"

Liz looked up and raised an eyebrow. "Well, it's unnerving to know that a little human is growing inside you. Sometimes I feel like that movie *Alien*," she said. When Casey laughed openly, Liz thought how nice her laughter sounded. It changed Casey's demeanor, making her even more appealing. Liz quickly dismissed her thoughts and continued, "But it's a miracle, and at first, honestly? There was a part of me that hoped the insemination wouldn't work."

"Why?" Casey leaned forward.

"Because right after we had it done, we found out about Julie's cancer. I hate to sound selfish, but after the shock of the news, my next thought was of this pregnancy."

There was a moment of silence and Liz looked at Casey, trying to gauge what she was thinking. She was frowning while she stared out into the darkness. Liz wasn't sure what to say next.

"Had Julie gone to the doctor previously? I can't imagine she wouldn't know or you couldn't see any changes in her."

The suspicious tone was unmistakable; Liz bristled with anger once again. She didn't know if it was her hormones or just the arrogance of this woman.

"Julie was always a healthy woman. Perhaps you remember that."

Casey shot Liz a look; Liz returned it with a challenging glance. "I remember Julie very well. And yes, she was a very fit woman."

"Well, I'm not a doctor, but the type of cancer she had was…" Liz stopped. All at once, she didn't want to have this conversation. She gently ran her hand over her belly, trying to calm the anger that was teeming inside. She took deep breaths and slowly exhaled. When she looked at Casey, she saw the confused look.

"My doctor in New Mexico advised deep calming breaths when I feel the onset of stress."

Casey, still frowning, nodded. "Stress that you think I'm causing?"

Liz blinked several times. "No. This situation alone is stressful. You've done nothing to add to it. Although, I wish you'd get that accusatory tone out of your voice." Liz felt her voice rise with each word.

"I'm not accusing anyone," Casey said. She started to say something, then stopped.

"Look, I'm sorry we're in this situation. Trust me, I wish I had somewhere to go. I probably should have stayed in Albuquerque." Once again, she took deep breaths.

"It's a little late for that now," Casey said, running her hand over her face in an exasperated gesture. "I don't understand…"

Liz cocked her head and waited; when Casey didn't continue,

she said as calmly as she could, "What don't you understand?"

"Nothing."

"Casey, this is going to be a long four months if we can't at least be honest with each other. Please tell me what's on your mind."

"I-I...I suppose it's just all bad timing. The insemination, then finding out Julie has a cancer raging through her."

Liz gave her a skeptical look. "Somehow, I think there's more on your mind than you're telling me." She stopped and watched the moonlight sparkling on the lake. "I'm grateful for your help. I'm grateful for my family's sake."

She turned and opened the screen door. Glancing back, she saw Casey still frowning; she shook her head. "If you ever decide to tell me what's on your mind, I'll listen. I know we're unlikely companions for these next few months. I hope we can at least be civil to each other."

Liz didn't wait for, nor did she hear, Casey's reply as she walked into the dark living room and made her way to the bedroom. She fought the tears of anger and frustration as she quietly closed the door.

Chapter 6

The next morning, Liz sat in the kitchen watching Skye make a mess of her pancakes as Casey stood by the piano, examining her sheet music. They had barely said good morning to each other.

"So I'll call you."

"Do you have to leave so early?" Liz asked as she wiped Skye's mouth, hands, elbows, and dimpled knees. How she got maple syrup there, Liz did not know.

"Well, I've got to meet with Niles. He's at the studio at four. Then I've got a....dinner engagement. Tomorrow, I'll be at the studio all day and the next," she said, sliding the sheets into her leather briefcase.

Liz noticed Skye was watching Casey. When she saw Casey pick up her keys, Skye tried to get off the chair. "I go Cafey."

Liz once again struggled with her. "No, sweet pea. Casey has to go to work," Liz explained, and all of the sudden, Skye's mouth drooped, her bottom lip quivering.

Casey watched Skye, not knowing what to do. "It's fine, Casey. Just go," Liz said with a smile.

"I go," Skye whimpered. She put her head down and cried.

Casey put down her briefcase and winced. She gave a pleading look to Liz. Skye was not hysterical or screaming; she was just plain sad. Casey walked up to the chair and knelt down.

"Hey, Shortround," she said. Liz smiled affectionately at Casey's tenderness with her child.

"No, I go too..." Skye said with her head on the table.

Casey grimaced and awkwardly put her hand on the soft blond curls, smoothing them back. "Please, don't be sad. I'll be right back. Then we'll go swimming and eat hot dogs."

Skye raised her head, her rosy cheeks flushed with tears that were streaming down her face. Liz saw Casey's shocked look and thought for sure she saw a tear welling in her green eyes.

"Pomise?" Skye sniffed.

"Sure I do. I'll even bring you a present," Casey said, ignoring Liz as she shook her head. "Deal?" She stuck out her hand.

Skye giggled, put her little hand in Casey's big one, and shook.

"Dea..." She giggled and grabbed Casey around her neck.

"Okay, you're strangling me now," Casey said with embarrassment as Skye pulled back.

"Kiss me," she said and Casey blinked. "Peas."

Casey gave her a wary grin. "Just like all the women in my life." She leaned down and dropped a kiss on her cheek. "Now be good for Mommy," she said, trying to sound firm while avoiding Liz's grin.

"Have a safe trip," Liz said and ran her fingers through her hair. She looked up into Casey's eyes.

"Thanks," she said. "Look. I'm sorry about last night. This is just all so bizarre and I'm trying to get a handle on it, I guess."

Liz heard the uncertainty in her voice, and still, she felt there was something on Casey's mind. "It's an adjustment for all of us, Casey."

"Mama, give Cafey a kiss bye," Skye said from her chair.

Liz's eyes widened; she felt the color rush to her face. Letting out a nervous laugh, she stepped away from Casey and sat next to Skye. "Finish your breakfast."

"I all done, Mama."

Liz looked down at the empty plate in front of her daughter; she couldn't even look at Casey. However, she heard her laughter as Casey walked out.

"Goodbye, ladies," she called over her shoulder. "See you in a few days. Don't burn the cabin down."

When she heard the front door close, Liz hid her face in her trembling hands. "Good Lord."

Casey sat in the studio with the headphones on listening to the recording. She shook her head angrily. "No, no, no!" She growled and took off the headphones. "Niles, get in here, peas," she said and stopped. "Please."

Niles ran his fingers through this blond hair as he walked in and waited. "The second refrain, am I right?"

"Yes. It's way too fast, and the brass is too loud. Can we get them back for another take?"

"Sure, they're scheduled for tomorrow morning. You have them all day. The producers want this done yesterday," he warned.

"I know." She looked at her watch. It was four thirty. By now, Skye would be up from her nap. All of the sudden, she wanted to be there and take the little dwarf fimming. She laughed out loud.

Niles gave her a wary look. "Are you all right? Usually when the conductor messes up this badly, you're ballistic," he said, watching her.

"I just had a good thought."

"You did?"

Casey raised an eyebrow at the incredulous tone. Niles folded his arms across his chest and leaned against the desk. "What's the good thought?"

Liz Kennedy's blue eyes flashed through her mind. She felt her heartbeat race for a moment.

"What in the world are you thinking about? You're all flushed," Niles said. "And if you don't tell me, I'll—"

"See you in the morning."

"Got a hot date?"

Casey waved as she walked out the door. "Good night, Niles," she said and slammed the door.

"God, I've missed you," Suzette said as she walked into the tenth-floor apartment. She wrapped her arms around Casey's neck and kissed her deeply. "Mmm. You taste good," she murmured into Casey's mouth.

"It's my toothpaste," Casey said, her green eyes dancing. "C'mon in," she said and turned.

Suzette pulled her back and quickly started unbuttoning her shirt. Casey raised an eyebrow as she allowed Suzette to disrobe her. "Or we can have sex right in the foyer."

They eventually made it to the bedroom. With a trail of clothes, at least they would be able to find their way back to the front door. Both flopped down naked on the bed. Suzette really missed Casey. She ravaged her, kissing up and down Casey's neck pinning her beneath her.

"I should go up north more often." Casey gasped as Suzette lay between her legs.

Suzette lowered her head and kissed Casey's breast. Her tongue slowly flicking, encircling the aching nipple, she then took it into her mouth and roughly sucked as her other hand wandered down the length of her torso.

Without a word, Suzette made up for lost time...

Much later, they lay in bed sipping champagne. "You should stay in Chicago. There is so much more to do here. Your Northwoods are so woodsy," Suzette pointed out as Casey lay on her side watching her. "Or you should take me more often."

"I like woodsy and my solitude," Casey murmured and took a drink of champagne. Before swallowing, she engulfed Suzette's breast and sensually licked the bubbly spirits away. "The only way to drink champagne," Casey admitted and lowered her head.

Once again, the phone rang.

"Didn't this happen last time?" Casey grumbled and Suzette reached for it. "Don't you dare."

"It might be Jeffrey," Suzette said, getting to the phone before Casey.

"Hello?" Suzette sighed as Casey nibbled at her shoulder. "Yes, she is. Who's calling?" She stopped and gave Casey a heated look. "It's a Liz Kennedy." Suzette smiled sweetly, then tossed the phone at her.

Casey juggled it like a hot potato and glared at Suzette. "Liz?

Is everything all right? Is Shortround okay?"

"Y-yes. Everything is fine. I know I'm interrupting, but it's only six and I, well, I didn't think. Well, I thought it would be okay to call."

"It's fine. What's the matter?" Out of the corner of her eye, Casey caught Suzette downing a glass of champagne.

"I feel so stupid. It's raining and the lights went out. I called Marge, but there's no answer."

"Shit, I'm sorry. Look in the kitchen, there's a breaker box."

There was silence for a moment when Liz replied, "Okay, got it."

"Flip the breaker on." Another moment passed before Casey asked, "Did it work?"

"No, I flipped the switch and nothing happened."

"Okay, it's not unusual. It must be raining hard."

"Like cats and dogs."

Casey sat up on the edge of the bed. She could hear the fear in Liz's voice. "Okay, I'm coming back."

"No, don't. God, I feel like an idiot calling you in the first place," Liz said quickly. "Wait. Hold on."

"Liz?" Casey heard nothing. She jumped up and paced, naked by the bed. Suzette was on her second glass of champagne as she watched. "Liz? Damn it."

Now all sorts of ugly scenarios flashed through her mind as she heard Skye crying in the background. "I knew I shouldn't have left them." Her heart raced as she waited.

"Casey?" Liz asked through the crackling phone line.

"Sweetie, what's going on?"

"It's okay. Marge is here. I just don't know where everything is here. We're fine, please go back—" She stopped and Casey blushed. "We're fine. I'm so sorry I bothered you."

"You call me. I don't care what time," Casey said firmly. "Understand?"

"Y-yes, I will, thanks, Casey, bye. Oh, wait, Skye wants to talk to you. Is that okay?"

"Sure, put her on." Casey instantly grinned. She looked at Suzette, who raised her champagne glass. Casey turned away.

"Cafey, light go out. I scared," Skye whispered. "Mama scared. Mama say damn."

Casey laughed out loud. "Don't be scared, Shortround. The lights will come back on when it stops raining. You take care of Mommy, okay?"

"'Kay. Come home," Skye pleaded. "Peas."

"I-I will, Shortround. You be good for me?"

"'Kay."

"Let me talk to Mommy, sweetie," Casey said. She wanted to say "I love you." Why didn't she? Why would she? she asked herself. What right does she have to even—

"Casey, again I'm sorry." Liz's voice was full of concern.

"Don't be, it's fine."

There was silence for an instant. Casey's mouth went dry; she swallowed once but said nothing.

"Skye misses you."

Casey heard the softness in Liz's voice and her heart continued to race. "That's because she wants a present." Both laughed, easing the tension between them.

"You know my daughter too well, Ms. Bennett," Liz said, still chuckling. "Well, bye. We'll see you in a few days?"

"Yes, I'll be home soon. G'bye, Liz."

Casey hung up the phone and looked at it for a moment. She then looked up to see Suzette holding an empty bottle of champagne. "Suzette, my pet. Put that down," Casey said slowly.

"I should object," Suzette sighed as Casey crawled back onto the bed, taking the champagne bottle out of her hand.

"That would be most objectionable," Casey assured her as she nibbled her way down the length of her torso. She kissed the soft dark curls as Suzette parted her legs, letting out a deep groan as Casey nestled herself between her legs.

She kissed her inner thigh, nipping up and down, eliciting small gasps from Suzette, who was holding onto the headboard for dear life murmuring encouraging words as Casey leaned in and parted the thick folds with her tongue, easily gliding up and down. Suddenly, Liz Kennedy's face flashed through her mind and she stopped in mid-glide. She blinked a few times, then shook her head.

Suzette whimpered, "Don't stop."

Casey tried desperately to concentrate. Finally, Suzette moved quickly and Casey looked up, dumbfounded.

"That does it. I know your touch, Casey Bennett," she said evenly and started gathering her clothes.

Casey was still stupefied as she sat up and just watched.

"Why don't you go back up to the Northwoods and do whatever you have to do? Seduce her, sleep with her, but get it out of your system," she said, now more angrily. "We have no commitment, and that's the way I like it, truly. However," she said as she dressed. "I would like to think that when you're fucking me, you're at least thinking about me."

Casey's eyes widened in shock. "Wait, it's not like that. I mean, yes, her face flashed through my mind, but, Suzette, she's pregnant."

"What?" she bellowed, then gave her a sick look. "You're fantasizing about a pregnant woman?"

Casey rolled her eyes at Suzette's horrified tone. "It's not like that. She has a little girl."

"What?" Suzette exclaimed again and threw up her hands. "She's pregnant and has a kid? Are you sick?"

Now Casey was angry. "No," she said, trying to gain some credibility. "I am not sick. It's not what you're thinking. She's very attractive, but I-I'm not attracted to her."

Suzette rolled her eyes as she buttoned her blouse. "Casey Bennett, don't try to blow smoke up my ass. If you want to fuck her—"

"Don't talk like that about her."

Suzette raised an eyebrow. "You just made my point," she said, chuckling as she slipped on her shoes. "You need to think about this one, Case. This isn't your run-of-the-mill Casey Bennett fling."

As Suzette walked away, she turned back to Casey. "A pregnant woman with a kid. Is she gay?"

Casey nodded, trying to collect her thoughts. This was too much reality at one time.

"Well, that's a point in your favor," Suzette said, seeing the confused look on Casey's face. "I have never seen you confused or confounded. You look…" She stopped and struck a thoughtful pose. "Vulnerable," she said as if it were a vulgar word. "I'll see you tomorrow at rehearsal. Do not yell at me this time. Just because we're lovers doesn't mean you can pick on my playing."

Casey gave her an even look. "Just because you're sleeping with the composer doesn't mean you can play your cello like crap," she said seriously, her eyes challenging the irate cellist.

"You called her sweetie," Suzette said. Casey winced as Suzette stormed out, slamming the front door.

Casey sat on the bed and stared at nothing in particular. "Okay. Three days ago, I was carefree, having great sex with a gorgeous woman. My life was my own. Now I'm sitting here naked, alone, with a pregnant woman and her child in my cabin," she said, then shook her head. "I need a drink." She picked up the champagne bottle… It was empty.

She flounced back on the bed and stared at the ceiling. "I called her sweetie?"

Chapter 7

"She called me sweetie?" Liz put the phone down, ignoring the fluttering sensation in her stomach. The baby is active, she thought, though she heard the concern in Casey's voice once again.

Marge lit several lanterns. "This happens all the time up here, don't you worry. Now Casey told me to check up on you," she said. "You must be someone special because nobody, and I mean nobody, has ever stayed in this cabin for longer than an evening or at the most a raucous weekend," she said, still chuckling.

Liz laughed along, avoiding mental images of Casey Bennett and any other woman.

"She made me promise to look in on you," Marge said and looked at Liz's stomach. "When are you due?"

"December 3. I feel like it's tomorrow."

"Had three and I know what you mean." Marge looked at Skye, who was holding onto Liz's neck. "Well, aren't you the cutie? I can see what Casey likes in both of you," she said with a wink. "I've known Casey for ten years. She bought this property then and cleared most of it herself with a few friends. It took her almost eight years to complete this. She worked hard and she played hard. She's had the..." She stopped and turned red.

Liz laughed. "I'm aware of Ms. Bennett's reputation."

Marge gave her a curious look. "I like you. You'd be good for Casey. Settle her down."

61

"Well," Liz started, knowing she was blushing. "Casey is just helping me until the baby comes. When I'm able, I'll get a job and we'll all start our lives."

Marge hid her grin. "Is that why you're all flushed?"

Liz immediately put her hands to her cheeks. "Am I?" She laughed nervously. "I suppose the arrogant Ms. Bennett has that effect on many women. Well, Skye and I will soon be on our own once again. Right, sweet pea?"

"Right, Mama," Skye said with a supportive nod.

Rehearsal was agonizing as Casey listened to her composition the orchestra was playing. She closed her eyes, then groaned. She heard Niles do the same. "Niles, it's not me, is it? Can't you hear that?"

Niles winced and nodded. "I hate to say it."

Casey leaned forward and buried her head in her hands. "It's Suzette. She—"

"Stinks," Niles offered.

Casey raised her head and narrowed her eyes. "Niles, stinks is not a professional term."

"Sucks?"

"Infinitely better," Casey said. "Now let's get Jeffrey out of here before he commits suicide. We need to regroup."

Niles mumbled as she walked away, "We need another cellist."

Niles knew Casey realized she needed to make a decision. Jeffrey knew it, as well. They convened in the empty studio; Casey sat at the piano, absently plunking away at the keys.

"Casey, you're exhausted. You rewrote half the score just to keep her. It's not right and you know it," Niles said.

Casey stood and stretched. "I know. I've got to tell her."

"Take a few days off. I've stalled the producers. Actually, it's a good time for this. The director is at Betty Ford. It'll be two weeks, at least. Go up north and relax. Come back with a clear head." Niles patted her shoulder.

Jeffrey gathered his briefcase. "I don't envy your position, Casey. However, I do agree with Niles on this one. Good night."

Niles waved goodbye as he watched Casey, who nodded sadly in Jeffrey's direction. Casey Bennett could be a very aggravating woman, he thought. It was her creativity, he figured, that made her so arrogant and a pain in the ass. However, she was a good woman. She was kind and generous, though she never let anyone know it.

All week, she had been talking to some woman. Every time she got the call, it transformed her face completely. He never saw Casey Bennett like this before. Usually, she was all about control, and when she worked, she was cold steel. Nothing got in her way and nothing distracted her. However, when she got those calls, she became quiet and well, female, Niles hated to say. Though he had to admit, Casey Bennett was a woman. Was she not?

"I'm sorry, what?" Niles asked, brought back to reality.

"I said, if you want to come up to my cabin, you're more than welcome."

Niles blinked stupidly. "Me? You're asking me? Me, to your cabin?" He reached over and felt her forehead. Casey glared down at him through angry green eyes but said nothing. "Well, I'll be. Maybe I will."

Casey grinned sheepishly. "You can bring Brian."

Niles put his hand to his heart. "Brian will be flabbergasted."

Casey grinned, running her finger under her nose in a seemingly awkward gesture.

"My God. Is Casey Bennett blushing?"

"Don't press your luck."

"Okeedokie," he replied quickly and threw his hands up. "So do I get to meet the one who's been putting you in this generous mood?"

Casey frowned. "There is no one. I just thought you've never seen my cabin. It would be a good break for all of us."

"Then who have you been talking to for the past couple days?" He sat next to her at the piano and placed his fingers on the keys. "I wish I knew how to play this thing. You make it look so easy."

Casey laughed and started playing. Niles moved to give her room. He said nothing as he watched her smiling face while her fingers elegantly danced across the keys.

"Now," he said. "Answer my question."

"Do you remember Julie Bridges?"

"Yes, your ex who wanted kids."

Casey nodded as she played. "She died a few weeks ago, cancer."

"I'm so sorry."

"Thanks. She left behind a partner who's pregnant with their second child."

"Good Lord," Niles exclaimed. "Second?"

He noticed Casey's smile then. "Yeah. They have a three-year-old, or four. I'm not sure. Her name is Skye, and she's full of life and has the devil in her blue eyes."

Niles leaned away from her and grinned, as well. "Skye? She sounds adorable. How do you know she has blue eyes?"

Casey gave him a side glance before answering. "Apparently, Julie's partner, Liz Kennedy, is five months pregnant and now finds herself in a financial pickle. Julie wrote a letter to me before she died asking me to help Liz and her family until she has the baby." She shrugged and continued playing.

"So you offered your cabin to them. That was very thoughtful of you."

"I know, how unlike me, right?"

Niles raised an eyebrow at the sour comment. "No, you're the only one who thinks that, sweetie. I happen to think you're a very caring woman. Now tell me what Liz Kennedy is like."

Casey snorted. "Now you sound like my grandmother."

"How is Meredith?"

"She's fine. She wants to meet Liz."

"So do I."

"I will tell you what I told her." She looked at Niles, who waited. "No."

Niles sported a smug grin. "So then why do you want me and Brian to come to your cabin? Will you hide this woman and her child?"

Casey felt the color rush to her cheeks. "No. I—"

"Admit it. You want us to meet this woman."

Casey looked to the heavens and shook her head.

Niles laughed openly and patted her shoulder. "Okay, okay. But you know I'm not going to let this go. Now tell me about her."

Casey stopped playing for a moment and stared at nothing in particular. Niles again waited; he was surprised when Casey smiled and shook her head. She started playing again, a different song, however. He raised an eyebrow when he heard the familiar chords.

"She's tough," Casey started. "And she's a good mother. She has a great relationship with her daughter and worries about their future. I can tell she hates being in this position, but I can't help thinking she put herself in it. I mean, why do this?" She looked at Niles, who shrugged. "Two kids and alone."

"Well, I'm sure this is not how she wants it to be."

"I know, but it smacks of irresponsibility. One kid? Sure. But two? What kind of expense is that, for chrissakes?"

"Why are you getting angry over someone else's decision?" He was quiet in his concern. "Is it because she's at your place?"

"No, well, at first, I was irritated. I guess if I was honest, I didn't want to have to think about Julie again."

"I know you cared very much for her."

"I did. But she made such a damned issued over having kids."

Niles noticed she stopped playing her unfinished composition. She took a deep breath and closed the lid on the keyboard. "Well, that's ancient history."

"That's being brought back to the present in the form of Liz Kennedy."

They sat in silence for a moment or two before Niles spoke. "Do you find yourself caring for this woman?"

Casey blinked and looked at him. "I…No. I, well…" Her voice trailed off and Niles once again saw the confusion in her green eyes.

"Can I make an observation?"

Casey grinned reluctantly. "Could I stop you?"

"I doubt it," Niles said. "Usually, when I ask you about the women in your life, you describe them by looks. One was a hottie.

One had gorgeous legs. One—"

"Get on with it."

"With Liz Kennedy, you described how she is and what she does. How she thinks. You never mentioned how she looks. Want to know why?"

"No."

"Because you view this woman as a person, not an object of your lust."

Again, silence. "Want to know what else—"

"No," Casey said quickly, then shrugged. "What?"

Niles laughed. "I think I'll save this for another time. You'll get the bends if we talk about this anymore."

"Well, thanks for talking anyway. I needed to bounce this off someone, or I'd go nuts," she said, running a hand through her hair.

"I'm flattered that the confident Casey Bennett wants my opinion."

"We both loved Julie," Casey whispered.

"I know. It's something you have to deal with now."

Casey nodded and stood, stretching her back.

"So what does she look like? You have my curiosity on edge," Niles said.

"She's got beautiful blue eyes and soft auburn hair. And when she smiles, it lights up her face, like she's genuinely happy." Casey shrugged.

"But that doesn't matter, does it?"

"Nope." Casey picked up the loose sheets of music and shuffled them. "Liz Kennedy might be younger than I am, but she definitely has more life experience." She stopped and laughed. Niles watched her and couldn't help himself, he laughed along with her. It had been quite some time since he had seen Casey laugh from her heart. It was captivating.

"Now you have to tell me what has you looking so happy," Niles said, leaning on the side of the piano. "Again."

Casey, still grinning, continued. "Liz's daughter, Skye. Her vocabulary is amazing. At least I think it is, but then I'm not around many three-year-olds. She's adorable, and Liz has done a remarkable job as her mother. They're wonderful to watch. You can see the love between them."

She stacked the sheet music and glanced at Niles. "You're gonna need Freud for what I'm about to say next, but she reminds me of my mother in this regard."

Niles laughed. "You don't need psychoanalysis for that. I met your mother, remember? She was a wonderful, kind woman who loved her daughter."

Casey said nothing; Niles could tell she fought the tears. "That Liz reminds you of her is just fine. And you haven't played that in ages."

Casey looked up and frowned deeply. "What was I playing? I don't even know."

"You were playing that composition you never finished."

"Really?" Casey asked with a laugh. "You're right. I haven't played that in a long time." She fell silent for a moment as she ran her fingers over the piano top. "I-I find myself in a very foreign world now, Niles."

Niles cocked his head and grinned. "Are you in love with this woman?"

"I-I have to say no. Only because I have no idea what really being in love is like. She was in love with Julie. I loved Julie. All of this is very strange, yet...I don't know, it seems so natural. Why?"

"Wow. This is completely foreign for you. Tell me something. Are you talking to me because Brian and I are married?"

Casey stole a glance and nodded. "I just thought you might shed some light."

"Well, I'd like to meet both of them. But not now," Niles said. "You need to really think about this and you need to do it on your own. Does this woman feel anything for you?"

"Probably not. Why am I thinking about this?"

Niles raised an eyebrow at the helpless tone in her voice. Casey Bennett was not a helpless woman. "Honey, this is the first time in a very long time that you are feeling anything remotely close to love. I mean, usually, you're all about control and sex and a good time and—"

"I get it, Niles," she said with a deep frown and sat on the piano bench. "I don't know anything of love, really."

Niles heard the dejected tone and sat next to her. "Before I met Brian, I was quite the playboy. Most gay men are until they meet the right man. Come to think of it, men in general are."

"So you met Brian and fell in love?"

"Yes, but I fought it tooth and nail. No one was going to pin me down even if he was the yummiest man I had ever met."

"Yummy?"

Niles nodded and flipped the top of the keyboard open and started playing "Chopsticks." "You need to go home and test the waters, but don't dive in too soon. These waters could turn into a tsunami."

Casey frowned and gave him a confused look. "There's a point somewhere in that mess of an analogy, isn't there?"

"I have no idea."

"Hmm. Tell me," she asked and started playing along. "What should I get a precocious three-year-old?"

"I have no idea."

The day before she was to go home, for some reason, Casey strolled the downtown streets of Chicago, absently looking into shop windows.

"What am I doing?" She shook her head, though she knew exactly what she was doing. It was the "why" that confounded her. She stopped at a storefront window and looked at the toys. Scratching the back of her neck, she chuckled and opened the door.

"May I help you?" a woman's voice called out.

Casey swallowed and nervously looked around. "I'm, uh, looking for a gift for a three-year-old."

"Boy or girl?"

Casey was absently looking at the shelves of stuffed animals. "Oh, uh, girl." She picked up a teddy bear, then replaced it.

"Birthday?" the clerk asked softy as she watched Casey.

"No, just a gift to—" Casey stopped, not knowing what to say. She gave the clerk a helpless shrug.

"To say you care?"

"Yeah. She's adorable and cute. Smart as a whip and—"

It was then she saw it. She grinned and picked up the stuffed animal. "I'll take this, please."

The woman laughed as Casey followed her up to the counter. "That was fast. You must know this girl very well."

Again, Casey shrugged and picked up the sunglasses. She laughed when she saw how small they were. "They actually make sunglasses for little kids?"

The woman laughed along. "You must not have any children or you would never have asked that." She held her hand out and gave Casey a questioning glance.

"Well, yeah, okay. I guess these, too." She picked up a baby rattle off the counter and gently shook it back and forth. Casey absently examined it and looked at the clerk. "This too maybe." Casey ran her finger under her nose and avoided the grinning clerk as she rang up her purchases.

She walked out with her bag, realizing she was grinning as she walked down the crowded street. She came to an abrupt stop in front of the maternity store and raised an eyebrow. Oh, this is not a good idea, Casey, she thought. However, she cringed and braced herself as she opened the door. She met a very pregnant woman walking in at the same time. Casey could not believe how big this woman's stomach was. She must have had an incredulous look on her face as she quickly backed out of the woman's way; the woman glared.

"Yes, I'm huge and I'm overdue," she said, sounding as if she were challenging Casey to comment at all.

Casey smiled weakly, held the door for her, and meekly followed the woman in. Once again, she had no idea what in the hell she was doing. Was she actually thinking of buying Liz something? And if so, what? "This is another bad idea, Casey," she mumbled. When she turned to leave, she bumped into the pregnant woman.

"Oh, shit, I'm sorry," Casey said, steadying her.

"We have to stop meeting like this," the woman said. Casey laughed nervously. "I'm assuming you're buying maternity clothes, though you don't look pregnant."

Casey blinked and stammered, "No, no, I'm not. A-a friend is. She's pregnant, gonna have a baby."

"Yes, that's what usually happens when you're pregnant."

Casey felt the blood drain from her face as she laughed. "Yeah, well…"

"Buying something for a friend?" the woman prodded. When Casey merely nodded, the woman grinned. "Come with me."

"Well, I…" Casey obediently followed this stranger through the small store. She stopped when they came to a chair. The woman, groaning loudly, eased into the chair. Casey offered her assistance, but the woman was already seated.

"Now how far along is she?"

"Uh…" In her mind, Casey was trying to do the long math. The women laughed. "When is she due?"

"December," Casey answered quickly. "First week or so."

"Hmm, okay. Dress or slacks?" the woman asked and held out her hand. "Karen."

Casey took the offering. "Casey. And slacks, I think." She had no clue.

"How much weight has she gained?"

"I-I have absolutely no idea."

The woman narrowed her eyes. "This will not be easy. See all these women?"

Casey looked around the store and for the first time, noticed how many pregnant women were in there. It was amazing. "Did they bus them in?"

Karen laughed out loud. "Pick one who is the same size as…"

"Liz," Casey replied, still looking at the women. She then saw a woman who was relatively the same size as Liz. "That woman." She pointed to the woman in question. "I feel like a jackass."

"Well, you should. Now knowing how much weight your partner had gained. You're supposed to take care of her."

"She, Liz is not my… I mean, she's staying with me and…" She stopped, knowing she sounded ridiculous.

"Take care of her," Karen said again. "Don't argue with a

pregnant woman. We're all on the edge and would kill for a pint of Häagen Dazs."

Casey swallowed and nodded. What am I doing? She thought and helplessly looked around.

Chapter 8

All the way home, Casey felt sick to her stomach when she thought of her conversation with Niles. Suzette's angry face flashed through her mind and she groaned openly. Actually, she had a good relationship with Suzette. There were no strings, no attachments, none of the trappings of emotions or jealousy. Well, this last incident showed Casey that Suzette could be the jealous type. However, Casey couldn't blame her. If the roles were reversed, Casey would be just as irritated. Or would she? What if Suzette was seeing someone else?

"I have no idea what the hell I'm doing anymore," Casey said as she drove. "I was happy and content, and now look at me."

She glanced down at the wrapped packages and rolled her eyes. "What am I doing?" She let out a helpless groan and watched the white lines on the highway zoom by. She couldn't help but compare it to her life as she knew it.

After she spent the trip arguing with herself, she pulled down her access road, smiling as the cabin and lake came into view. She actually missed all of it—the cabin, the lake, and her two houseguests.

She heard Skye's voice as she took her luggage out of the trunk.

"Cafey...Cafey!"

At the sound of Skye's happy voice, Casey grinned widely and whirled around. She saw the pint-sized human running toward her and trip. Skye let out a grunt as she dusted off her hands.

Casey ran up to her, and at the same time, Liz came running around the corner of the cabin. They both got to the groaning child at the same time. "I faw down."

"Are you okay, Shortround?" Casey asked.

Skye nodded happily as Liz dusted off her bottom. Liz looked up at Casey and smiled. "Hi," she said breathlessly.

"Hey," Casey said.

For a moment, neither woman said another word.

"Did you have a good trip? You look tired," Liz said, breaking the silence. "Well, Skye's happy to see you."

"It was productive." Casey scratched the back of her neck.

Liz cocked her head and smiled. "That's good."

"I have no idea," Casey said with a nervous laugh and picked up Skye. Casey threw her over her shoulder, and her pint-sized friend squealed with laughter.

"Did ya miss me?" Casey asked and glanced at Liz.

"Uh-huh. I miss you." Skye giggled as Casey tickled her on the way down. Casey held her on her hip as she picked up her duffel.

The three walked up onto the deck and Casey set Skye down with a groan.

"I go fimming," Skye said happily, then looked at her mother.

"You did? With Mommy?" Casey saw the stern motherly look from Liz as Skye looked down at the ground and put a finger in her mouth.

"Okay. What's going on?" Casey asked.

"Skye Marie?" Liz said in a firm voice.

Casey raised an eyebrow. Skye Marie? That cannot be good, she thought.

"I go fimming. By mineself," Skye mumbled in a small voice.

Casey's eyes widened in shock. "By yourself?" she squeaked out.

All at once, Casey had images of this little thing lying facedown in the lake. She knelt down, put a finger under Skye's chin, and lifted. "Sweetie, don't ever go down to the lake by yourself. Promise me," Casey said as her heart pounded in her ears. She looked up at Liz.

"You let her go down to the beach by herself?"

Liz's blue eyes blazed with anger. Casey saw the stupefied look and realized she said the wrong thing. Liz said nothing as her nostrils flared with anger. "I hope you had a good trip."

"Liz, I—"

"I was just starting lunch. C'mon, sweet pea, time to eat."

Skye looked as though she was going to cry and Casey smoothed back her blond curls. "Go with your mom, Shortround. I'll get washed up for lunch."

Liz took Skye by the hand and disappeared around the cabin. "Damn it," Casey said, angry with herself and her outburst. She picked up her bag and followed them into the cabin.

Lunch was silent and awkward. Liz was still seething as she cut Skye's sandwich and placed it in front of her. As if Skye could sense her mother's anger, she said, "Thank you."

When Liz placed the plate in front of Casey, Casey said, "Thank you, Mama."

Liz's head shot up; she glared into Casey's eyes for a moment. Casey tried not to laugh, but Skye did not. "She not your mama, Cafey."

Casey shrugged, and in the next minute, they all laughed, breaking the tension. She drank her iced tea and watched Skye, who was playing with her bologna that was covered with ketchup. She grimaced at what that combination would taste like.

"Cafey? We go fimming?"

Casey wiped her mouth on the napkin and looked at Liz. "I dunno, Shortround. It's up to your mother."

Liz glanced from Casey to her daughter. "Of course you can go swimming. But you must listen to Casey and do as she says. We don't want anything to happen to you. Casey will take you swimming whenever you want, but you can't go in the water by yourself. Understood?"

Skye's bottom lip quivered at the reprimand, but she nodded. Casey cleared her throat. "Now if I remember, I promised you a present."

Skye's eyes widened as she watched Casey walk into the living room and return with her duffel. She pulled out her sunglasses and put them on, avoiding Liz's curious look. Casey then pulled out a little pair, handing them to Skye. Her eyes widened as Casey helped her put them on.

"Mama. Like Cafey," she exclaimed and Casey laughed.

Liz shook her head. "This is what I need, a smaller version of Casey Bennett." She looked at the pair of them in sunglasses and had to laugh. "You look adorable, sweet pea."

"Like Cafey?"

Casey looked over her sunglasses at Liz, who gave her a smirk.

"Oh, more than Casey, sweetie," she assured her.

The air went out of Casey's ego balloon with a definite *pffft*... She grunted childishly and reached in her duffel and handed Skye the package. Skye looked up at her mother, who smiled and nodded. She then ripped at the wrapping.

"Mama... It a fith!" Skye screamed in delight as she adjusted her sunglasses. She held up a stuffed animal that had blue and orange fins and hugged it close.

Casey sported a superior grin. My idea, thank you very much, she thought.

"I see. It's beautiful, sweet pea, you can sleep with it," her mother said enthusiastically.

Skye nearly jumped out of her skin, she was so excited. She jumped out of her chair to give Casey a hug around the neck. "Thank you, Cafey."

"You're welcome, Shortround."

"Cafey. Go fimming now?" Skye asked, pulling at Casey's shorts.

"Your mom went to all the trouble to make this great sandwich, Shortround, and I'm gonna finish it."

"Skye, Casey's tired. How about a nice nap, then we'll all go down to the lake?"

Skye stamped her foot.

"Skye," Liz warned and the independent three-year-old frowned.

"I want fim," Skye said stubbornly.

Casey raised an eyebrow, trying not to laugh as she finished her sandwich. "Feisty little curly top," she mumbled into her iced tea glass.

Liz glared at her then and whispered, "Will you back me up on this?"

Casey nodded as she wiped her mouth on the napkin. She knitted her eyebrows together and looked down at Skye, who reflected her frown, looking way up at Casey.

"Nap..." Casey said.

Skye looked from one to the other. She then picked up her stuffed fish and pulled at Casey's hand. Casey laughed as she stood. Then Skye pulled at her mother's hand.

"Cafey tired, Mama tired," she said, pulling at both women.

Casey avoided Liz, hoping she couldn't tell she was blushing.

"Well, it's a big bed. We can put her in the middle, that way she won't fall out." Casey looked into her blue eyes.

"Y-you do look tired, and that couch really isn't long enough for you," Liz offered.

The whole time, Skye was looking up from one to the other. "Nappy," she insisted and pulled both women out of the kitchen.

Casey easily flung Skye onto the bed and set her in the middle. Liz lay down and sighed with relief as she stretched out.

When Liz struggled to sit up, trying to kick off her sandals, Casey walked around the bed. "Hold on, you turtle," she said as she reached for the sandals.

"I can do that, please—"

"Keep still," Casey whispered and slipped off the sandals, her fingers lightly running over the soft skin on her ankles.

Liz put her head back. "Thanks," she said. "I bet you miss your own bed. I'm sorry."

"Mama, read. Peas," Skye asked and cuddled to her side. The girl reached back for Casey and pulled her shirt. "Mama read to uth… "

Casey grinned and moved closer to the middle of the bed and cuddled Skye close. She settled in as Liz picked up the book of poetry.

"What shall I read?"

Skye took her thumb out of her mouth. "The kiss one, Mama," Skye urged and wrapped her arm around her mother's.

Liz looked down at her daughter and smiled. "The kissing one again? How about something else?"

Casey was still watching her and wondered what caused her face to instantly flush. Must be a pregnancy thing, Casey thought as she leaned on her elbow, propping her head on her hand. "The kissing one?"

Liz hid her smile and nodded as she thumbed through the pages. "How about the other book, sweet pea? Dr. Seuss or maybe—"

"No, Mama, peas, the kiss one," Skye pleaded.

Liz chuckled nervously. "Skye, I don't know why you like this poem so much, and Shelley no less."

Suddenly, Skye looked back at Casey. "Mama read."

"I know. I can't wait, Shortround," Casey said, meaning every word.

Liz avoided her look, cleared her throat, and started in a low lilting voice. "The fountain mingles with the river, and the river with the ocean. The winds of heaven mix forever, with a sweet emotion."

Liz's soothing voice lulled Casey so much she missed the next few lines. She watched Liz's face as she recited the end of the old poem.

"And the sunlight clasps the earth, and the moonbeams kiss the sea. What are all these kissings worth, if thou kiss not me?" Liz stopped and looked over at Casey. "What's the matter? Don't you like poetry?"

Casey blinked. Her mind was a thousand miles away; she did not dare try and figure out where. Casey knew she was gazing intently as Liz. "No, it was beautiful."

Skye was holding on to her mother's arm and hugging her fish. "'Gen, Mama," Skye said sleepily.

"Skye—"

"Yes, please. Again," Casey agreed in a low quiet voice. And again, their gazes locked for a moment before Liz started.

As she read, Skye fell sound asleep before she finished. Liz gently rested the book on her chest and looked down at her daughter. "This happens every time I read to her," she whispered. "It must be my voice."

"It's very soothing," Casey whispered.

"Oh, I don't know about that."

"Liz, I'm sorry about the swimming thing."

Liz shook her head. "I know. It's okay."

"No, it's not. I have no right to—"

"We can talk about it later. I don't want to wake her up."

Casey nodded, then yawned. Liz smiled and closed her eyes as Casey watched her fall asleep. In a moment or two, she was surprised to find her eyelids growing heavy; soon she followed mother and daughter into a peaceful sleep.

Once again, something poked Casey in the eye. She jerked and woke to see the sleepy little blonde once again nose to nose.

"Cafey. Go fimming," she whispered.

Casey stretched as she looked at her watch. It was two thirty. It was amazing; Casey couldn't remember a time when she took a nap. She shook her head at the idea, although she felt completely rested and rejuvenated. She looked over to see Liz lying on her side, facing them, still sound asleep. Casey watched her thinking how peaceful she looked. As she gazed at Liz, she couldn't ignore her racing heart. Liz was beautiful, even pregnant. Maybe it was because she *was* pregnant and happy. Motherhood was foreign to Casey, but Liz Kennedy took to it naturally. Liz was a good woman and Casey Bennett did not know many good women. She wondered what was to come of all this. What was Liz thinking?

"Cafey," Skye insisted in a whisper.

"Okay. Shh. Let's let Mommy sleep for a while longer. C'mon..." Casey whispered and slid off the big bed. She put her finger to her lips. So did Skye.

"Mama seeping?"

Casey nodded and picked Skye up, quietly walking out of the room.

"Geesh, Shortround, will ya hold still?" Casey struggled with Skye's bathing suit. Once on, Casey sat back sporting a confused look. "Why doesn't this look right?"

Skye grimaced and reached around, pulling at the bottom of her suit as she frowned. It was then that Casey noticed the tag... It was in the front.

"Shit," she said and Skye frowned.

"Not nice, Cafey," Skye scolded.

Casey was actually ashamed—a three-year-old shames Casey Bennett, she thought, shaking her head. "You're right. I'm sorry. Now let's get this suit on right before your mother gets up and thinks I'm a bigger idiot than she already does."

It was almost four o'clock when Liz woke to the soft sounds of the piano. Feeling rested, she struggled out of bed and slipped on her sandals, rolling her eyes as she remembered Casey slipping them off her big, fat, swollen feet. However, she enjoyed the warm feel of Casey's strong fingers on her feet. I bet she gives a great massage, Liz thought as she walked out into the hallway. She stood there unnoticed as Casey played the piano while holding Skye in her lap.

"Put your fingers here, here, and here," Casey said and pressed her fingers onto the keys playing the chord. "See? You're playing the piano."

Skye looked up. "'Gen, Cafey, peas."

"How can I resist those baby blues? They're like your mother's. Okay, again."

Liz stood there watching and curiously raised an eyebrow at the blue eyes comment. Julie never did these things with Skye. She was never home long enough, and when she was, she only played what she wanted. It was like having two children. Casey Bennett was right. Julie was in love with the idea of having children, not the reality. Liz only hoped having this child would change that. She guiltily ran her hand over her stomach. Was she wrong to want a child? She shook the question from her mind, instead thinking of Casey's attitude toward parenting. Casey Bennett let Julie go instead of having children. She was mature and intelligent; Casey knew it would end in disaster. Liz wondered what it would be like now if Julie were alive. Liz felt a pang of guilt waft over her again as she looked at Casey, smiling and laughing with her daughter.

Skye then saw her mother. "Mama, I paying pinano!" Skye cried out in delight.

"I hear you, it's beautiful, sweet pea." She glanced at Casey, who was smiling slightly as she watched her.

"You look rested," Casey said.

Liz knew the color was once again rising in her cheeks as she put a hand to her hair and walked up to the piano. "I look awful."

"You look just fine," she said as Skye reached up and grabbed Casey's cheeks, forcing her to look at her.

"'Gen, Cafey," Skye insisted. Casey raised a dark eyebrow. Skye watched her face. "Peas?"

"Sure, ya dwarf."

"Stop calling her a dwarf," Liz insisted, and Casey laughed out an apology. "Do you like annoying me?"

Casey cocked her head. "Yes, sometimes," she said and laughed again as Liz glared at her. Casey lifted Skye off her lap and set her on the piano bench. Skye immediately started to bang on the keys. Casey, wild-eyed, cringed as she turned to her and gently grabbed her hands.

"Gently, gently. This is a fine musical instrument," she explained to the feisty blonde. "And expensive."

Liz rolled her eyes and stepped up to Skye. "Sweet pea. No banging or you can't sit there," Liz said in a concise motherly fashion. Skye pouted, then looked up at her mother's stern unwavering face.

"'Kay, Mama," Skye said and gently poked the keys.

Liz gave Casey a superior glance. "Fine musical instrument. She can't even say it," Liz said sarcastically.

Casey narrowed her eyes. "I'm going to make some iced tea, then take a shower."

Liz sat outside with Skye, who played with her fish. Liz handed her a slice of orange and Skye happily took it, shoving it into her mouth.

"Skye? You…you like Casey, don't you?"

"Mmm-hmm. I fim. She bide me sungasses. She bide me a fith. I pay pinano." Skye rattled off her list.

Liz smiled, thinking how her daughter's vocabulary was getting better day by day.

"You like Cafey, Mama?"

Liz grinned. "Yes. I like Casey," she said as she handed her another slice of orange.

"Cafey say Mama piddy," Skye said, and as she reached for the orange, Liz pulled it back.

"What? Did Cafey, uh, Casey say I was pretty?" she whispered to her daughter, then looked at the door. "Did she say that, sweetie?"

Skye nodded happily and reached for the orange. Liz grinned and sat back. "When, sweet pea?" She should feel guilty grilling her own daughter.

"Fimming. Mama, peas." Skye whined and reached for the orange slice.

"Oh. Sorry, sweetie," Liz said and handed her the piece of fruit.

"What, uh, what else did Casey say, sweetie? Can you remember for Mommy?" Liz peeled another piece of bait. She pulled Skye up on her lap, groaning as her back ached.

Skye gave her an adult, thinking pose that had Liz affectionately rolling her eyes. "Blue eyes," her daughter said as she ate the orange.

"Casey said I have pretty blue eyes?"

Skye nodded and ate another slice. Liz's heart raced at the idea. Get a hold of yourself, Kennedy, she thought. This woman is way out of your league. Being nice to your daughter is one thing, being attracted to a pregnant woman with fat, swollen feet is quite another. She let out a dejected sigh. Oh, well, she thought, it was a nice dream.

"Cafey piddy, Mama?" Skye looked up at her mother.

Liz stared off, thinking of those long legs and that body in a bathing suit, the green eyes dancing, and the smile. "Yes, sweet pea. I think Casey is very pretty."

Just then, Casey walked out onto the deck and Skye grinned. "Cafey, Mama, say you—"

Liz stuffed an orange into her daughter's mouth and smiled sweetly at Casey.

Casey gave them a curious look. "You two look as guilty as sin."

Skye wrenched her face away from her mother. "Present!" she exclaimed as she saw the wrapped boxes behind Casey's back.

"Casey, you'll spoil her," Liz said, noticing the awkward grin as Casey looked down at Skye.

"Sorry, Shortround, these are for your mom."

Liz swallowed with difficulty. "For me?"

Casey shrugged and handed her the boxes.

"Hurry, Mama!" Skye cried out and clapped her hands.

Liz prayed that Casey did not see her hands shaking. She pulled at the wrapping paper and opened the box. "Oh, Casey. It's gorgeous," Liz exclaimed as she held up the blouse; it was cobalt blue and silk.

"God, I hope it fits. I had some poor pregnant woman helping me," Casey said nervously and scratched the back of her head. "I think she wanted to kill me after a while."

"I'm sure it will," Liz said and looked up. "Thank you."

"Mama, more. Open…" Skye insisted.

Liz gave Casey a helpless look. "More? You shouldn't."

Casey blushed deeply, and once again, Liz saw the embarrassed pose and smiled inwardly. The urge to touch her crimson cheek was overwhelming.

Liz looked down at her daughter. "Okay, sweet pea, help me," she said, and Skye eagerly ripped off the paper. Liz held up a pair of tan linen maternity slacks. Liz knew what they must have cost. "Oh, Casey," she said in a small grateful voice.

"Well, you don't seem to have many maternity clothes, and I just figured you'd be more comfortable, a-and I—"

"Cafey, what this?" Skye asked. She held up the baby rattle. Casey's eyes bugged out of her head, and she avoided Liz's shocked glance. She had completely forgotten about it.

A smile then tugged at the corner of Liz's mouth as she raised an eyebrow in question.

"It's a baby rattle," Casey said to Liz.

"For baby?" Skye asked and shook the rattle.

Casey threw her hands up in defeat and chuckled. "Yes, Shortround." She looked at Liz, who had tears in her eyes. "I-I saw it on the counter and..."

"Thank you," Liz whispered, then inexplicably burst into tears.

Casey's eyes flew open in alarm. Skye flung herself onto her mother's lap. "Mama..." she exclaimed.

Liz could not control herself; she was blubbering like a fool and holding on to her daughter.

Casey smiled and knelt down in front of both. "It's okay, Shortround, your Mommy's just happy, right?" she asked and covered Liz's shaking hand with her own.

Liz looked up and nodded as she cried.

"See, I'm getting the hang of this pregnant thing," Casey said proudly.

Liz suddenly reached up and grabbed Casey around the neck. For an instant, Casey was stunned. She recovered quickly and put her arm around Liz.

Liz then stopped and immediately released Casey. "I-I'm so sorry. Thank you, Casey. This was quite unexpected," she said and dried her eyes.

"Well, I hope they fit because you're wearing them tonight. C'mon, I'm starved, we're going out to eat," Casey announced, and Skye clapped her hands.

"Hot dogs?" she asked happily.

"Well, sure. Whatever you want, Shortround," she said as she ruffled the blond head.

Chapter 9

Liz and Casey laughed as Skye scrunched up her face as Casey fed her the asparagus.

"Yucky, Cafey." She pulled back as Casey tried it again.

"Shortround, life is not all hot dogs and macaroni and cheese."

Liz rolled her eyes. "You have to start thinking like a three-year-old, not just acting like one," Liz said as she sliced the hot dog up in little pieces.

Casey opened her mouth to say something sarcastic, then stopped as she looked at Liz. She wore her auburn hair down and flowing. The blue of the blouse matched her eyes perfectly as Casey knew it would. She then remembered how Liz hugged her earlier. Relax, Romeo, she thought. Liz was grateful, that's all. She sighed and shook her head.

"Goodness, that was a heavy sigh," Liz said as she fed Skye, then concentrated on her plate of pasta.

Casey hid her grin as she watched this woman eat. Eating for two was no lie, and Casey was amazed at how much she could eat and how little weight she gained.

"Hey, don't you have to go see a doctor?" Casey asked as she ate one last bite of steak and pushed the plate away. Liz glanced at her plate. "Go on, I'm stuffed."

"Well, I was looking in the phone book," Liz said, pulling

Casey's plate in front of her. "With the little money left, I've been paying a healthy premium for my insurance. So I can go to any obstetrician—"

"Whoa. You can't just go to any doctor," Casey said, then flipped out her cell phone and dialed. "Roger, Casey. Who is Trish's obstetrician?" she asked and scribbled on a napkin. "Thanks. What, oh, it's..." She blushed as she glanced at Liz. "It's going all right," she grumbled. "Good night, ya hack."

"Okay, tomorrow you call Dr. Lillian Haines. Roger says she's the best O-B something."

"OBGYN," Liz said dryly. "Obstetrics and Gynecology. And I appreciate your help, but I'd like to pick my own doctor."

"Why? She's the best. Now don't argue it's your last semester and—"

Liz put her head back and laughed out loud. Skye followed suit just because her mother was laughing. Casey sat there and watched. Then she started laughing, as well, not knowing what she was laughing at.

"What? What's so funny?" Casey asked as she laughed.

"It's...trimester... Last trimester," Liz said through her laughter.

Casey stopped abruptly. "It's not that funny," she grumbled and drank her water.

Liz then stopped and dried her eyes. "I'm sorry. You're right." Liz cleared her throat.

Skye was still laughing. "Cafey funny, Mama?"

"Eat your hot dog, sweet pea," Liz said and fed her daughter.

Skye fell asleep in her new car seat. The two women drove in silence until Liz cleared her throat. "Thank you for tonight, for the gifts, and the car seat," she said as she put her head back.

Casey glanced over and smiled. "Well, $250 is a lot of money to keep shelling out," she said, both laughing as they pulled up to the cabin.

Casey got out, and without a word, she walked around, opened Liz's door, and helped her out. "Turtle woman," she mumbled playfully.

She got Skye and held the sleeping girl. Liz stumbled as they walked up to the porch; Casey reached out to steady her. Liz held on to her arm as they walked in the darkness.

"Better hold on to me. I don't want you falling. I forgot to turn on the porch light," Casey said as Liz wrapped her arm around Casey's forearm.

When they got to the front door, Liz felt Casey watching her; she tried to avoid the look and her racing heart. The romantic moonlight flooding the porch didn't help. The moonbeams illuminated all three of them as Casey opened the screen door. Liz thought Casey was about to say something when Skye woke and wriggled in Casey's arms.

"I better get her to bed," Liz said in a soft voice. She saw Casey shiver instantly and inwardly smiled.

"I not tired, Mama," Skye grumbled.

Liz sat on the couch, too tired to argue. She slipped off her shoes and painfully wriggled her toes.

"Mama feet," Skye said and rubbed her feet.

Liz put her head back and laughed. "Thank you, sweet pea." She sighed and closed her eyes. Then she felt a stronger pair of hands lifting her feet.

"Here, Shortround, let an expert show you how it's done."

Liz quickly lifted her head to see Casey sit on the couch. She placed Liz's feet on her lap and gently rubbed.

Liz sighed and laid back. "You've got exactly one year to stop that."

Casey laughed as she massaged her tired feet.

"Uppie," Skye said and yawned. Liz groaned and tried to sit up, but Casey stood first.

"Relax. I'll put the dwarf, er, Shortround to bed. I'll be right back," Casey said firmly. "Skye, say good night to your mom."

Skye stubbornly crossed her arms across her chest. "I not tired..." she grumbled.

Casey looked down at Skye and put her hands on her hips. "How can I take you fishing tomorrow if you don't go to sleep?" she asked, then folded her arms across her chest, as well.

Liz watched from the tall woman to the little blonde and said nothing. Skye looked at her mother, who shrugged. "If you want to go fishing, you'd better get to bed."

Skye grabbed her fish, kissed her mother good night, and took Casey by the hand. "What do you wear to bed?" Casey asked.

"PJs." Skye looked up. "You wear PJs?"

"Never mind," Casey answered as they disappeared down the hall.

Liz wondered what indeed Casey wore to bed. The fleeting image of Casey naked left her when she heard Casey mumbling a good night to her daughter; she realized she was still lying on the couch. "What am I doing?" she whispered and struggled to sit up.

Casey stood in the hallway. "What are you doing?"

Liz blushed deeply. "I just felt awkward waiting. Y-you don't have to..."

Casey walked over and assumed the previous position, including the contented sigh from Liz. "I have no idea what it's like to be pregnant," Casey said as she massaged Liz's foot. "But sometimes, you just look dog-tired. Besides, I am a master masseuse. Some people would pay big bucks for this."

"Like the woman you were with the other night," Liz blurted out, then her eyes flew open. "I'm sorry."

Casey's green eyes danced wickedly as she gently rubbed her ankles. "No, Suzette does not pay."

"Suzette? Her name is Suzette?"

Casey hid her grin and merely nodded.

"Are you serious about each other?" Liz asked as she put a pillow behind her head and watched Casey.

Casey frowned for an instant. "Well, if you're asking are we a couple, then no. Is that your question?" Casey's strong fingers worked the instep of one foot, then the other.

"W-well, I suppose yes. I mean if you're sleeping with someone—"

"Liz, there is very little sleeping," Casey said and quickly continued, "Besides, I'm afraid my days with darling Suzette may soon end."

Inwardly, Liz did the happy dance for some reason. Outwardly, she was the picture of concern. "Why is that?"

"Well, Suzette plays the cello—"

Liz let out a short, barking laugh and stopped when she saw the look on Casey's face. "Sorry, I thought that was a joke."

"She's a studio musician. We met two years ago when I was working on a movie. We started seeing each other. Then I got this chance to do a really good composition and I, well, I needed a cellist."

"So you naturally picked the best one."

Casey turned five shades of red, avoiding her smug grin. She rubbed the foot a little too hard for an instant. "Nepotism, no other word will do."

"So what's the problem?" Liz asked as she yawned.

"She stinks," Casey said succinctly.

"And now you have to tell her she isn't very good and when you do..."

"It's bye-bye, Suzette."

Liz noticed the confused looked on Casey's face. "It seems she ought to understand. If you say it the right way, that is."

Casey glanced over at her. "What's that supposed to mean?"

"You're not the most diplomatic person I've ever met."

"Hey, didn't I get Skye to bed? Didn't I get her to take a nap?"

"Isn't she three?"

Casey opened her mouth, then shut it. "Suzette has a bigger ego than I do."

Liz grinned mischievously. "As big as that, huh?"

Casey took a foot in both hands and squeezed. Liz laughed when Casey then grabbed the foot and started to tickle. "No! No!" Liz shrieked.

"Shh, you'll wake the child," Casey said. When Liz put a hand to her stomach, Casey immediately let go of her foot. "Are you all right?"

Liz nodded and bit her lip. "She's just moving." She reached for Casey's hand. "Here, feel this."

Casey retracted for an instant, then cautiously offered her hand. Liz gently took it and placed it on her belly. "There," she said and they waited for a moment, still another moment passed as they sat in silence.

Suddenly, a fluttering wave shot through Casey's hand; her eyes flew open. "The baby?" she whispered.

Liz grinned and nodded. "We probably woke her up." Casey just stared at their hands on her stomach. "They say the baby can hear things," Liz whispered.

Casey shook her head in awe. "I'm a grown woman, and I've never experienced anything like this. Thank you, Liz."

Liz smiled affectionately. "My pleasure, Casey."

For a moment or two, they sat there with hands on her stomach waiting for the next movement. "I think she's asleep."

"Amazing." Casey sighed and shook her head. She looked up to see tears in Liz's blue eyes. "Hey, what's wrong?"

Liz blinked back the tears and shook her head. "Nothing really. I'm just very happy right now, right at this moment."

"So am I. I don't know how to explain it. I'm so grateful to be a part of this. You're an extraordinary woman. When I think of all you've gone through in your young life."

"Well, you're not so old, you know," Liz countered in a soft voice.

Casey rested her arm along the back of the couch. Her other hand still on Liz's stomach, she caressed back and forth. Liz swallowed with difficulty. It had been so long since another woman had touched her.

Suddenly, Casey seemed to realize what she was doing and pulled her hand away as if scalded. "I'm sorry. Rubbing your stomach like that," she said apologetically.

"I don't mind. I like it actually." Liz wasn't at all sure she should have said that, but she swore she saw a hopeful look on Casey's face.

"Liz, I know…" Casey stopped when they heard Skye crying.

Casey bolted up and helped the turtle woman as they ran down the hall. Skye was crying in her sleep as they sat on either side of her. Instinctively, the girl latched onto her mother, who gently rocked her back and forth. "Shh, sweet pea. Mommy's here."

The three of them sat there in the darkness until the deep breathing lulled all of them. Gently, she placed her in the middle and smoothed back her hair.

Casey frowned and looked at Liz. "Is she okay?" Casey tried to whisper. However, it came out in a low voice, waking Skye. Liz sighed while Casey gave her an apologetic grin.

"Cafey? Seep," Skye said and reached up for her.

"Hey, kiddo, go back to sleep," Casey whispered.

"Seep. Peas," Skye said through a yawn and held on to her shirt.

"Why don't you sleep in here? I'll take the couch," Liz offered in a whisper.

"Nothing doing. We can both sleep in here," Casey whispered. "I'll go lock up."

"It's okay, Skye. Casey will be right back," Liz whispered as Casey walked out of the bedroom.

Liz got undressed as quickly as her stomach and swollen feet would allow. She did not want Casey to come back into the room.

"How sexy would that be?" she whispered as she desperately struggled into her nightgown, letting out a painful groan. "Throw myself into early labor just so she won't see me in a nightgown." She then slid into bed next to Skye.

When Casey came back into the dark room, Liz heard her open the drawer. Liz tried to remain quiet and keep her eyes closed. However, her curiosity got the better of her. She cracked one eye open and watched as Casey undressed in the moonlight. She swallowed so deeply she thought for sure it would wake up Skye. In the filtered moonlight, the silhouette of the curve of Casey's breasts was enough to send a tingle down Liz's spine. She continued to watch in awe; Casey had a beautiful body.

When Casey quickly changed into what Liz thought was a pair of boxers and a tank top, Liz heard her chuckling as she slid under the covers.

"What's the joke?" Liz whispered out of the darkness.

"Sorry, I didn't mean to wake you." she whispered across Skye. Liz turned her head to see Casey's face, half hidden by the moonlight. "I don't own a pair of pajamas, but I didn't want to give Shortround an early education in anatomy," she whispered with a chuckle.

"Well, thank you for that," Liz whispered back. "Good night, Casey."

"Good night, Liz."

She heard Casey yawn, and in a moment, she heard the soft deep breathing. For a few moments, Liz listened in the darkness to Skye and Casey as they slept. She smiled and cuddled the blanket around her and stifled the chuckle that threatened to overtake her. Liz wanted to tell Casey that Skye's mother received the anatomy lesson instead, while Casey had undressed in the moonlight.

In the early morning, Liz woke. A soft breeze blew the curtain, allowing the early morning sunlight to stream into the bedroom. Liz looked for her daughter and was amazed to see her on top of Casey, who was lying sprawled out on her back. To add to her amazement, Liz must have rolled over in the night. She was lying on her side, her head resting on Casey's shoulder and her arm protectively lay across her daughter's back.

I should move, Liz thought, but she was honestly too tired and much too comfortable and content. The late summer breeze wafted over her and she instantly fell back to sleep.

As they sat at the breakfast table, Liz noticed a worried look on Casey's face as she put the plate in front of her.

"Thanks," she mumbled absently.

"What's wrong?" Liz asked. Fine, she thought, she'll realize this was all a mistake. One night sleeping with her and her daughter was enough reality for Ms. Bennett.

"I was thinking about Suzette," Casey said.

Liz rolled her eyes as she fed Skye. All at once, Liz was cranky. She felt it rising and could not stop it. God, I cannot wait until I have control over my hormones, she complained to herself.

Skye was being a fussy three-year-old and pushed Liz's hand away. "No..." she grumbled.

All three women were in foul moods.

"Well, it seems you've got two choices," Liz said as she

tried to feed Skye again. "You can either tell her that her musical skills are not up to par or continue to have sex with her." The irrational, hormonal anger seeped out of every pore. "Gee, there's an important decision: integrity or sex? Hmm, which one will the egomaniacal Ms. Bennett choose?"

Casey glared at her. "What the hell is the matter with you? Thanks for the helpful advice." She tossed down her napkin. "Shit."

"Fit," Skye said.

Liz glared at Casey.

"Damn it, Shortround," Casey scolded.

Skye laughed. "Damment."

"Casey!" Liz argued.

Casey growled and pushed her chair back. "Well, don't you have any control of her? Christ."

"Quieste…" Skye laughed again and stopped at the scowl she got from Casey.

"Just stop talking if all you're going to do is swear," Liz said.

Casey got up and stormed into the living room with Liz hot on her heels. She turned Casey around and glared up into the now angry green eyes.

"It's hard enough to try and raise a three-year-old—" Liz started.

Casey let out a loud rude laugh. "Three? Who are you kidding? That kid is three going on forty," she said childishly. "And leave Suzette out of this. It's none of your concern who I sleep with."

"Thank God for that. Fine, go sleep with your tone-deaf cellist. You deserve each other," Liz bellowed.

"Fine, I will!"

"Fine!" Liz yelled, damning the tears that flooded her eyes.

Casey swallowed and took a step toward her.

"Don't you dare..."

Now Skye was crying, as well. Casey ran her fingers through her hair. She stormed past Liz and put on her running shoes. She ran out the door, hearing Skye crying out her name.

Liz tiredly walked up to Skye and picked her up. "I go...

Cafey..." Skye said and struggled against her. She ran to the front door and laid her head against the screen.

"Cafey!" the little blonde cried out and banged the screen.

Chapter 10

Casey ran faster, trying not to hear Skye as she called for her. This was much too much emotion for her. She ran as fast as she could. It was something Casey Bennett did all too well.

While she ran, she thought of Julie, and her anger mounted. If it weren't for her, none of this would be happening. She'd have her life back; she'd be…what, she thought as she slowed down. She stopped running and bent over, feeling as though she might vomit. She stood and took a deep breath and started walking down the gravel access road, taking in the beauty of the woods.

All at once, she turned to go back and stopped. Running a hand through her damp hair, she continued walking away from the cabin.

Did she truly want her life back? What life? Suzette, who really didn't care for her? Oh, the sex was tremendous, but that was quickly becoming unimportant to Casey. She stopped and laughed openly. "What are the odds of that happening?" She shook her head and took a small path leading into the woods.

Julie, she thought. Julie Bridges was a force of nature, that was true. When they first met in the airport in Chicago, Casey was hooked. They both hailed the same cab at O'Hare Airport in a rainstorm.

Casey held her briefcase over her head, trying to keep dry as she whistled for the cab. She barely noticed the pilot next to her doing the same. When the cab quickly pulled to the curb, the pilot and Casey reached for the door. Casey thought the pilot would be a gentleman and let her have the cab. She was pleasantly stunned to see a pair of soulful brown eyes angrily staring back at her.

"I saw it first," the woman said and reached for the door.

Casey grinned and opened it. "Look, it's pouring, let's share it before we drown."

The woman narrowed her eyes for a moment, then slipped into the cab. Casey followed her and wiped the rain out of her face. "What a downpour."

The cabby looked over his shoulder. "Where are you ladies headed?"

"The Drake Hotel," the woman replied first.

Casey raised an eyebrow and looked at her. "The Drake, huh? Pretty snazzy. I think I'll go there, as well. I love the restaurant in that hotel." She looked back at the smirking pilot. "Would you like to join me for dinner?" Casey offered her hand. "Casey Bennett."

The pilot took the offered hand. "Julie Bridges."

For a moment, they just looked at each other. The cabby coughed. "The meter's running. So the Drake?"

Julie never took her eyes off Casey. "The Drake."

Casey grinned and settled back.

"This is a nice restaurant," Julie said as she drank from her water glass. "Thank you for waiting while I changed."

Casey nodded. "You're welcome. You were more soaked than I was."

Julie shrugged. "I offered you my room to get dry."

Casey looked up from the wine list. "Which was very nice of you, perhaps I'll take a rain check." She then concentrated again on ordering the wine. "Would you like some wine?"

"Yes, please. Go right ahead. I have no idea about wine."

The server approached their table and Casey ordered the bottle of wine. It was not until he walked away that Casey spoke. "So tell me about yourself, Julie Bridges."

"Not much to tell. I was born in Indiana. An only child, I

have loving parents, but I missed having friends. My father was in the military so we traveled a lot."

"A pilot as well?" Casey asked. The server brought the bottle to the table and opened it. Casey tasted it and nodded.

"Yes, he was a colonel in the Air Force," Julie said and lifted her glass when Casey offered hers.

"Well, here's to rainy nights in Chicago," Casey said with a smile.

They touched glasses in silence. Casey watched Julie's lovely face as she drank her wine. Her shoulder-length blond hair shimmered in the dimly lit restaurant, and her brown eyes sparkled. She had smooth flawless skin that Casey instinctively knew would be soft to the touch.

"You're staring, Casey," Julie said; she grinned, as well.

"I can't help it," Casey said. "You're very attractive. I'm sure you've been told that before."

Julie looked into her eyes and searched her face. "As I'm sure you have."

Casey's arousal level raised several points as she drank her wine. "How long are you in Chicago?"

"I have a flight tomorrow night at nine," Julie replied quickly.

Casey nodded but said nothing. Julie grinned and leaned forward. "Still want the rain check?"

Casey sat on a huge boulder and lifted her face to the morning sun as it filtered through the trees. She closed her eyes and remembered the sexually charged evening and next morning with Julie. Their relationship started that fast. From then on, they saw each other whenever Julie was in Chicago and whenever Casey could get away and meet her for a long weekend. During that time, Casey knew she was falling in love, but something held her back. Perhaps it was Julie's almost childlike attitude, her cavalier approach to responsibility. Living the life of a single, carefree pilot was not unlike her own life as a single carefree composer.

Julie and she were evenly matched in many ways, and at the time, Casey followed her heart and wanted more. So did Julie, but it was her wanting children that threw Casey a curve.

"Honey, we're not equipped for kids," Casey tried to explain.

Julie lay in her arms and looked up. She swiped the blond hair away from her face. "You don't want children? You said you liked the idea."

"I said, if the situation was different, I would like the idea," Casey gently corrected her and sat up. "Honey, look at our lifestyles. You're a pilot who is constantly on the go. You're never in a place long enough."

"You're grounded, Case. You've got a wonderful apartment here. It's huge, and you're in Chicago now more than ever. You'd be around all the time. We could get a nanny—"

Casey cocked her head in confusion. "A nanny?"

Julie went on before Casey could continue. "Yes, once you have the baby, you'll—"

"Me?" Casey asked in amazement. "Okay, we need to regroup here and talk seriously." She slipped out of bed and into her sweats and a T-shirt. Julie did the same.

Julie sat at the bar in the kitchen while Casey made coffee. She set a steamy mug in front of Julie, who pouted severely. Casey shook her head and sat across from her. She reached over and took Julie's hand in hers. "Now let's be honest. You and I have only touched on this topic once, and that was last year. Honey, my biological clock is ticking, and I really don't care. I do not have a maternal need to bear a child. Yes, I like children. Would I like to be a parent? Perhaps, someday when I'm married or in a secure, stable relationship."

Julie pouted still as she drank her coffee. Casey smiled sadly. "Which we do not have, Julie."

Her head shot up then and she glared at Casey. "Are you saying you don't love me?"

Casey rolled her eyes and drank her coffee. "Julie, think of what you're asking here. To bring a child into this world, with two women who barely see each other and who have no idea how to raise and nurture a child. It's completely unfair and childish of you to want that simply because you were an only child and now being a grownup you need a playmate." She knew the words would sting, but they needed to be said. In the past year, Julie was indeed showing signs of her spoiled childhood, where her parents gave her what she wanted, more than likely out of guilt for traveling around the country and the world, never giving her any stability.

Julie glared at her. "You missed your calling. You should have been a psychiatrist instead of a composer. Why do you stay with me if I'm such a neurotic mess? I love children and I thought you felt the same. Apparently, you don't."

"Julie, we've talked in-depth about your childhood and your parents. You've blamed them for dragging you all over the world, but, honey, you're a grown woman now. Stop blaming them and start living your own life—"

"I am," she said angrily. "I want children. I have a need for that, Casey. Deep inside of me. Can't you understand that? Or are you too selfish?"

Casey bristled at the accusation; the urge to continue this hurtful path was overwhelming. Instead, she countered softly, "If you have this need so deep inside you, why am I expected to have the baby?"

Julie's anger mounted. She stood and paced back and forth like a caged tiger. Casey drank her coffee and waited; she knew when Julie felt trapped.

"Fine. I-I'll have the baby," she said simply and gave Casey a challenging look.

Casey sighed sadly. "Honey, this is not a challenge. I'm trying to explain that we are not a good match for children. You say you want a child, but you won't put yourself physically through the process." Casey now felt the anger rising. "Damn it, it's an enormous responsibility that I know we cannot handle. And if you were thinking about this clearly, you would agree. I will not bring a child into this world with two strikes against them to appease your selfish need to rewind your biological clock."

Julie's back stiffened. "This is a deal breaker, Casey."

Casey stared at her in disbelief and shook her head. "Then it is what it is."

Casey remembered how the topic was indeed a deal breaker. They stayed together for another six months, but both knew it was a losing battle. It ended in Denver. Casey was angry and sad, but deep in her heart, she knew it was inevitable. Of course, she thought their relationship was great. They were never challenged, never tested. This was their test. Casey came away broken-hearted, but she knew she was right. If she had to do it all over again, she would have done the same thing.

Now she had Julie's partner, pregnant and with a three-year-old, living in her cabin. And to make matters worse, or better, depending on how she looked at it, Casey was attracted to Liz. Suddenly, Casey felt completely confused. She had no idea what to do. Liz's face, as she slept next to her, flashed through her mind. Skye's contagious laughter had her chuckling.

However, she wouldn't take on the responsibility with Julie. Could she with Liz? Did she even want to? "Damn it," she said angrily and started jogging back to the cabin.

The more she thought about it, the faster she ran. Casey didn't know if she was running from or to Liz and her family. She wasn't sure if she wanted to know.

An hour later, Liz got Skye to calm down. The poor little thing hyperventilated and got the hiccoughs. "C-Cafey c-comin' back?" she asked as Liz rocked her on the porch swing.

"Yes, sweet pea. Casey will be back. She was just mad."

"Mama yell at Cafey."

Liz winced and held her close. "I know. That was wrong of me, Skye. Mommy has to tell Casey she's sorry."

"Cafey make Mama cry."

"Well, Mommy cries very easily these days. Casey and Mommy just had an argument. Like when you don't want to take a nap or eat your breakfast."

"I fim," Skye offered and Liz nodded.

"Right, like when you wanted to swim."

With that, they heard the back door open.

"Cafey home..." Skye cried out and scrambled inside.

Liz sat there, her heart racing, feeling horrible about the stupid argument.

"Mama, Cafey hurt." She heard Skye's voice call from the front door.

"Hurt?" Liz bolted up as quickly as she could and dashed into the cabin.

Casey was leaning against the counter with a frozen package of hamburger against her head. There was dirt and smudges all over her clothes and scratches on her legs and arms.

"What happened?" Liz exclaimed as she took the frozen package away. A large red welt was forming above one brow. "Sit down," she ordered.

Casey eased herself into the kitchen chair. Liz put ice in a towel and placed it on her forehead. "I-I tripped," Casey said angrily and Liz bit her bottom lip as she held the ice. "Go ahead. I can almost hear the peal of laughter coming."

"Cafey faw down?" Skye asked as she patted Casey's leg.
"Uh, yes, sweetie. Don't bother Casey right now," Liz said as she could see Casey's anger rising once again.

"I was running." Casey stopped and breathed heavily. "For my life," she added sarcastically, and Liz hid her grin as she held the ice to her head; her other hand caressed the back of her damp neck. "I ran too fast on the way back and twisted my ankle on a rock and went flying in a fu... I fell in a ditch."

Liz looked down at her swollen ankle. "Okay, let's get you to bed. You need to put that foot up and I need to clean those scratches."

"I'm fine," Casey countered.

"Casey Bennett, get into bed," she ordered.

Casey looked up and grinned. "Well, I've never had to be ordered to the bedroom before. You're so forceful, Mommy," she added dryly.

Liz felt the color once again rising in her cheeks. Casey stood painfully and looked down into the blue eyes. "I'm sorry. It was my fault."

"No, I'm sorry. It's none of my business, you were right," Liz said teary-eyed.

"This pregnancy is having an effect on both of us, Liz," Casey said, and out of the blue, she put a gentle hand to her cheek. "I should know better. I'm sorry. I'm just not used to being around a woman, great with child."

"This is new for both of us, you're right there."

Liz gently examined Casey's ankle. "I don't think it's broken. You can move it. Just a bad sprain and a little edema," she said almost to herself. Casey watched her curiously as she expertly wrapped the ankle. "Not too tight?" She looked up and Casey shook her head.

"You did that pretty quickly and very professionally," Casey said. "Where did you find the ACE bandage?"

"It's what I did part time," Liz said and put her ankle up on a pillow. "And I found it in the mess you call a first-aid kit in the bathroom."

"Oh." Casey winced. "What did you do?"

"I'm a nurse. An RN actually," she said and sat on the edge of the bed.

Casey nodded. "I can see you as a nurse. You're very gentle, very considerate. Did you work at a hospital?"

"No, a clinic in a rotten area of Albuquerque. The pay was horrible."

"But you didn't do it for the pay," Casey said; it was not a question.

"No, I didn't. If I did, I probably wouldn't be in this situation."

Casey then shifted uncomfortably and Liz leaned back.

"Are you in pain?" she asked, noticing again the confused, clouded look. "Are you?"

"No, I'm fine," Casey said, still looking as though she wanted to say something.

"Okay, well, what's wrong?"

"Nothing."

"Casey, every once in a while, I get the impression you want to say something. I can't make you, but I truly wish you'd say what's on your mind." And again, Liz felt her anger rising. She took the antiseptic and doused a few cotton balls. "This is going to hurt."

"That sounds like a threat." Casey winced as Liz cleaned the scratches on her leg.

When she finished, she tossed the remains of the first aid in the wastebasket by the bedside.

"I hurt too, Mama," Skye whimpered as she crawled up on the bed.

Casey was lying on her back; Skye lay next to Casey and looked up. "Mama make it better?"

Casey looked up at Liz and shrugged. "I guess."

Liz snorted sarcastically at Casey, then turned her attention to her daughter; she cursed herself for her trembling hands. "You hurt too, sweet pea? Let me see. Where?" she asked; Skye offered her unblemished knee.

"I faw too."

"Aw. I am so sorry. Does it hurt, sweetie?" Liz asked tenderly.

"Mmm-hmm, kiss it, Mama," Skye said and Liz laughed and leaned over Casey to kiss her knee.

"There. All better?" she asked.

Skye nodded happily and watched her mother. "Sit still while I clean your forehead," she said to Casey. Afterward, she placed a Band-Aid above her brow.

"There. All better," Liz said, oozing sarcasm.

"Ha, ha," Casey said and felt her brow. She looked down at Skye's curious look. "I guess we're lucky, Shortround." Casey glanced at Liz, who shook her head.

Skye stared up at the Band-Aid on Casey's brow. "Mama, kiss it," she said seriously and pointed to Casey's forehead.

Liz's back stiffened, and she knew she was blushing. "Casey's a big girl, Skye."

"I'm not that big," Casey said.

"Mama..." Skye insisted.

Liz looked back and forth between the two children. She saw Casey's challenging gaze and rolled her eyes. She then bent down and kissed Casey's forehead. From the look of surprise on her face, Liz knew Casey did not think she would do it. Liz pulled back and both women stared at each other.

"Mama make it better, Cafey?" Skye asked.

Liz didn't know what to make of the look on Casey's face.

"Yes, Shortround. More than she knows."

"You shouldn't be on that ankle," Liz said.

Casey, clad in her bathing suit, grabbed Skye around the waist and hauled her up. "I'm fine. The water will be good for it," she said stubbornly.

Liz gave up. It was hard enough with Skye. Casey was just a taller, albeit much more attractive, version.

"C'mon, you little sack of potatoes, let's go swimming." She hauled Skye up over her shoulder and limped down to the beach. She turned back. "You gonna be all right up here?"

"I'll be fine." Liz smiled and nodded. "Go on."

As she watched Casey head down to the beach to play with her daughter, she couldn't get a handle on what was going on in Casey Bennett's mind. One minute, she was kind and generous with her gifts, then the next she was distant and arrogant. The only constant was Liz's uncertainty about Casey Bennett—and the uncertainty of the future.

Chapter 11

Liz watched Casey and Skye playing in the late afternoon sun; she decided to make something cool to drink. She rose with a deep groan, and as she headed inside, she heard a car pull up the gravel access road. She peered out the kitchen window to see an impeccably dressed elderly woman exit the luxury car and stretch. "I wonder who that is."

She was going to get Casey, but this woman seemed to know where she was. Liz opened the back door and the woman smiled. Liz saw a vague resemblance to Casey and held the screen door open. "You must be Casey's grandmother."

"Very good. Now if you can just give me the lottery numbers for tonight's game, we'll be all set."

Liz laughed and stepped back to allow her into the kitchen. "I'm—"

"Liz Kennedy. I'm Meredith Casey." She offered her hand. "Casey has told me of your situation."

"She has?" Liz frowned.

Meredith held up her hand. "Only the basics." She looked at Liz's stomach. "How are you feeling? I told that idiot granddaughter of mine I wanted to meet you."

Liz laughed as Meredith walked into the living room and sat with a groan. "That is one long drive."

"Can I get you something? I was just going to make some iced tea."

"That would be heavenly, thank you."

Liz returned to find Meredith smiling as she looked out the big picture window. She knew she was watching Casey with her daughter. "Here you go, Mrs.—"

"None of that. It's Meredith, please," she said and took the glass. "May I call you Liz?"

"Of course." Liz looked out the window, as well. "Skye adores your granddaughter."

Meredith raised an eyebrow and drank her tea. "And how are you getting along with her?"

Liz felt the color rush to her face, trying to hide it as she drank. "Casey is being very kind and generous to let me and Skye stay here until my child is born." She watched Skye with Casey and absently put her hand on her stomach.

"Let's sit, shall we? My feet are killing me." Meredith eased into the recliner. "One thing about Casey, she knows creature comforts."

Liz said nothing as she sat on the couch, though she felt Meredith's gaze upon her.

"I am sorry to hear about your partner," Meredith said. "Though it was quick, it must still have been a shock."

"Thank you. It was a shock and still is in some ways. And in another, it's…" Her voice trailed off as she drank her tea. "I don't want to bore you with my situation."

"Not at all, dear. I can imagine you haven't talked to anyone but my granddaughter, and even that may not help."

Liz laughed along with Meredith. "I can't blame Casey. She was thrown into this situation, pretty much emotionally blackmailed by Julie into helping us. I didn't want to leave and come out here. But I couldn't stay in New Mexico alone. Not with having Skye and being pregnant. I know this is inconvenient for Casey. I only hope I can make it up to her somehow."

"Don't be ridiculous. Casey needs someone to take care of, something in her life other than that idiot savant cellist."

Liz had the glass to her lips; she spewed the tea out of the glass and started choking and laughing at the same time. Meredith laughed heartily as she kicked off her shoes. "I take it you know of what's-her-name?"

"Suzette," Liz said, wiping her chin.

"Ah, yes, Suzette. Have you met?"

"No, I have not had the pleasure." Liz shook her head, still chuckling.

"What in God's name?"

Liz looked up when she heard the curious tone to see Meredith looking out the window. Liz followed her gaze and blinked several times. Casey stood on the porch with a small inner tube over her head with one arm through it; the inner tube was a bright red and blue with fish all around it. Skye was slowly climbing up the steps behind her.

"Go get your mother, Shortround," Casey said in a strangled voice.

"'Kay, Cafey."

Skye ran into the living room and up to her mother. "Mama, Cafey stuck." She then noticed Meredith and frowned.

"Hello," Meredith said. "What happened to Casey?"

"She stuck," Skye repeated and pulled on her mother's leg.

Liz groaned and stood. "Now what?"

"This I have to see," Meredith said.

Casey whirled around, her eyes bugging out of her head. "Gram? What are you doing here?" she asked, desperately trying to wriggle out of the inner tube.

"Waiting for the floorshow. How on earth did you get stuck in that thing?"

"Casey, what are you doing?" Liz tried to pull the inner tube. She only succeeded in wedging Casey's arm tighter.

"Ouch, for godsake," Casey said. She glared down at Skye as she laughed. "This is your fault."

"Oh, fine. Blame a three-year-old," Liz said.

"Well, it was her idea—"

"Who's the adult?" Liz asked angrily as she pulled at the tube.

"Um, may I offer my assistance?" Meredith asked and stepped forward. She took the long fork from the barbeque stand and punctured the inner tube.

They all stood there as the air hissed and deflated the tube. Meredith then motioned to her granddaughter. "May I?"

Casey took a deep angry breath and nodded. Meredith then lifted the deflated rubber tube over her head and handed it to her. "Perhaps you should stick to playing the piano."

Casey glared at her. "Who invited you?"

Casey emerged from the shower in shorts and a tank top, her hair damp and a red mark around her neck and shoulder. Meredith exchanged glances with Liz, who bit her lip in an effort not to laugh. Skye sat in her booster seat at the table, eating a slice of cucumber. She looked up when Casey walked into the kitchen.

"Cafey? Cooclumber," she said and offered the one she was eating.

"Thanks," Casey said and took the half-eaten wobbly cucumber and started to pop it into her mouth; it then fell onto the floor. "Oops." She picked it up and tried again.

Liz's mouth dropped as she snatched it out of her hand. "Are you insane? Don't eat that after it fell on the floor." She tossed it in the garbage.

Casey frowned and looked at her empty hand, then to Skye. "It dirty, Cafey."

Meredith sat back and watched as Liz prepared the salad for dinner. "Can I help, Liz?"

"Oh, no, Meredith. You just sit."

"How about a martini, Gram?" Casey asked. "And then you can tell me why you drove six hours without telling me. I would have picked you up."

"I'd love a martini, and I'm a grown woman," Meredith said. "And I wanted to meet Liz and her adorable daughter." She reached over and chucked Skye under the chin. Skye giggled and squirmed in her seat. "And you may call me Grandma."

Liz glanced at Casey, who frowned for an instant, then concentrated on her cocktails. The frown was not lost on Meredith, nor was the worried look on Liz's face.

"So tell me, Liz. How are you feeling? Bloated, hot flashes, raging hormones?" Meredith asked, then smiled wickedly. "Back spasms? Heartburn?"

"And the list goes on," Liz said over her shoulder while munching on a carrot. "And my appetite."

"There's nothing wrong with your appetite," Casey said and handed Meredith the long-stemmed glass. As she walked away, Meredith beckoned her back with an "ah, ah." Casey rolled her eyes and plopped a few olives into the glass.

"I know. That's the problem. I'm eating like a horse."

"Well, you look fine." Casey took a long pull off the bottle of beer she opened.

Meredith watched both with interest. Casey absently put the bottle cap on the counter; Liz automatically tossed it into the garbage while Casey poured an iced tea and set it on the counter next to Liz. Liz looked at the glass. "Could you…?"

Casey had already retrieved more ice and added it to her glass. Liz said a quiet "thanks."

"Welcome," Casey said, placing her hand on Liz's shoulder as she walked by.

She glanced at Meredith, who raised an eyebrow and sipped her martini. "What?" Casey asked.

Meredith just smiled. "Yes, you are very attractive, Liz. Motherhood agrees with you. Don't you think, Casey?"

Casey looked at Liz, who was facing the counter. Meredith watched her granddaughter as her gaze traveled up and down Liz's body.

"Yes, she is, and it does," Casey said.

"I just want to be healthy so the delivery goes well and I recover quickly." Liz placed the bowl of salad on the table. She looked at Casey, who was still watching her. "What?"

Meredith watched the exchange while feeding Skye a piece of celery.

Casey blinked. "What?"

Liz dried her hands on a towel. "You look as if you wanted to say something. It's getting annoying."

Meredith watched the color rise in Casey's cheeks. She looked like a thermometer. "No, I-I don't have anything on my mind."

"Liar," Meredith mumbled as she fed Skye.

"Well, are you manning the grill?" Liz took the steaks out of the fridge. "Good thing you bought enough."

"Oh, sure."

Casey had the coals red hot; she tossed three steaks on the sizzling grill and stepped back. "I have no idea what I'm doing," she called into the kitchen and held the tongs in the air.

Meredith laughed along with Liz, who was still munching on cucumbers, and for every slice of tomato that went in the salad, she had eaten two. "Don't worry. If you burn them, Liz has already eaten dinner," Meredith said dryly and shook her head. "Let me make sure she doesn't burn the porch down."

Out on the deck, Casey sipped her beer and looked up from her task when Meredith walked out.

"Well, well, you look positively domesticated. It suits you."

"What are you doing here? Not that I don't love seeing you."

"Niles called me all a-twitter," Meredith said. "Don't you know any straight people?"

"Ha, ha. Niles likes you." Casey took a long pull from the beer bottle. "He liked Mom, too."

Meredith heard the forlorn voice and sipped her martini. She sat in the lounge chair and crossed her legs. She watched Casey for a moment as she stared into the kitchen window. Liz could be heard laughing with Skye.

"I miss Mom," Casey whispered. She looked at Meredith and shrugged.

"I do too." Meredith put her head back and studied Casey. "I know I have not been as supportive of your lifestyle as Eleanor was. Your mother had a very giving and open heart, much like her father." She laughed. "Your father was more like me, and we weren't even related. Funny how that works."

Casey nodded and gazed into the woods beyond the cabin. "You've been much more supportive in recent years, Gram."

Meredith grunted. "That's because I'm trying to buy my way into heaven."

Casey laughed then. "No, you're not. You're kinder than you let on."

"And if you tell anyone, I shall disinherit you."

"I thought you had no money…"

"You'll get my martini shaker."

Casey leaned against the porch railing and looked out over the lake as Liz and Skye's playful banter could be heard in the background.

"What are you thinking?" Meredith asked.

Casey smiled. "I love to get away from Chicago and the rat race and hide here."

"Alone?"

Casey struck a thoughtful pose. "You know my lifestyle."

"Is that what you still want? Brief encounters. The novelty of someone new? It's fleeting at best."

"I'm not sure I'm equipped for anything else. Julie was the only one I came even remotely close to it all with. And she…"

"Wanted a family."

Casey nodded. "I was right not to have a family with Julie. She wasn't ready. I wasn't ready."

"And now?"

Casey's head shot up; she stared in disbelief. "Now? What do you mean?"

Meredith motioned to the kitchen. Casey's mouth dropped. "Liz? Oh, good grief, Gram. I, she…" She finished her beer with one long gulp.

"You haven't thought of it?" Meredith gently prodded.

"No, well, yes, but no." She stopped and let out a long sigh. "Gram, am I fond of them? Yes. Is Liz attractive? Certainly. She's more beautiful pregnant."

"Really? Have you told her this?"

"Shit, no."

"Why not? I'm sure in her condition she'd love to hear it."

They were silent for a moment. "I have Suzette."

Meredith groaned deeply and rolled her eyes. Casey continued. "Really, Gram. While Suzette might be shallow, she knows what she wants from me."

"Nothing," Meredith chimed in.

"No strings. No attachments, no—"

"Love."

Casey's shoulders sagged and she hung her head.

"I'm annoying, aren't I?"

"You have no idea."

The giggling heard in the kitchen from mother and daughter brought a contented grin to Casey's face once again. Meredith laughed and put her head back, gazing at the twilight sky. "I'm sorry, Casey. I shouldn't butt into your life. You're a grown woman with a fabulous career and a carefree lifestyle. The last thing you need is a ready-made family." She lifted her head and noticed the faraway look in Casey's eyes. "But you're doing a good thing here, dear. I sincerely mean that. It's not an easy situation for you or Liz. Perhaps a wonderful friendship may be forged from this. That in itself would be very good for both of you."

"Maybe." Casey shrugged and lifted the lid to the grill and put it on the ground. "I wonder if these are done."

"Casey? Did you check the steaks?" Liz called out from the kitchen.

Meredith let out a wicked laugh then. "She's reading your mind now? Interesting."

Casey glared and drank her beer; she noticed the bottle was empty. "Shit."

Skye appeared at the screen door. With her nose pressed against the screen, she cupped her hands around her face and peered at Casey. "Cafey, Mama—"

"Tell your mother I'm not stupid," Casey said as she poked at the steak.

"Mama! Cafey say she not stupid."

Casey completely avoided Meredith, who nearly spit up her drink. She wiped her chin. "What a waste of good vodka." She smiled sweetly at Casey.

"Well, I didn't say she was," Liz called back. "Oh, good grief, that stubborn…"

"She's got your number." Meredith held up the empty glass.

Casey groaned helplessly and took the glass. "Who invited you?" She walked to the opposite side of the deck and looked out at the woods. She couldn't think anymore; this was too much emotion, too much—

"Casey?"

When she heard her grandmother's voice, she groaned. "Gram, I know what you're saying and—"

"Do you know where we could order a pizza?"

"Mama! Fire!"

Casey whirled around when she heard Skye's scream to see flames shooting out of the grill. "Shit!"

Meredith calmly sat in the chaise lounge and watched as Casey dashed off the deck and grabbed the garden hose.

The screen door flew open and Meredith now looked at Liz, who ran onto the deck with a pitcher of iced tea. Meredith, feeling like she was at a tennis match, looked back when Casey ran back with the garden hose and pointed the nozzle at the flames, just as Liz stood back and heaved the pitcher of tea at the grill; the iced tea missed the grill but doused Casey—lemons, ice, and all.

Blinded by the tea, pelted by the ice cubes and lemon wedges, Casey tried to get liquid out of her eyes and turn on the hose. "This damned thing!"

"Casey, I'm so sorry," Liz exclaimed.

Meredith looked to the heavens and shook her head; she stood with a groan and picked up the lid, placing it on the grill. Skye was giggling. Casey was breathing like a bull, completely soaked. Liz stood there holding the empty pitcher of tea and waving the smoke out of her face.

The aroma of charred beef filled the air.

Meredith dusted off her hands. "Now about that pizza."

"I found a doctor in Rhinelander," Liz offered as they ate dinner. "I have an appointment day after tomorrow in the afternoon."

Casey looked up from her pizza. "Is this a normal appointment?"

"Yes, don't worry." Liz blew at the steamy pizza.

"If I'm still here, dear, I'll take you." Meredith smiled at Liz, who glanced at Casey.

"Thank you, Meredith. Unfortunately, I don't have a car."

Casey wiped her mouth on the napkin. "I would've taken you.

You only had to ask."

Liz felt the blood rush to her face. She hated feeling this helpless, and once again, she heard the critical tone in Casey's voice. It was really getting annoying. "I've interrupted your life so much as it is. I—"

Casey snorted sarcastically.

Meredith's eyes flew open. "Casey Bennett!"

Liz threw down her napkin and wiped the pizza sauce off Skye's mouth. "C'mon, sweet pea, time for a bath."

Meredith put her hand on Liz's arm. "Let me. I haven't bathed a child in years." She looked at Skye, who giggled. "How about, Skye, can Grandma give you a bath?"

"Sure," Skye said and struggled off the chair. She pulled at Meredith's hand. "Come, Gamma. I show you fith."

Liz was fuming as she watched Skye and Meredith disappear down the hall. She pulled herself out of the kitchen chair with as much dignity as her stomach would allow and reached for the dishes.

Casey held onto her hand. "I'll clean up."

"No, thank you. I'd like to earn my room and board, Ms. Bennett." She angrily wrenched her hand away and picked up the plates and glasses.

Casey tossed down her napkin and walked out of the kitchen. Liz whirled around. "Enough of this."

She followed Casey into the living room. Casey was kneeling by the hearth, preparing to start a fire. I'll give her a fire, Liz thought.

"Okay, Casey. You and I need a heart to heart."

Casey's brow furrowed deeper. She then tossed the kindling and wood on the fire and angrily struck the match. "I have nothing to say."

"Oh, yes, you do. You've been on the verge of something since the day you picked us up at the bus station. Now we're having this out. I can't live on pins and needles like this. One minute you're adorable and sweet, and the next you're an ass." Inwardly, she wanted to kick herself in the ass, if she could get her foot that high, when she let the adorable comment slip.

Casey was breathing deeply; Liz could tell she was controlling her anger.

"Look, I know this is an inconvenience and I know you weren't expecting your life to be like this. But, damn it, neither was I!"

Casey whirled around to her. "Then why?"

Liz blinked at the obscure question. "Why what?"

"You seem, or seemed, like a logical, well-adjusted person. You know how Julie was, how irresponsible she was."

Liz bristled at the accusation. "I do not owe you any explanation. How dare you? What right do you have to question a decision made about a family and a relationship? What do you know of love, Casey Bennett? Or of a commitment?" She walked up to Casey and stood in front of her. "I don't think your life has been so exemplary that you can question mine. I had a partner who loved me. Was she irresponsible? Perhaps."

"Perhaps, that's almost laughable. Julie was like a child. She had no idea how to be a parent."

"And you have vast experience in that department?"

Casey looked down into Liz's eyes. "No, I do not. But I will admit to it and not go off and selfishly have two children. I can only imagine the cost of that, and you working part time as it was."

Liz shook her head. "Wait a second, what are you talking about two children?"

"Why would you do this? Twice?" Casey asked. Liz heard the pure confounded tone. Casey raised her hand. "Look, I apologize. It's none of my business."

"Is that what has been bothering you all this time?" Liz asked. "You thought Julie and I had two inseminations?" Liz sighed deeply, then laughed. She looked up to see the curious, almost scared look on Casey's face. "So you think I'm irresponsible, as well, is that it?"

"Like I said, it's none of my business."

"You're very arrogant and pompous. You do realize that, don't you?" Liz heard the muffled laugh coming from the direction of the bathroom.

"Let's skip it."

"No, this is important. I'm going to tell you, Ms. Bennett. Then if you still feel me irresponsible, I will gladly pack my bags and leave." She turned and faced the fireplace. She shook her head and laughed again.

"Twice?" Liz repeated. How could Casey Bennett know? "Casey, Skye is not my biological daughter."

Chapter 12

Casey shook her head as if to clear the cobwebs; she painfully pinched the bridge of her nose. "I beg your pardon?"

Liz sighed. "I'm going to need to sit for this one." She eased into the chair by the fireplace. Casey awkwardly reached out to assist her; she was too late and pulled her hand away.

With that, Skye came dashing down the hallway, completely naked. "Gamma give me bath. She read to me."

Meredith entered the living room, running her fingers through her silver hair. "Only pulled her out of the drain once." She laughed and held out her hand. "C'mon, you little guppy, kiss your mother and Casey good night."

Liz let out a groan as she leaned down to kiss Skye. "G'night, sweet pea. I love you."

"Ni-ni, Mama." She ran to Casey who knelt down. "Ni-ni, Cafey."

"G'night, Shortround," she whispered and kissed her flushed cheek. "Sweet dreams."

Liz felt the tears well in her eyes when she saw the forlorn look on Casey; she swore she saw tears in her green eyes, as well. She looked back at Meredith. "Thanks for this, Meredith."

"My pleasure, dear."

"Um, Meredith?"

Meredith cocked her head as she held onto Skye's hand.

"PJs?" Liz pointed to her naked child.

Meredith snapped her fingers. "I knew I forgot something. Casey used to sleep naked all the time. I believe she still does."

Casey's eyes bugged out of her head; she avoided Liz, who laughed. The silence that filled the room lasted for only a moment before Liz started again.

"Okay. Where do I start? I'm Skye's godmother. My best friend, Barb, and her husband, Steve, died in a car accident when Skye was about two months old. We had planned that I would be her legal guardian and would adopt Skye should something like that happen. Of course, we never dwelled on it or spoke of it again. They had no relatives to speak of. I thought I would have a problem with Steve's parents, but they didn't seem to mind. Don't you think that's strange? A grandparent not wanting their granddaughter?"

Casey shrugged. She was just trying to keep up with all this. "I would think so. When my mother died, Meredith just took over. I know I was grown and in college, but I can't imagine her not wanting to be in my life." She stopped and stared at the fire.

"How did you mother die?" Liz asked.

Casey looked up and shrugged. "Cancer. Seems to be the popular way to go." She stopped, realizing what she said. "I'm sorry. That…"

"I understand, and you're right. Did you have much time with her?"

Casey nodded. "Yes, but she was so sick throughout college. She wouldn't let me quit and come home. Gram said she wanted me to finish and not have to take care of her. I-I wish…"

"You had more time with her," Liz said, finishing for her.

"Yes," Casey said. "Sorry, please finish about Skye."

"Well, after the funeral and finalizing the paperwork, Skye came home with us. Barb's parents were deceased and Steve's parents were there for the funeral, then they flew home. I think they live out of the country, well, they did at the time. I felt there was no other choice. Besides, Julie was thrilled. Skye is a beautiful little girl, full of life."

"And the devil," Casey found herself saying with affection. Liz had to agree. "I feel like a heel. I thought you were irresponsible, spending a boatload of money on not one but two artificial inseminations, then Julie dies and you're stuck with no money."

"I can see where you would think that." Liz groaned slightly as she shifted in the chair. Casey pulled the ottoman over and lifted her legs onto it. "Thanks," Liz said with a tired sigh. Casey sat on the hearth and leaned against the stone wall. She stared at the dancing flames; Liz saw the contemplative gaze and for the first time really thought how attractive Casey was. Oh, not in the "ohmygod, you're gorgeous," which she was. But in a quiet subtle way—like now. Casey didn't know, or didn't let on, that Liz was watching her. She looked vulnerable; it was a definite aphrodisiac to Liz.

"Perhaps I should feel like a heel, Casey."

Casey blinked slowly and looked at her. "How so?"

"Julie broached the topic of artificial insemination. At first, I said no. We had a child, but Julie wanted another. 'To keep Skye company,' she had said. Julie, if you remember, was an only child and had a very lonely, sad childhood. I used that as an excuse. I was trying to keep Julie, I think."

Casey said nothing.

"She was constantly gone, always flying here and there. Never spending time at home with Skye…or me. So I foolishly thought she wanted a baby between us, to feel more like a family and to be more responsible. It was so stupid of me."

"I can't believe she's dead," Casey said, then shot a look at Liz. "Shit. I'm sorry. What an asinine thing to say."

"Don't be. I agree. However, you know, she'd been away for so long that I don't know, it somehow made this easier. Does that make sense? I mean, I did love her, and I do miss her, but the last six months have been so overwhelming and I've had so much to deal with." She stopped and glanced at Casey. "I'm not looking for sympathy."

Casey smiled slightly. "I know. That's the one infuriating thing about you."

Liz glared, then saw the lips twitching with amusement. She laughed along. "I have a fierce independent streak." She watched Casey, who nodded emphatically, then stared at the fire again.

"What are you thinking?"

"I was thinking about Julie. She wanted kids, but I knew she wasn't responsible and I couldn't conceive of doing that to a child, not when you have a choice. Being gay, you have to be so careful. Even straight, having a child is an enormous responsibility."

"Too much for you?"

Casey thought before answering. "No, it's not. Just not with Julie, and I don't mean to speak ill of her, Liz. I-I loved Julie..."

"You don't need to explain. I know exactly how you feel. I loved Julie, as well," Liz said, laughing as she shook her head. "There was something about her."

"Yes, there was. I will be honest, though, I'd never even consider having a child unless I was married to my partner," she said and frowned. She hadn't thought of this topic in five years. "But that's another story. I am not in the market for a family or a relationship. I-I like my freedom," she said, feeling uncomfortable with this topic.

Liz nodded and put her head back. "I don't blame you. You seem to have a good, comfortable life. You come and go as you please, though you don't eat right. I imagine you're not wanting for the company of a lovely woman. Don't you get lonely? I mean at night to have just one someone to hold on to, to wake up and start the day with?" When Casey did not reply, she continued, "No, I guess you don't. I envy you, Casey Bennett," she said and yawned. "Well, things happen for a reason, a good reason. I believe that." She sighed and closed her eyes.

"Can I tell you something?"

Liz lifted her head and nodded. Her stomach fluttered with anticipation at what Casey was about to say.

"Just now, you look young, too young to have two kids and go through a companion dying, friends dying, and, hell, you look pretty good for all that life. You're an attractive woman, Liz."

Liz felt her face grow warm; she knew she was blushing. Casey grinned and looked away.

"Thank you. I don't feel very attractive."

"Gram said you'd feel like that," Casey said. "Look, I'm sorry I'm not in touch with all this. I want to help, and now that I know the whole story and feel like a jackass, maybe we can start over."

Liz grinned. "I'd like that. Skye, well, she really adores you."

It was Casey's turn to blush. She laughed and scratched her forehead. "She's a handful, but I really get a kick out of her."

They both laughed and enjoyed the comfortable silence for the first time between them. "So tell me how you got stuck in that inner tube."

Casey laughed. "I was trying to show her how to put it on, so she could stay in the water without me holding her. She's a lot like her mother, very independent."

"God help you, Ms. Bennett."

"I think He already might have."

Liz shot her an incredulous look and grinned.

"Well, you're both still alive," Meredith said as she walked down the hall. "Skye is sound asleep. I had to read her Shelley. For godsake, Liz, doesn't she know 'One Fish, Two Fish, Whatever Comes Next Fish'?" She waved them off while they laughed. "I need a drink."

Chapter 13

"You must come for a visit to Chicago," Meredith said as they walked to her car.

"I'd love to, Meredith. Thank you so much," Liz said with tears in her eyes. She hugged Meredith and kissed her cheek.

"You'll take care of this idiot, won't you?" Meredith motioned to Casey, who rolled her eyes.

Liz laughed as she wiped the tears away. Skye's bottom lipped quivered as she reached up. "Goodbye, my little darling."

"Bye, Gamma," Skye said. "You coming back?"

Meredith chucked her under the chin. "You try and keep me away." She reached for Casey, who hugged her fiercely.

"Good grief, Gram. I'll see you when I go back to Chicago."

"And bring the girls." Meredith lightly slapped her cheek. "Behave until then."

Casey picked up Skye and waved as Meredith's big car maneuvered down the access road. "Don't kill anyone!" Casey called out.

Liz slapped her arm and took Skye from her. "We'd better get going, too. My appointment is in an hour." She looked at Casey. "Thanks for driving me and taking Skye."

"We'll have fun," Casey said. She waited patiently for Liz to get ready.

It was a short drive to the clinic. Casey parked in front of the doctor's office in town.

"Skye, be good for Casey," Liz warned as she kissed the blond hair. She looked at Casey. "Casey, be good for Skye," she added with a chuckle.

"Amusing," Casey countered and couldn't hide her grin when she saw Liz's blue eyes sparkling. Casey had a hard time looking away. She then felt her shorts being tugged.

"C'mon, Cafey." Skye groaned and pulled.

Liz laughed. "You'd better go. I shouldn't be more than a half hour or so."

"We'll meet you back here," Casey said.

"Be careful," Liz said, trying to hide her concern.

"What could go wrong?" Casey asked as Skye pulled her down the street.

Liz sat in the examining room afterward while the old doctor scribbled on the chart.

"Everything looks good, though you need a little more weight on you. How is everything else? Your husband—"

"I'm not married, Doctor," Liz offered.

The old man looked at the chart again. "Ah, I see. I'm sorry to be presumptuous. Nowadays, you just don't know. Well, you're doing just fine, keep it up. Is your…?" he hesitated and Liz saw the color rise in this face. "…are you living alone?"

Now it was Liz's turn to blush. "N-no. I'm staying with a friend for now. Perhaps you know her, Casey Bennett."

The old doctor raised an eyebrow, and Liz had a good idea that Dr. Martin knew Casey.

"She's been a tremendous help," Liz continued, then smiled thinking of the burnt dinner from the night before and how Casey had helped with Skye. "More than she realizes," she said absently as she remembered how all three lay in the big bed while Liz read to them. She also remembered the look she got from Casey. Her green eyes seemed to look right through her. Perhaps she only wanted it to be so.

Liz took a deep contented sigh and realized Dr. Martin was watching her. He smiled as she cleared her throat.

"I know Casey Bennett. If she can make you look that happy

and content, then I hope you stay with her until the baby comes," he said and patted her hand. "As I said, keep up the good work and—"

"Doctor, um, we have a woman," the nurse said as she poked her head into the room, "with a small girl…"

Liz bolted up. "Blond girl? Tall dark-haired woman?" she asked nervously.

The nurse nodded and doctor and mother quickly followed the nurse to the other examination room.

Liz rushed in to find Casey lying on the table with an icepack on her knee. Her jeans were ripped at said knee and her elbow was scraped raw. Skye was standing on a chair holding Casey's hand.

Skye turned to Liz and grinned. "Mama! Cafey faw down 'gen."

Liz rushed to Skye's side. "What happened?" she asked as she checked Skye for injuries. Her little face was flushed with excitement.

Casey tried to sit up, but Dr. Martin put a hand on her shoulder. "Hold on, let me have a look."

He took the icepack off and saw the small abrasion on her knee. Between him and the nurse, they got to work. "What did you hit?" he asked and he poked and prodded.

"Well…" Casey started and winced.

Dr. Martin said nothing as he listened to the three females. He saw the look of concern in Liz's blue eyes and the embarrassment in Ms. Bennett's green eyes.

He stepped back as the nurse cleaned Casey's knee and elbow. As he watched, he glanced at the blond girl and stifled a hearty laugh. He listened to her mature explanation.

"Cafey faw off fweeng."

Liz tiredly rubbed her face. "Fell off a swing?" She looked down at Casey, who nodded and just stared at the ceiling. "How did you manage that?"

"It was far easier than I ever thought it could be," Casey said and Liz laughed out loud. Skye joined her.

"Tell me."

"Can we discuss this at home?" Casey pleaded, stealing a

glance at the smirking doctor and nurse.

"Oh, no. I want to hear this." Dr. Martin pulled up a chair. He sat at the counter and scribbled. "You're fine, nothing broken, just a few scrapes and a wounded ego. So... Continue."

Casey took a deep resigned breath and stared at the ceiling again. The doctor noticed how Liz had her arm around her daughter; with her other hand, she caressed Casey's arm.

"We were swinging," Casey started and looked at Liz. "I had Shortround in one of those kid's swings, she was safe," she said quickly.

Liz smiled. "I know."

"Well, your daughter wanted me to go higher."

"Cafey go so high, Mama!" Skye interjected with enthusiasm.

"I can imagine, sweet pea."

"I got my foot stuck in the dirt and kinda flew off the swing."

"Cafey fly like birdie, Mama," Skye exclaimed.

"Can we get out of here now?"

"Not just yet, I'd like Dr. Martin to X-ray your head," Liz said.

"Why? I didn't hit..." Casey stopped and glowered at Liz. "Very funny."

Dr. Martin laughed as he stood. "You're fine. Stay off the playground for a few days. Why don't you take the little one out and get her a sucker? I want to talk to the big one for a moment."

He saw the worried look on Casey and Liz as he ushered them out of the room. He turned back as Casey sat up and flexed her knee. "Don't tell me it's worse than you thought," Casey offered with a grin. It immediately faded when she saw the stern look on the doctor's face.

"I had a nice talk with Liz, says she's staying with you until the baby comes." He stood in front of Casey, who nodded. "I'm not sure how much experience you have with pregnant women...May I call you Casey?" he asked and Casey nodded again. "There will be mood swings during her pregnancy." He walked over to the desk and picked up a few pamphlets. "I suggest you read these. It may give you a little insight into the pregnant woman's psyche. There's also a wonderful book at the library." He scribbled on the prescription pad and handed it to her.

Casey took the offering and leafed through the pamphlets.

"That is if you want insight," he said and watched her.

"Yes, Doctor, I want insight. I want to help with this pregnancy. Liz and Skye...well, they're...I mean, I've come to... I'm not sure what Liz has told you," she stammered helplessly.

"She's told me enough to understand her situation. I'm not sure why you're helping her, Casey, but I hope you're in it for the duration. She's going to need you. She needs you now."

The magnitude of what he was saying seemed to hit home as he watched her. Casey took a deep confident breath and nodded. She slipped the pamphlets into her back pocket.

"Thanks, Dr. Martin. I'll take care of her and Skye. I'm not sure if I know what I'm doing."

Dr. Martin patted her on the back as they walked out. "You'll be fine. Having a baby is as natural as falling off a swing," he said and pushed her out the door.

Chapter 14

"Stay," Skye begged as she clung to Casey's pants leg. Liz fought the tears that stuck in her throat as she watched her daughter.

Casey put her briefcase down and pulled Skye up in her arms. "Shortround, it's just like before. I'll be back before you know it. Please don't cry," she whispered and kissed her cheek. "You have to take care of your mom while I'm gone, okay?"

"'Kay," Skye whispered. "You coming back, right?"

"Yeah, Shortround, I'll be back. I promise. Now eat your breakfast."

"Bye, Cafey." Skye kissed her cheek.

They walked in silence, side by side, toward the car. "She's really fond of you, Casey."

Casey turned to Liz and smiled. "I'm fond of the little dwarf, as well. I just wish she wouldn't get so upset when I have to leave."

"I think somehow she remembers Julie. She would promise to come home, but she was always delayed. Skye would sit in the window and wait until I had to carry her to bed. I don't know why Julie did that," Liz said pensively, looking down and kicking at the dirt. "She asked Meredith the same thing."

Casey leaned against the car as she watched her. "I'm coming back, Liz."

Liz looked at her then. "I hope so, you live here."

Casey laughed and shook her head. "I'll be back by Friday. Call me or Marge if—"

"I know the drill, General." Liz offered a mock salute.

They stood there in awkward silence. Liz was playing with her hair and absently rubbing her stomach. Casey was holding her briefcase and looking out at the lake.

"Well... So..." They both said at the same time and laughed. Casey opened the car door.

"Have a safe trip," Liz said and backed up.

"I will. Liz..." Casey started as she closed the door. She had no idea what she wanted to say or if she should say anything.

"I know, Casey. Now get going. See you on Friday."

She watched the car pull down the dirt road. Casey stuck her hand out the window and waved. Liz smiled and waved in kind.

Liz groaned as she picked up Skye's toys and stretched her back. She had just gotten her to bed, and for the hundredth time, she had to reassure her Casey would be home the next day. Liz began to like that idea as much as her daughter. She wondered what Casey was doing in Chicago when she wasn't in the studio. For some reason, she wanted to meet the gorgeous cellist.

"Why?" she whispered. "What difference would it make?" She put Skye's toys on the couch and lumbered into the kitchen to put the kettle on for tea. "I'm sure Casey Bennett would rather be with her than a fat pregnant woman." She puttered around the kitchen until the sound of the whistle gently told her to make the tea and get off her feet.

"I do miss her," Liz said, almost in awe of the idea, though the thought of it made Liz smile. She picked up her teacup and gazed out at the lake; it was twilight. With the stars just appearing in the early evening sky, the moon would soon be rising above the trees. It was beautiful in these woods. She felt safe and content. Suddenly, a wave of anxiety wafted through her. She wasn't sure what the future would hold for her unborn child. Casey Bennett's face flashed through her mind and she smiled.

She gazed out at the quiet lake and sipped her chamomile tea.

On Thursday night, Casey stood by her big window overlooking Lake Michigan. It was a rough day at the office for her. Nothing sounded right, the music was all off, or perhaps she was off. She glanced around the plush apartment and sighed pensively. Chicago held nothing for her anymore.

She wondered why that was and realized the answer might be six hours north of there. The answer to what, though? she thought. Liz's face flooded her vision more and more. Then Skye's happy face came into view, and she laughed out loud. "What the f...heck is going on with me?" She sipped her wine and gazed out at Lake Michigan.

The chimes from the doorbell brought her back to reality. She glanced at the clock on the mantel and groaned. "Please don't let this be Suzette." She opened the door and shook her head. "What are you doing here?"

Meredith, somewhat out of breath, waved her off as she pushed past her.

"Did you take the stairs?" Casey put her hand under her arm and guided her to the couch. Meredith sat with a grunt.

"No," she said with a wheeze. "But your apartment is so far from the elevator."

Casey sat in the chair opposite the couch. "You scared the life out of me. Hey," she said. "How did you know I'd be home...and alone?"

"I called Niles. He told me you had a touch of melancholy earlier. So I knew you wouldn't be with the savant."

"I was not melancholy. And will you quit calling her that?"

"Of course, dear. There have been many other names that have been rolling around. How about—"

"Never mind. Would you like a drink?" Casey didn't wait for an answer.

"You ask the oddest questions. Speaking of odd, isn't melancholy an odd word?" Meredith kicked off her shoes and wriggled her toes.

Casey returned with the chilled stemmed glass and handed it to her grandmother. "Thank you, dear. You are now back in my will."

Casey smiled and sat by the fireplace and watched the flames.

"You look so much like your mother. She had that same pensive look when she was confused."

"I'm not confused," Casey said, looking up. "What do I have to be confused about?"

"Liz, Skye," she said, then whispered, "falling in love."

Casey's mouth dropped. "You're senile," she said and reached for her drink.

Meredith laughed and took a sip from her glass.

"Gram, I'm not in love with Liz."

"Not yet, you're not."

"Gram..."

"Case..."

Casey groaned and laid her head back against the flagstone fireplace. "Please don't read anything into this. Don't get your romantic knickers in a twist. There's nothing between Liz and me. Shit, Gram, I practically called her a gold-digging bitch who was irresponsible and selfish."

"But you were wrong," Meredith reminded her. "What did Liz call you?"

"Arrogant and pompous."

"Ah, yes. Hit the proverbial nail right on the head, didn't she?"

Casey said nothing but took a long pensive breath and let it out slowly.

"And before this is done, you'll irritate each other, and you'll probably do something or say something really stupid and you'll have to apologize all over again. But in the end, dear, you'll realize just how much you need Liz Kennedy and her family."

Casey blinked several times as if trying to register what the hell her grandmother was saying. "I am not in love with Liz. She is not in love with me. I'm only helping her until the baby is born and she can get back on her feet. I'm sure she wants to get her life back and go home."

Meredith snorted and ate an olive. "Hogwash."

Casey shook her head. "I—"

The doorbell had Casey groaning as she stood.

"I wonder who that could be?" Meredith asked.

"I just wanted a nice quiet evening."

"Thinking of Liz."

Casey growled and opened the door. "C'mon in," she said and stepped back.

Niles entered and smiled happily when he saw Meredith. "Meredith! How nice to see you."

Casey glared at him. "Like you didn't know she'd be here."

"Oh, shush. Yes, I'd love a glass of wine." Niles slipped out of his coat. He took Meredith's offered hand and kissed it.

"Brian is one lucky sonofabitch," Meredith said.

Niles laughed as he sat next to her. He took the glass of wine from Casey, settling back against the deep cushions. "So what have we been talking about?"

"One guess." Casey resumed her place on the hearth.

"Have you convinced her?" he asked Meredith, who shrugged and swirled the olive in her glass. Niles looked at Casey. "You're not convinced?"

"I am not in love with Liz Kennedy."

"Of course you're not…yet."

"That's what I told her." Meredith set her glass on the end table. "What's this?" She picked up several pamphlets. "Know What to Do When It's Time?" She leafed through one, then absently handed it to Niles, who studied each one Meredith gave him.

"What?" Casey said, feeling her embarrassment rising. "She, well, Liz will be here for a few months. I have to know what's going on. Don't I?"

Both nodded without looking up as they read. "I didn't know this." Niles pointed to the pamphlet. Meredith looked over and read the passage.

"Well, you're not a pregnant woman, dear."

They read in silence; it was annoying Casey to no end. She bolted up and sat next to Niles on the couch. Without looking at her, he handed her a pamphlet.

Casey took it and read. "I didn't know this."

Niles and Meredith exchanged glances but said nothing. Casey felt a bad headache coming on.

The next morning, before she headed back north, Casey pulled into the Chicago Library parking lot. The quiet in the huge building was deafening. She walked up to the counter and took the paper out of her pocket. A young woman behind the counter smiled.

"May I help you?"

She spoke so softly, Casey barely heard her. She cleared her throat and handed the woman the paper. "I need to get this book."

The woman glanced at the paper, then back at Casey. "For your wife?" she asked with a knowing smile.

Casey felt the color flood her cheeks. "Uh, no, no. I have a friend who's pregnant, and I'm helping out and—"

"You had a long talk with Dr. Martin, and he suggested this book."

Casey was amazed. "How do you know Dr. Martin?"

The woman presented the paper. It was then Casey realized Dr. Martin had scribbled the information on a prescription. She laughed nervously. "Something like that."

"I can find this book for you. Come with me."

Casey followed the woman up the stairs, then down a few aisles until the librarian stopped. She searched the shelves and stopped. "Here we are." She handed the book to Casey.

"Have, um…"

"Yes, I've read it. My wife and I had a baby two years ago. This helped Gina," the librarian said. "Enormously. She had no clue."

Casey laughed. "I think your wife and I are in the same boat."

"You have a library card?"

Casey winced and shook her head. The librarian held out her hand. "My name is Dorie. I'll need some identification."

Casey shook her hand and pulled out her wallet.

Casey leafed through the book while Dorie typed her

information into the computer. "So, um, how…I mean, if you don't mind…"

Dorie looked up over her glasses. "I don't mind at all. You can ask anything you like."

Feeling much more at ease, Casey leaned on the counter. "Did you have mood swings and cravings?"

"Oh, God, yes. I thought Gina was going to leave at one point. And as for cravings? For a while, I craved Chinese food and potato chips."

"Well, that's not so odd," Casey said.

Dorie stopped typing. "At the same time."

"Oh."

"So how far along is your friend?"

Casey heard the hesitation in Dorie's voice when she said friend. "She's due in December." She realized that was only a couple of months away. All of the sudden, she felt sick; her stomach was in knots and the room felt as though it was closing in on her. She pulled at the collar of her sweater, feeling the sweat form on her brow. She didn't realize Dorie had come around from behind the desk, guiding her to a nearby chair.

"Are you all right? You looked like you were about to faint."

Casey took the offered paper cup of water and gulped it down. "I'm fine. I don't know what happened."

"Reality." Dorie patted her shoulder.

Casey looked up in confusion when Dorie laughed. "You're just realizing the magnitude of the situation. Gina had the same reaction, right about this time, as well, if I remember correctly."

With her heart rate returning to normal, Casey laughed along. "Weren't you ever scared?"

Dorie struck a thoughtful pose for a moment and it happened. She smiled and the look on her face was the exact look Liz had many times. Casey has seen that look—the look of utter bliss. She envied Dorie and Liz.

"I was at first. Then all of the sudden, it became clear as a bell," Dorie said. "I was going to have a baby, and I was happy." She patted Casey on the shoulder again and walked back to the desk. "And Gina wanted to vomit."

Casey thought about Dorie, all she read, and all that Niles and her grandmother had talked about the whole long drive up north. She couldn't think anymore. Even the radio did nothing. She couldn't get it out of her mind. Was she falling for Liz? Was that possible? Did she even want that? She'd asked herself these questions over and over; she prayed for an answer. Casey was sure of this much—the thought of Liz Kennedy made her stomach flip and her heart pound in her chest. Was that love?

At nearly four in the afternoon, she pulled onto her access road, and her heart skipped a beat. The last time she came home, Skye was so excited she tripped and fell. She remembered Liz's blue eyes, filled with concern for her daughter, and what for Casey? Anything? "Oh, God, stop this!" she begged and parked the car.

She heard their voices down by the beach. As she made her way toward them, she nearly laughed out loud. There was Skye. Liz had her in small inner tube in the shallow water. Liz wore a blue tank top, oversized of course, and shorts. She stood in knee-deep water pulling her daughter around near the shore.

Liz wore sunglasses and a baseball cap, her long hair pulled through the opening in the back. Casey found herself gazing at her body. Her thighs were muscular and her upper arms were firm. Casey wondered what she did before she was pregnant. Was she athletic? Did she work out? Or was she naturally in good shape? Keeping up with Skye most likely helped her keep fit. Though, this didn't matter to Casey. Liz was beautiful, not because of her looks, but because of who she was. Her smile came from deep within. Liz was a confident, caring woman. Suddenly, Casey felt inept and shallow. When did she become so cavalier about love? Was sex all she would ever have? She jammed her hands into the pockets of her shorts and felt the wave of self-pity ripple through her.

When she heard Skye giggling, she couldn't help but laugh; her mood instantly lightened. "Thanks, Shortround," she whispered to no one.

Skye looked past Liz and shrieked, "Cafey!"

Liz whirled around and smiled so widely, Casey just beamed in return.

"Hey," Casey called out with a wave and walked down to the beach. Skye struggled out of the shallow water and past her mother. With the inner tube still around her waist, she dashed toward Casey, trying to wriggle out of the inner tube.

"Now you know how I felt," Casey said and offered her assistance. Skye jumped into her arms; Casey held on tight.

She looked at Liz, who was slowly making her way out of the shallow water. Casey met her halfway and offered her other hand.

"Hi," Liz said breathlessly.

"Hi," Casey said. Skye wrapped her arms around Casey's neck.

"Sweet pea, you're all wet and you're strangling Casey."

"It's okay. It feels good." She looked down at their hands, then let go. "You look good."

Liz stopped smiling for an instant, the crimson started in her neck. She nervously put her hand to her neck and laughed. "Well, thanks, but I think I've been out in the sun too long."

Casey noticed the sunburn as she set Skye down. "Mama," Casey scolded playfully.

"Cafey, fim," Skye said and pulled on Casey's leg.

"Let me go change. Unless you're tired," Casey said, looking at Liz.

"No, please, this is wonderful. Go change. We'll be here."

The cool lake rejuvenated Casey as she dove off the pier. Liz sat on the pier under an umbrella and watched Skye play in the sand. This would definitely be a bath night. She turned and watched Casey as she swam. Good Lord, what a body, she thought. Watching her, Liz tried to get a mental picture of Casey and Julie together. Not in a sexual way, but in an intimate way. Liz could see what attracted Julie to Casey. She was confident, sexy, and intelligent. Liz shivered when she remembered hearing Casey play the piano that afternoon when she woke. The music was so sensual, so romantic. She then remembered how irritated Casey was. Must be the artistic temperament, she thought. Liz closed her eyes and imagined Julie listening to Casey as she played; she almost envied her. What must it feel like to know someone is playing a song for you and only you?

She rolled her eyes and laughed inwardly. You're a romantic fool, Kennedy, she thought. It was a nice dream, but as all dreams, it wasn't real. The reality struck her then. She would have her baby, get on her feet, and...and what?

The cold water in her face broke her reverie. Skye laughed as Liz shrieked when Casey splashed water again. "Oh, you!"

Treading water, Casey grinned evilly. "You have to catch me first."

"You just wait, Ms. Bennett. Once this baby is born, paybacks are a bi—"

"Ah, ah." Casey wagged a finger in her direction as she walked out of the water. She absently reached behind and pulled at the bottom of her suit. Liz stared at Casey's firm backside and felt the tingling sensation she hadn't felt in quite some time.

After a wonderful dinner of hot dogs and hamburgers, and a good bath, Skye was sound asleep before the sun went down. Liz left the bedroom door ajar, then found Casey on the porch leaning on the railing, watching the sunset.

For an instant, she stood at the screen door and just watched her. The sounds of late summer echoed through the woods; the crickets chirped, the night birds called, and the light summer breeze whistled through the birch trees. Liz smiled and walked out onto the porch.

Casey turned to her. "Shortround was pooped."

"Yes, she was. She had a full few days. I had to really keep her busy. She missed you very much."

"I missed her, too," Casey whispered. "I-I missed you, as well, Liz."

"Thanks," Liz said and avoided her face. "I missed you, too."

Casey hid her grin as she turned back to look at the lake. Liz tried not to smile, but she couldn't help it; she was happy. She then saw the tube of ointment lying on the railing. "What's that?"

Casey followed her gaze. "Oh, it's a lotion I use when I get sunburn. I thought you could use it." She laughed and pointed to her shoulders. "You're really red."

Liz strained to see the back of her shoulders. "God, I nearly smothered Skye with it all week."

"And completely forgot about yourself." Casey reached for the tube. "Here, let me."

Liz put her hand out to take the tube and Casey gently brushed her hand away. "Let me. You can't reach it. Turn around."

"Oh." Liz did as Casey asked. She looked to the heavens to help her composure when she felt the cool lotion on her shoulders.

"It would be better if you didn't have this tank top on," Casey said in a low voice.

"Are you flirting with me, Ms. Bennett?" Liz asked, knowing her voice trembled. She tried to avoid the fluttering sensation in her stomach.

"I don't know. Would that be a bad thing?"

"I don't know."

There was a moment of silence, then both women laughed.

"I guess this will have to do."

"I guess." Liz winced as a long sigh escaped at the same time. She immediately missed the gentle fingers when they finished. The spell was broken.

She turned around to find Casey frowning deeply. This was not what she expected to see. Liz had hoped at least to see Casey breathing heavily or perhaps her hands trembling.

"Thank you. I feel better already," Liz said.

"You're welcome."

"It's a beautiful sunset," Liz whispered and stood next to her. "The lake is as smooth as glass tonight."

"Maybe tomorrow we can take the rowboat out. Skye would like that."

"Yes, she would." Liz looked at Casey, who was looking at the lake. "Thank you, Casey."

Casey looked down into her eyes. "For what?"

"For all you've done for me and for Skye. I'm not quite sure where I'd be right now."

"Julie is to thank for that. I had no idea you existed."

"I thought Julie told you about me."

Casey cocked her head and thought about that. She smiled then. "Yes, she did. I suppose I had no idea that Liz Kennedy, compassionate mother and friend, existed. I had an abstract idea, but now I know you, how you are, what you think." She shrugged and continued. "So, yes, I had no idea you existed."

Liz said nothing for a moment. "You have a way about you, Ms. Bennett. I can see what Julie loved about you. I suppose we both should thank Julie." Liz felt the tears well in her eyes. She desperately didn't want to break this mood by blubbering like a fool. "I'll thank her in my prayers tonight, along with you." She felt as though she should leave before her hormones got the better of her and she said something she would regret.

"I will too," Casey said.

Liz smiled and placed her hand over Casey's. "I think I might turn in. Good night, Casey."

Casey nodded. "Sleep well, Liz."

Later that night, as Skye slept, Liz lay in the big bed and stared at the ceiling. She ran her hand over her stomach while wiping away her tears with the other. Though she and Casey were getting along better and they had a wonderful day, her head pounded, trying not to think of all that was to come and how she would manage alone. Though, if she were honest, Liz was always alone. Julie was constantly on the go. Being a pilot took her away more than Liz wanted, but she was never sure if it bothered Julie as much. She grunted sarcastically, apparently it did not. Liz's pleading fell on deaf ears.

In the beginning, it was wonderful, as she imagined most new relationships were. Julie was an ardent lover and Liz reveled in her tenderness. Liz thought she found someone whom she could love and build a life with. Julie Bridges certainly seemed to fit the bill. However, in the following year, when Julie took the longer schedule and route with the airlines, it started to change. It was a slow, subtle change that seemed to take Liz by surprise. Perhaps she wasn't giving Julie enough attention. Skye came into their lives early in their relationship. They had only been together for about two years when Barb and Steve died in that car accident. Everyone's lives changed after that.

Liz had no idea how to be a mother, and though saddened by her parents' death, Julie loved the idea of being a mom for Skye. Liz shook her head, staring now out the bedroom window—Julie loved being Skye's playmate was more accurate.

Although motherhood had been thrust upon her, it came easily to Liz, easier than she could imagine. When she saw those adorable blue eyes, she fell in love with Skye. From that day, her well-being was paramount. It was just an enormous responsibility; she knew she was hard on Julie at times. And truth be told, Julie did try. There was a period of adjustment for all of them. Then things seemed to fall into place and they were happy. Julie took the job with the airlines because it was more money—money they needed. Yes, Liz thought and sighed tiredly, they were happy, they were a family. Then it all fell apart.

Her eyes grew heavy, lulled by Skye's deep breathing. She reached over and placed her hand on Skye's shoulder just to make contact. As she drifted off, Casey's face crowded her mind and invaded her dreams.

"How much do you weigh?" Casey asked as they ate breakfast. She handed Skye a sausage link and the little blonde nodded enthusiastically as she took the offering.

Liz narrowed her eyes at Casey. "She can use a fork."

Casey looked up and grinned. When she saw the scowl, she quickly took the sausage from Skye and cut it into little pieces, then handed Skye the fork.

"And I have no idea how much I weigh. Why do you ask?" Liz asked abruptly. She looked at her hand and flexed it a few times.

Casey heard the terse tone in Liz's voice and could tell Liz was probably trying to control her raging hormones. By the way she was examining her hand, Liz more than likely felt bloated. She glanced down the hall to the bedroom, quelling the urge to run into the bedroom and find the correct chapter Dorie had advised her to read in *Understanding Her Pregnancy*.

"I just want to make sure you're gaining enough weight, that's all. Dr. Martin said you needed to keep an eye on it," she said, feeling awkward and inept. Honestly, Casey had no clue what she was doing. This whole pregnancy thing was so beyond her.

Liz tossed down her napkin. "Will everybody relax about my gaining weight?"

Casey was shocked, and as she glanced at Skye, so was she. She wanted to say something but wisely shut up.

Liz took a deep breath. "I would love a cup of coffee, not decaf, regular coffee with cream and sugar! I want to be able to stand up without holding on to the table. I want to be able to walk and not waddle," she continued, her voice rising with every word.

Casey and Skye just sat there gaping.

"I want to sleep through the night without shuffling to the bathroom every hour. I want control of my emotions once again. Yesterday, Skye and I were watching 'The Three Stooges,' and I started crying when Moe poked Curly in the eyes! I want to see my feet again," she bellowed and buried her face in her hands.

Casey glanced at poor Skye, who was watching her mother with great curiosity.

Okay, mood swings, mood swings, Casey thought, reaching over to put her hand on Liz's arm.

"I'm sorry. I'm fine, sweet pea," Liz said as she sniffed and wiped her eyes with the napkin.

Skye lifted her bare foot. "Mama see my feet!"

Casey and Liz laughed outright. "Yes, baby, I see your feet." She reached over and took the little foot in her hand and kissed her toes. "I love these toes," Liz exclaimed and Skye shrieked with laughter.

Liz was still laughing while she struggled out of her chair. As she gathered the breakfast dishes, Casey stood. "Sit, I'll clean up."

"No, no. I want to. You play This Little Piggy with Skye," she said with a challenging grin.

Casey felt the color rush to her face. Skye clapped her hands as she presented her bare foot to Casey. "Piggy, peas."

Casey cleared her throat and glanced at Liz, who had her back to them as she washed the dishes.

"Okay, Shortround, here goes," she started and held the little foot in her hand. "You have small feet," she said in amazement, emitting a small giggle from the owner. "Anyway, this little piggy went to market—"

"Why?" Skye asked with a frown.

"I-I really don't know," Casey said and looked to Liz, who shrugged. "We'll come back to that one. This is good. Now this little piggy stayed home and I don't know why," she added before Skye could ask. "This little piggy had roast beef. Maybe that's why the other piggy went to market. This one," she said and playfully tugged the wriggling toe, "ate all the roast beef, 'cause this one," Casey announced with a self-satisfied air, "had none."

Liz had turned off the water and leaned against the sink to hear the rest of Casey's logical rendition. Casey sported a confident smile as she continued. Liz watched her daughter, who looked from her foot to Casey with great interest.

"Now this little piggy goes wee, wee, wee all the way home. Not quite sure why, though. Maybe she was at the market with the other one and…" She stopped abruptly, realizing how ridiculous she sounded. She looked at Liz, who had one eyebrow raised in smug fashion as she dried her hands on the towel.

"Mama plays better," Skye whispered.

Casey smiled sheepishly and sat back. "Well, it's been a while since I played that game," she conceded and drank her coffee.

She watched as Skye struggled to get out of her booster chair while Liz tried to help. "Mama, I do it by mineself," Skye argued. Liz stepped back.

Skye slipped down from her seat and ran from the kitchen.

"When did that start?" Casey asked with a chuckle. "She sounds so much older."

"Two days ago. Her independent streak is starting. This will be interesting," Liz said with a groan. "Her vocabulary is growing every day."

Casey looked up and noticed how tired Liz looked. Her blue eyes still sparkled, but she looked pooped. She stood and guided Liz to the couch. "C'mon, take a load off and put your feet up for a while. I'll clean up."

When she finished, she walked into the living room to find Liz sleeping peacefully on the couch, her feet up and her head back.

"Mama," Skye called from the hallway.

Immediately, Liz's eyes flew open and she tried to sit up. Casey went to her. "I'll see what the little urchin wants. I think I'll take her for a walk in my woods."

"Okay, Skye. Let's go for walk," Casey offered and took the girl out. On the way out, she winked at Liz. "Be right back, we're gonna check out the woods."

Liz smiled gratefully, appreciating the quiet time and appreciating that Casey could sense this without being asked. She hated to ask anything of Casey; she had been so good and so considerate. It was nice to have someone take care of her daughter, just for a few minutes.

An hour later, Liz was getting worried. She paced back and forth in the cabin. Then she heard them talking as they walked onto the porch. She threw her arms around Casey's neck.

"Where have you been?" she cried as her hormones flew all over the place.

Casey's eyes widened as she put an arm around Liz's waist. "I'm sorry. We went to pick wildflowers," she explained and Liz let her go.

"Sorry," Liz said and picked up Skye and started crying all over again.

Skye gave her mother a strange look and looked up at Casey, who shrugged and motioned her to give her mother a kiss.

Skye put her hands on either side of her mother's face and went nose to nose. "Don't ki, Mama," she said in adult fashion and kissed her mother.

That did it. The water works started. Casey affectionately put her arm around her shoulders.

"Mama sad?"

Casey took Skye from Liz and led Liz to the couch where she sat next to her. Skye crawled up and sat on Casey's lap.

"No, Shortround. Mommy is just happy. She loves you very much."

"I love you, too!" Liz cried out.

Casey was stunned.

Skye clapped her hands together. "Mama vuzz Cafey!"

Casey laughed and reached over, brushing the tears off Liz's cheek.

"Cafey vuzz Mama?" Skye asked and yanked on her shirt.

Liz looked into Casey's green eyes; she had no idea what she saw there. Well, she had an idea, and it scared her to death.

"Yes, Shortround. I love your Mommy, too," she said as she handed Liz the wildflowers.

Chapter 15

When it was time for bed, Skye pulled at Casey's hand. Liz laughed and tried to pick up her daughter. "It's time for bed, sweet pea."

"Cafey come too," Skye said. "Read to me."

Casey laughed and allowed Skye to pull her down the hall. "I'll read to her. You relax," Casey said over her shoulder.

"Now you've done it, Ms. Bennett. You'll be reading to her every night," Liz called out as she made her way to the front porch. She eased into the rocker and put her head back.

Smiling, she heard Casey mumbling as she read to Skye. Liz looked out at the lake and watched the evening stars fill the sky. She put her head back and closed her eyes as she gently rocked in the chair.

When she woke, she looked around in a panic. "What time is it?" She stifled a groan as she went back into the house. It was nearly 9:00 by the clock on the mantel. Where was Casey? She walked down the hall and went into the bedroom; she smiled and shook her head. There lay Casey on her back sound asleep with her arms over her head. Skye was sitting up next to her, looking at the book. She looked up when Liz walked into the room.

Skye put her fingertip to her lips and Liz nodded. "Cafey faw asleep."

"I see," Liz whispered. "Why aren't you?"

"Mama sleep."

Liz raised an eyebrow as she glanced at Casey, breathing deeply in her sound sleep. She looked so peaceful, Liz thought, so vulnerable. Liz held out her hand, and Skye handed her the book. "Time for you to get to sleep, sweet pea."

Skye scrunched her nose, then lay back against the pillows. Casey in her sleep put her arm around Skye, who in turn cuddled closer.

Liz changed and locked up the cabin. She went back into the bedroom to check on Skye. She was going to sleep on the couch, but as she looked at the firm mattress that looked so inviting, her back told her otherwise. She bit at her bottom lip as she gently pulled back the sheet and eased under them. She let out a contented sigh as she stretched out on her back. Liz closed her eyes, and just before she drifted off, she reached over, resting her hand on her daughter's leg.

Liz woke the next morning to find Casey gone. She slipped out of bed, mindful not to wake Skye, and threw on her robe. She walked out into the living room finding Casey nowhere in sight. Then she looked out the big window and saw her swimming; she was naked.

"Oh, God." She stood rooted to the spot and stared. "I should be looking away," she whispered, but she couldn't take her gaze off the tanned hips as they bobbed out of the water as Casey swam. She had a beautifully toned body. Liz sported a sour look. "I remember those days," she said dryly.

Just then, Casey changed directions and swam to shore. Liz swallowed and tried to look away, truly, she did. No, she didn't. She wanted to see Casey's body.

Casey walked out of the water, running her fingers through her thick short hair, then shook it like a dog. Liz tried to find some moisture in her mouth as she watched the muscular, yet distinctly feminine body gracefully walk to the robe and slip it on.

"Damn..." Liz sighed and fanned herself. She quickly went into the kitchen and started breakfast.

Casey was reading the paper as they finished breakfast. "Hey,

I know what we're doing today," she announced and put the paper down.

As always, Skye watched every move Casey made. Liz looked up and cocked her head in question.

"We're going to the Oneida County Fair. Hot dogs for Skye, ice cream for your mom, and my Kennedy girls for me," she blurted out, looking right into Liz's blue eyes.

Liz smiled and Skye squealed with excitement.

Skye was head and shoulders above the rest, literally. Casey hoisted her onto her shoulders and Skye hung on to her hair.

"Look, Mama!"

Casey winced. "Shortround, the hair..." she grumbled as she held onto Skye's sandaled feet.

Liz looked up and laughed. "You're way up there, sweet pea." Then she shook her head. Both wore their sunglasses; it was quite a picture.

As they walked around, Liz ate. Two caramel apples later, she nibbled at Casey's popcorn. "This was such a bad idea." Liz sighed as she took another handful.

"You haven't done this at all. Besides, you've only gained a little. Doc said you should have more. Are you still taking the vitamins?"

"Now you're an expert on pregnancy."

"Yes, I am. So don't sass me." Casey looked down into her eyes and cleared her throat. "I, um, I think we need to discuss the, well, when it's time. I don't like the idea that you're here and I'm in Chicago. I have to get back in a couple days. Well, why don't you two come with me?" she blurted out.

Liz stopped and gaped at her. "What? Come to Chicago with you?"

Casey rolled her eyes as she held on to the midget's legs. "Yes, why not? I'll be there for at least three weeks. I don't know if I'll have time to come back between them. Now don't get mad."

Liz narrowed her eyes at her and put her hands on her hips. "What did you do?"

"Cafey, what you do?" a little voice came from atop her head.

Casey raised her eyes and frowned. "Traitor," she mumbled. "I didn't do, well, I did, but I think it's a good idea."

"What is a good idea?" Liz asked slowly.

Casey grinned slightly. "I contacted Dr. Haines, remember her? I explained my…our situation, and she said she would be more than happy to see you while you were in Chicago. So it's all set," she said, grinning as she took a step back.

Liz took a deep breath but said nothing. Casey swung Skye off her shoulders and held her, whispering something quickly in her ear. The little blond curly top gave her mother a pleading look.

"Peas, Mama? I love Cafey."

Liz was astonished. "You, using a child!"

"What?" Casey asked helplessly. "Can I help it if the little urchin loves me?"

"Casey," Liz started as they walked through the fair. "This is, well, it's unexpected." She stopped and faced Casey. "Are you sure you want to do this? Skye and I are fine here."

"No," Casey said. "I don't like you being alone."

"Marge—"

Casey held her hand up. "I love Marge, and I trust her. But I have to stay in Chicago, and I'd rather have you there with me."

"Why?" Liz looked at the ground. Well, looked at her stomach anyway; someday she'd see her feet again. She wasn't sure going to Chicago was a good idea. When Casey didn't answer, she looked up.

Casey had an odd look on her face. Liz couldn't gauge what it was. Skye ate her popcorn, seemingly uninterested in the adult conversation.

"I don't want you…"

"Yes?"

Casey looked into her eyes. "I don't want you to be away from me that long."

Liz had taken a handful of popcorn out of the white paper cone and quickly looked up, dropping the popcorn to the ground. When she found she could speak, she said, "It will only be for a few weeks."

Casey shook her head. She tossed the popcorn in the nearby

trash and set Skye on the ground. Casey stood in front of Liz and put her hands on Liz's sunburned shoulders. "Liz, I'm not sure what's happening between us or if anything is happening."

"Is there?" Liz looked into Casey's eyes.

"I don't know. I-I hope so," Casey said. She stopped and laughed nervously; Liz did the same. "All I know is right now, the thought of you and Skye out of my sight is..." She stopped and swallowed. "Well, it's just something I don't want to happen. I want you to come and stay with me at my apartment while I'm in Chicago. It's plenty big enough and I'd feel better, and I..."

Liz smiled and put her hand on Casey's arm. "Okay, you win. Skye and I will come to Chicago with you."

Skye clapped her hands and Casey swung Skye around happily.

The rest of the day was glorious. Liz ate while Skye and Casey went on carnival rides; Skye threw up once. Casey only looked as though she might. She played all the games and Skye's hero won more stuffed animals for her.

Then as they were leaving, they passed a carnival game. It was then Casey saw the necklace. It was a Native American dream catcher charm on a gold chain.

"Wait," Casey said and handed Skye over to her mother. "How do I win?"

The man grinned evilly. "Just take that hammer..." He motioned to the old game. "Swing the hammer and hit the base, if it rises and hits the bell, you win whatever you want."

Skye screamed with delight. Liz hid her eyes as she adjusted her daughter on her hip. "I can't believe she's doing this..." she mumbled and looked through her fingers.

Casey spit in both hands and rubbed them together as she winked at Liz and Skye. She then heaved the heavy sledgehammer and took a mighty swing. It only rose halfway; so much for her ego. However, she was undaunted.

Liz gave her a smug grin and Skye laughed. "'Gen, Cafey, 'gen."

Casey frowned, her pride now on the line. She tossed a few dollars on the stand and the man let out a wicked laugh. "You're not gonna do it. One in a thousand..." he said in a challenging voice and Casey glared at him.

"Casey, you're going to hurt yourself."

Casey ignored her. "One in a thousand, huh?" She grunted and heaved the hammer over her head.

Skye was sleeping in the backseat, holding on to as many stuffed animals as she could. Liz was smiling slightly, her fingers caressing the gold charm that hung around her neck. Casey's green cat eyes danced wickedly as she sported an arrogant grin.

"One in a thousand... Ha!" She let out a self-satisfied grunt as she pulled up next to the cabin.

Liz laughed out loud as Casey took Skye out of her seat, handing the sleeping bundle to Liz.

Casey collected all the winnings for the day and dumped them onto the couch. "I'm going to need another room for all this."

"You're our hero," Liz said as she set the sleeping child in the bed.

"She needs her own bed. Don't you think?" Casey asked.

Liz nodded. "You only have one room, though, and I really don't want her to sleep in the loft."

"No, that's no good," Casey whispered, then took her by the arm and walked out.

Liz sat on the couch while Casey started a fire. "Autumn is finally here. It's getting a bit chilly. Coffee?" she asked and Liz scrunched her nose in disapproval.

Casey gave her an enticing smile. "Hot chocolate?"

Liz grinned. "Marshmallows?"

"I'll be right back, turtle woman."

They sat on the couch drinking hot chocolate. Liz had her feet up on an ottoman, warming them by the fire, the cup resting on her large stomach.

"You know, when we come back from Chicago, I could make the room here I use for my music into a small bedroom. It's across the hall from our...from the bedroom and Skye could sleep there. Then when the baby comes, she can sleep in the room with you," she said and cursed inwardly for slipping up.

She recovered quickly. "That way, Skye can have her own room, you can sleep with the baby, and when I'm here, I'll still have the couch. Or by then, maybe I can get a bed up in the loft and sleep there."

"The baby and I can sleep in the loft. You shouldn't be put out any longer, Casey. It is your bedroom after all, and by the spring, I'll start thinking about getting a place of my own..." Her voice trailed off.

Casey's heart sank at the thought of them not being around anymore. "Or we can stay in Chicago," she offered in a hesitant voice, then quickly continued, "We've plenty of time to think about that. Let's just concentrate on the present. I don't want you worrying about anything but having your baby."

Liz looked at her and smiled. "Thank you. I can't believe how lucky Skye and I are. She...she loves you very much," Liz said in a soft whisper.

"I love Skye, too. She's in my heart, Liz," she said and took the chance of a lifetime. "And so are you."

Liz said nothing as she stared at the flames.

"Liz," she started and stopped.

"Yes?"

"Nothing. I...nothing," she said and felt like an idiot.

"I'm very grateful for all you've done, Casey, eternally grateful," Liz said in a soft voice.

Casey shrugged. "It was easier to do than I ever imagined." She laughed then and continued, "Like falling off a swing."

Liz smiled and reached for her hand. "You've been very kind."

"It's not just out of kindness."

She glanced at Liz, who stared at their hands. "What was it then?"

What was it then? Casey asked herself as she caressed Liz's warm hand. Usually, Casey was sure of herself and confident with women. However, she never felt this way for any other woman, and she knew it was more than the physical attraction. However, make no mistake, the physical attraction was definitely there. Was she falling in love; had she already? Liz was a good woman, with a family and a future. Why in the world would Liz want anything to do with her?

"What are you thinking, Casey?"

Casey looked into the blue eyes and took the leap. "I was thinking how I'm floundering here. Usually, with a beautiful woman, I'm very..."

"Arrogant?" Liz offered with a grin.

Casey let out an embarrassed laugh. "I guess."

They sat in silence for a moment. "I don't feel so beautiful right now."

"Oh, Liz. You are, believe me. You may not feel it, but you are." She was stunned to see the tears well in Liz's eyes. "I'm worried that I might be falling in love with you."

"W-worried?"

Casey nodded. "I have no idea what love is, really. And now I find myself caring for you deeply...and Skye."

When Liz sighed deeply, Casey glanced over, giving her a worried look. "Is something wrong? You shouldn't have eaten two caramel apples. Damn it, Liz. It was probably that stinking cotton candy. I told you," she scolded in a worried voice. This was much easier to deal with than the "what was it then" scenario. "How about I make some tea or maybe you should take a hot bath? Wait, no, no baths, you can't. I forgot. How about..."

Liz rolled her eyes, then reached over, took Casey's face between her hands, and kissed her... Right there on the couch.

Casey was shocked and gasped openly as she felt Liz's warm lips against her own. Inexplicably, she pulled Liz closer and returned her kiss. Their lips blended in a soft, tender kiss that was amazing to say the least. The electricity sparked between them as their lips moved easily against one another; Casey reluctantly pulled back.

Liz smiled. "That was a kiss," she exclaimed.

Casey immediately stood and paced. Her heart and mind were racing. "Hold on now. I don't, I mean, this is...we need to. Okay, will you let me finish?" she said nervously.

Liz smiled and watched her sputtering.

"What did you say?"

"I didn't say anything," Liz answered and smiled.

"Oh. I thought you said something. Well, anyway. Look, Liz. I, you…"

"Casey?" Liz asked in a quiet reassuring voice. "Come here and sit down."

Casey frowned deeply. She was completely out of control here and she loved it. She obediently sat next to Liz, who took her hand.

"It was just a kiss," Liz said.

Casey shot her an incredulous look. "It was not just a kiss, Liz. I-I…"

"What?" Liz held on to her hand.

Casey groaned. "Oh, I have no idea."

Liz patted her hand. She felt Casey studying her. "Why did you kiss me?" Casey asked.

Liz laughed nervously. "I have no idea."

It was Casey's turn to laugh. "Well, at least we both have no idea."

"Casey, there's a lot going on here, and I won't deny I've grown fond of you."

"I thought I was arrogant and pompous."

Liz looked up. "Oh, don't get me wrong. You are."

Casey didn't know if she should be indignant or laugh; she chose the latter. Liz joined her while they held hands like teenagers.

"I think it's time for bed," Liz said, looking at their hands.

"Would it be…?"

Liz looked up then. "Yes."

Casey grinned and let out a sigh of relief.

They lay in bed, with Skye between them; Casey rolled onto her side and looked at Liz. In the shadowy moonlight, she studied Liz's profile. "You're beautiful," she whispered.

With her eyes closed, Liz smiled. "Thank you."

After a few wonderful moments of gazing at Liz and listening to her own heartbeat, she heard Liz ask, "What are you thinking?" Liz opened her eyes and looked at her.

"I was thinking of the day you read that poem. It has been

running through my mind ever since. *Winds of Heaven*…That's what I think of when I think of you. I-I don't know why exactly." She stopped and smiled. "How did it start? The winds of heaven mix forever with a sweet emotion. Those winds brought you here, you and Skye."

Liz sniffed and placed her hands on her stomach. "Don't leave out this one. They say the baby can hear things."

With that, Casey got out of bed and walked around to Liz, who was wide-eyed. Casey sat on the side of the bed and placed her hands on Liz's stomach. "Can you hear me?" she asked as she leaned down. "You're gonna be a happy baby. You have a big sister who'll look out for you and a mom who loves you."

Casey looked up to see tears welling in Liz's eyes. Without breaking eye contact, Casey smiled and whispered, "I envy you that." She then lightly kissed the back of Liz's hand as it lay on her stomach.

Liz gasped and tried to swallow; she said nothing as Casey kissed her other hand, then walked around the bed, slipping under the sheet, careful not to wake Skye.

Liz looked as if she were in shock. "That was incredibly romantic, Casey."

Casey closed her eyes; a wide grin spread across her face. "We leave for Chicago on Saturday. You need to get some sleep."

"Yes, Casey," Liz said with a deep sigh.

"Wench."

"Don't push it."

Chapter 16

"I've never been to Chicago," Liz said as she looked out the window at the tall buildings. "It's impressive."

"Nah, they're just buildings," Casey assured her. Then she drove farther east down the Congress Expressway and touched Liz's arm. "That's impressive," she said firmly and nodded straight ahead.

Liz's eyes widened at the sight of Lake Michigan bursting into view. "Sweet pea, look, a huge lake," she exclaimed.

Skye strained in her car seat and saw the water. "I fim, Cafey," Skye said, and both women laughed.

"In the summer," Casey reminded her as she looked in the rearview mirror and saw the disappointed look.

They took the elevator to Casey's tenth-floor apartment.

"I can't believe you live here." Liz sighed as the elevator doors opened.

Skye clung to Casey's neck as they walked across the hall. Casey opened the door and walked in, followed by Liz, who looked around the huge living room.

"My God, it's as big as your entire cabin."

"I know. I'm trying to sell it. However, for the time being, it's home. So do whatever you like." She set Skye down.

Liz looked around the expansive living room. By the big window overlooking Lake Michigan stood a huge piano. The opposite wall was all fireplace with a huge couch comfortably placed in front of it. A dining area was off in the back, and the kitchen was to the right. All open, it looked like one huge studio apartment.

"Bedrooms are down the hall. Master has its own bath. The other is at the end of the hall." Casey said as she lit the gas fireplace. "Instant fire," she said. "But I like my cabin better."

"Me too. I love the smell of a wood-burning fireplace." Liz sighed as she stared at the flames.

All at once, Casey was inexplicably happy. She walked over to Liz and stood in front of her, cupping Liz's face in her warm hands. "I want to kiss you."

"I'd like that."

Casey gently kissed her and pulled back. She shook her head. "What's happening, Liz?"

"I'm not sure, but I like it."

"I do too." Casey kissed her again. This time, Liz pulled back and smiled as she walked over to the window.

Casey walked up behind her and placed her hands on Liz's shoulders. "What's wrong? Should I not have kissed you?"

Liz shook her head and wiped the tears from her cheeks. Casey gently turned her around. "Hey, what's wrong?"

"It's just my hormones, I think. Don't mind me," Liz said with a chuckle.

"Liz, I think I—"

"No, don't say it." Liz put her fingertips against Casey's lips.

Casey frowned and kissed her fingers. "I understand. There's a lot going on, and you know my reputation." She let out a sigh of resignation and walked away.

"Casey, it's not that," Liz insisted and followed her down the hall. Casey turned to face her. "There is a lot going on, that's true. But it has nothing to do with your past or mine."

"Yours?" Casey asked. "I don't care about the past."

Liz ran her hand over her stomach. "We have a good deal to talk about."

Casey glanced from her stomach and back to her face. "Yes, we do. And we will. I think I'm falling in love with you, Liz."

Liz closed her eyes and put her hand to her face. "You don't know what you're saying." She opened her eyes. "Look at me."

Casey smiled and leaned against the doorjamb. "I'm looking."

Liz's face turned crimson. "Don't say something you're—"

Skye came running down the hall. "Mama! Fith, fith," she cried out and tugged at her mother's pants leg. "Come."

"We'll finish this later," Casey said as they walked into the small bedroom.

An aquarium stood against one wall. Casey walked over and flipped the switch and the light flickered on, illuminating the tank.

Skye was amazed as she watched the colorful fish swimming around. Then Casey had a brilliant idea. She knelt next to her, running her fingers through the blond curls.

"Shortround, how would you like to have this as your bedroom? You can sleep in here and watch the fish. You can feed them and take care of them for me."

Skye's eyes widened, and she hugged Casey around the neck. "Mine own room. I feed fith?"

"Yep, but you have to take care of them," Casey reminded her, and Skye nodded and picked up the container of food. "I'll show you how to feed them later."

Skye ran to her mother. "Mama, mine own room."

Liz gave a suspicious glance in Casey's direction. "What's going on in that musical head?" She then turned her attention to her daughter. "That's great, sweet pea. Would you like your own room?"

Skye nodded and placed her stuffed fish on the bed and gently patted it. "Mine own bed, my fith."

"Well, it's all settled. Skye has her own room. Now we have to figure out where Mommy wants to sleep," Casey said as she pondered the question while scratching her chin.

Liz stood leaning against the door and looked to the heavens. "You big child," she said but couldn't help but grin.

"Hmm… Where should Mommy sleep?" Casey sighed and looked down at the curly top for help.

"Casey Bennett," Liz scolded half-heartedly as she watched her daughter mimicking Casey as she scratched her chin.

Skye frowned and looked at both women. "Mama sleep with Cafey."

Casey's mouth opened in a mock amazement. "No? You think Mommy and I should sleep in the same bed?"

Skye nodded emphatically. "Sure..." she said and dismissed the topic.

"Sure. I agree with Shortround." Casey nodded emphatically. "It's all settled. Mama sleep with Cafey," Casey said in a low seductive voice as she walked past Liz, who was blushing, and kissed her cheek.

"Okay, the fridge is stocked. I just have to make a quick trip to the studio. I'll be back in two hours, tops." Casey threw on her coat. She grabbed Liz around the waist and pulled her as close as the baby would allow. "Have dinner ready, wench," she said seductively and kissed her deeply.

Liz narrowed her eyes at Casey, who smiled sheepishly. "Or I'll pick something up. Oh, I almost forgot, here..." She handed Liz a cell phone. "If you go out with Skye and you need to call. Keep it on you." She kissed her again. "I like kissing you."

"Cafey kiss me. Uppie..."

Casey looked down, easily whisked Skye up with one hand, and kissed her.

"Kiss Mama 'gen." Skye giggled.

"My pleasure." Casey kissed Liz, then pulled back.

Liz sighed happily. "'Gen, Cafey." Liz sighed.

Casey set the child down and kissed Liz deeply. Both women sighed as Casey reluctantly pulled back.

"I gotta go. See you in a little while. Shortround, watch the fish." She winked at Liz and walked out the door.

Liz looked down at her daughter. "Casey is a nut."

Skye nodded, then ran down the hall to her new bedroom.

Niles watched Casey as she leafed through the music. She was humming. Casey Bennett was humming. She rolled her sleeves up and grunted. "Okay. What's the story here, Niles? How long..." she started and looked up at the grinning Niles.

"What the hell are you grinning at?" she asked and put her hands on her hips.

"Oh, nothing, nothing. So how are Liz and little Skye? God, I feel like I know them."

Casey now grinned. "They're fine. I-I brought them here. I figured I'd be tied up for at least a couple weeks and I didn't—"

"Want her out of your sight for that long?" Niles offered and Casey growled.

"No. I just didn't want her to be alone for that long. She's due in December. I... Well, I... Oh, shut up, Niles," she said rudely and rearranged the music sheets. "We've got work to do, smart ass." She growled and sat next to him at the control panel of the sound booth.

Niles smiled and leaned into the microphone. "Oh, Jeffrey, let's please the composer. She's in a snit."

Casey closed her eyes and counted to ten. "I'm going to murder you later," she grumbled.

Niles covered the mike with his hand. "I'll make a note of it. Okay, let's see how it sounds."

Almost three hours later, Casey was ready to strangle someone—not just anyone, Suzette. "Can it be possible that she could get worse?" Casey groaned and buried her head in her hands. She then yanked the microphone and bellowed. "Enough!"

Niles quickly grabbed the mike out of her hand before the onslaught of profanity started.

"Welcome back," he said as Jeffrey stormed into the sound booth.

"Either she goes or I go. I can't bear it any longer," he said angrily, and Casey waved her hand in acknowledgment. "Case..." he pleaded firmly.

"I know, I know." She looked at her watch. "Shit. Let's regroup. I'll talk to Suzette tomorrow."

"I'll find another cellist. Don't worry. Go home, you look pooped," he said.

Liz had the chicken in the oven and looked at the clock. Casey had said two hours. That was almost three hours ago. She looked at the cell phone and bit her bottom lip. She did not want to seem like one of those nagging women. Casey probably just forgot about the time.

Then the hormones kicked in. What if she was with the tone-deaf cellist? Casey had a healthy sex life and had a relationship with this woman. Could Liz blame her? This woman was probably gorgeous with a gorgeous figure and was not pregnant. She also knew exactly how to please Casey.

All at once, she felt the pang of insecurity. Pregnant, fat, and with swollen feet, she thought, and eased into the kitchen chair, pushing it back to allow for the trunk she carried in front of her. Why in the world would Casey Bennett want her? Skye, that was the reason. Casey loved Skye and felt a responsibility to help. Maybe Casey only said she loved her because of Skye. Maybe she didn't love her at all and was with that Suzette right now. Maybe Casey was like Julie, in love with the idea.

"Well then, Casey Bennett, you just sleep with your cellist. I'll have my baby and the three of us will go back to New Mexico," she said as the tears flooded her eyes.

With that, the front door opened. "Liz. Sorry I'm late," Casey's voice called out, and Liz struggled to her feet and angrily walked into the living room. She had a wooden spoon in her hand.

Casey immediately noticed the face. "Uh, Liz, put that down, it may go off," Casey said slowly as she took off her coat. "I'm sorry I'm late. I got caught up at the studio."

"With Suzette no doubt!" Liz exclaimed

Casey's eyes widened. Okay, remember, she's due in a month, she thought. You have read the books, stupid.

"Cafey!" Skye came from out of the bedroom and ran down the hall.

"Hey, Shortround," she said happily as she scooped her up and gave her a kiss. "Are you taking care of the fish?" she asked as she set her down. Skye nodded happily and ran back to her room.

Liz put a shaky hand to her face and Casey quickly walked up to her and put her arms around her. "Liz. I am sorry."

"No, I'm sorry. I hate myself," she exclaimed and gently pushed Casey away and walked into the kitchen.

Casey winced and followed her.

"Smells good. Look, why don't you go and sit by the fire? I'll finish dinner."

"It's all done. It was ready an hour ago," Liz snapped, then hated sounding like a nag as she sat at the table.

"Aw, Liz. I'm sorry. I'm not used to this. Please give me time. I should have called, I know." She knelt next to her and took her hands in her own. Liz took her hand away and ran it through Casey's thick salt and pepper hair.

"I shouldn't expect you to change your whole life. It's just this pregnancy, Casey. I'm scared."

Casey's head shot up. "Why?"

Liz put a hand to Casey's lips. "I'm just so tired all the time. I don't know. I'm sure it's normal."

"When's your appointment with Dr. Haines?"

"Day after tomorrow. I'll take Skye with me."

Casey dejectedly sat back on her heels and looked up into the blue determined eyes. "You don't want me to go with you," she said in a deflated voice.

Liz searched the sad green eyes. "I don't want to take you away from your work. You've done so much."

"Do you want me there? Because I want to go," Casey said seriously.

"Of course I want you there. I just never thought you'd want to."

Casey rubbed her tired eyes. "Let's eat, and after we get Skye to bed, you and I are going to talk. I mean really talk."

Casey barely tasted anything she ate. She and Liz exchanged nervous glances during the meal. Casey cleared the dishes as Liz got Skye to bed. She turned off the light in the kitchen, hating the fact that her mouth was dry and her heart was racing.

She nearly ran into Liz when she walked out of the kitchen;

Liz laughed as she held on to Casey's arm for support. Casey looked into her blue eyes; she gently brushed a loose strand of hair away from her face. "How about some hot chocolate?"

Liz shook her head and led Casey to the living room. They sat on the couch and stared at the fire. Casey knew Liz wasn't going to start this conversation since it was her bright idea to have it.

"Well," Casey said and glanced at Liz.

"Yes?"

"If you like to chime in at anytime…"

"Look, Casey, we don't have to have any kind of discussion."

Casey turned to her and listened as Liz continued. "As we've said, this is new for all of us. You were thrown into this, and I know it was not what you wanted. I don't want you to feel obligated to say something you may not really feel. I will admit I enjoy your company, and I love it that Skye adores you." She stopped, looking as though she was collecting her thoughts.

Casey leaned back against the cushion, still facing her. She realized how much she loved to gaze at Liz. She noticed the way her brow furrowed when she was deep in thought. How her smile seemed to come from her soul when she talked about Skye. How her heart ached when she was away from Liz. Nothing held much interest for her anymore.

"Are you listening to me?" Liz asked.

Casey heard the angry tone and blinked. "Oh, sure. Continue."

"What did I just say?"

Casey couldn't help the grin that spread across her face. "I think you were about to tell me you loved me."

Liz straightened her back; her look was that of utter astonishment. Casey liked this look, as well.

"What did you say?"

"I said you were about to—"

"I didn't say it."

"No, but you were about to." She reached over and caressed Liz's shoulder.

"I was not. I was giving you an out, Ms, Bennett. You arrogant woman."

Casey raised an eyebrow and sidled closer. "You think I want out of this?"

Liz took a deep quivering breath and looked down at her hands that lay in her lap. "I wouldn't blame you if you did."

"Well, that's true."

"Please don't play with me, Casey. Not now."

When Casey heard the sad tenor of Liz's voice, she was silent for a moment. She reached over and placed her fingertips under Liz's chin, turning her face toward her. She was shocked to see tears in Liz's eyes. For another long moment, they were silent. Casey searched her glistening blue eyes.

"Liz Kennedy, what have you done to me?" she whispered.

"I don't know, but whatever it is, you've done it to me, as well."

"I would never play with your heart, Liz." She needed to say this before she lost her nerve. "I love you."

Liz's gaze darted around her face, then inexplicably, she buried her face in her hands and desperately tried not to break down in a flood of tears. Casey knew it and winced happily. "Gonna cry?"

Liz only nodded and burst into tears and flung her arms around Casey's neck. Casey held on to her as Liz sobbed into her shoulder. Casey grinned and rocked her gently, kissing her hair. "So you love me, too, right?"

Liz nodded and sobbed, trying to talk. "I-I..." She stopped.

"And you thought the same thing when you read that poem? Because I thought I saw it in your eyes when we looked at each other," Casey asked.

Liz nodded again. "Y-yes. I n-never thought y-you'd—" She stopped, unable to continue.

"Feel the same?" Casey finished while Liz wept and nodded. "Well, I do. I just can't believe you love me," Casey said in amazement. "Someday, when you stop crying, you'll have to say it out loud, so I'll believe it. I hope it's before the baby is born."

Liz sniffed into her shoulder as the tears stopped. She pulled back and looked up into Casey's eyes, taking a deep quivering breath. "I do love you. I have loved you since I read that poem. I don't know why Skye loves that poem so much."

"Did you read it with Julie?" Casey asked, hating herself for asking.

"Good grief, no," Liz said and waved her off. Casey hid her grin as she continued. "Julie, God love her, was not the type. I was napping with Skye and she asked me to read, and it was the only book within reach. Then I remembered the poem. It's how I look at love, I suppose," she said and Casey kissed her head. "Skye just took to it."

"A little cupid I'd say." Casey put her arm around Liz and held her close. She leaned back and took Liz with her.

They sat in a comfortable silence for a time. "Casey..." Liz started and Casey gently stroked her hair.

"Hmm?"

"I won't always look like this. All bloated and fat."

Casey heard the worried tone and tightened her arm around her. "You silly turtle woman. You won't believe me, and I don't know if it's because we're both women and we can commiserate and understand on some basic level or because I'm overwhelmed by the entire situation. However, I find you extremely sexy and very desirable and I know you aren't feeling that way now. However, Ms. Kennedy, when you do... Well, I give you fair warning."

Liz looked up into her green eyes and gently touched her cheek. "Thank you. That was perfect."

"It's easy when it's the truth."

Again, there was silence. "W-what about when the baby comes?"

"What about it?"

"I mean, let's be realistic. You've been on your own and living a very carefree life. Are you sure you want to take on all of this?" Liz asked in a small voice.

Casey didn't hesitate. "Yes. For the first and only time in my life, I'm in love, and I love you, Skye, and the unknown dwarf."

"God, I'm really falling for you," Liz said and nuzzled closer. "You'll change your mind when you have to get up at two a.m. for a feeding."

"That's what you think. That babe will be suckling from your breast, sweetie, not mine."

There was silence again for a moment. "Well, you'll be in there somewhere," Liz assured in a small whisper, and Casey groaned happily.

"Does this mean you want to come to the doctor with me?"

Casey gently sat forward and faced Liz on the couch. She took both warm hands in her own. "Liz, please listen to me. I want to be a part of this. I am a part of this. I love you and the baby. I want to be there for everything and anything you need. I do not care about my work. Now I'm going with you for every appointment you have, I don't care when it is. Right?"

Liz gently pushed the thick lock off her brow. "Right."

Casey breathed a huge sigh of relief. "You had me worried for a minute there, Ms. Kennedy. Don't do that ever again." Casey could sense there was something else. "What, Liz?"

Liz blushed furiously. "I, I mean, we." She stopped and looked at Casey, who was trying to decipher what she was saying. "Right now, I mean being pregnant. Well, I'm not…"

Then it dawned on Casey. She chuckled and stopped when Liz glared at her. "I know what you're getting at, sweetie. Look, there's a whole chapter devoted to sex and the expectant mother."

Liz hung her head and groaned as Casey continued. "You're not feeling very sexual, right?"

Liz's head snapped up, giving Casey an incredulous look. "Do we have to discuss this now?"

"No," Casey said. "I think we've accomplished quite a bit so far tonight."

"I agree with you there." Liz nuzzled back into Casey's shoulder.

"You and I need to be alone, Liz. Not sexually, I know that, but intimately without the lovemaking. We need to get that connection, as well. The sexual part will come later," she said and grinned wildly.

Liz nervously looked down at her stomach.

"I know it won't be for a while, but I can wait," Casey whispered and kissed her stomach, her neck, and her lips. "So much to look forward to."

Both women were silent as they stared at the fire. Casey absently stroked Liz's hair. Liz looked up and cupped Casey's face. "Sleep with me tonight?"

Casey's heart thumped in her chest. She stood and offered her hand to Liz. "You check on Skye, I'll lock up."

Liz nodded and smiled as she walked away; she turned and pulled Casey in for a long kiss. "See you in the bedroom."

Casey stood there swaying as she watched Liz disappear down the hall. She quickly turned off the fireplace and shut off the lights. She met Liz in the darkened hallway, the only illumination was from Skye's nightlight in her room; Liz left her door ajar.

"Shortround still sleeping?" Casey whispered.

Liz turned to her and nodded. She then kissed her cheek. "Thank you."

"For what?"

"For coming into our lives and loving us."

"It's by far the easiest thing I've ever done," she whispered and kissed her forehead. "Now it's time for bed."

Liz smiled and took her hand and walked across the hall. Liz shyly took her nightgown and went into the bathroom. Casey grinned and slipped out of her clothes, and out of habit, she slipped into the makeshift pajamas.

Liz came back, looked at her, and laughed. "I think Skye and I have put you through enough," she said and motioned to the PJs.

"I don't want to seem like…" She stopped as Liz walked over to the opposite side of the big bed and took off her robe. Casey swallowed with difficulty as she gazed at the beautiful pregnant woman before her. The soft silky nightgown hung loosely over her body.

Liz grinned and raised an eyebrow. "What? You've seen me in a nightgown before, Casey."

"Y-yes, but Skye's always been in bed and now we're…" She stopped and walked around the bed and kissed her. "Lie down, you turtle," she said affectionately and pulled back the quilt. With a little assistance, Liz got into bed and Casey slid the slippers off her feet and pulled the covers over her. She then walked around and turned off the light.

Liz was almost instantly asleep as Casey cuddled close. "It's kind of odd not having Skye in the middle," Liz whispered.

Casey laughed and kissed her forehead. "I think we'll get used to it," she said. "What?" Casey asked curiously when she heard Liz laughing.

"Honey, take off those boxers." Liz laughed. "I've seen you naked."

"Great." Casey jumped out and quickly stripped off the PJs and gladly got back into bed and cuddled close behind Liz. "What do you mean you've seen me naked, when? I've been very careful not to," Casey whispered in her ear.

Liz reached back and put her hand on her cheek. "You went skinny dipping one morning and well..." She stopped and Casey grinned. She could almost feel the color rising in Liz's body.

"You shameless hussy, you," Casey said in a low voice.

"You have a beautiful body, please be patient with me," Liz said in a small voice.

Casey sat up and rolled Liz onto her back. "I think you're beautiful. Please don't worry about that. Trust me, to hold you like this, to be sleeping next to you is heaven. Good night," she whispered against her lips.

"Good night," Liz murmured.

She fell wonderfully asleep...for two hours. The baby was pressing on her bladder. Liz groaned and struggled out of bed and headed for the bathroom.

On her way out, she checked on Skye. She was sound asleep and holding her fish. Liz smiled and walked back to bed.

Casey was sprawled out on her stomach and Liz stood there for a moment and gazed at her lovely body. She then got into bed and let out a small groan.

Casey instantly woke and lifted her head. "Okay?" she mumbled as she sat up slightly.

Liz inched her way closer and lay on her back next to her. Casey sighed and slid closer, her arm draped across her chest, her head resting on the pillow so close Liz could feel her warm breath on her cheek.

Casey woke with a contented sigh. She opened one eye and smiled. Liz was still sleeping, her mouth slightly opened and her breathing deep and even. Casey took the time to marvel at Liz's body. She tentatively leaned over and placed her ear against Liz's stomach. "Can you hear me?" Casey whispered. "I love your mom. She's so pretty, and she loves you. Oh, my name is Casey."

"What are you doing?"

Casey looked up and grinned. "Good morning, Mommy. We're just getting acquainted. They can hear now, you know."

Liz laughed sleepily and stretched. "Are you going to be quoting from that book until the baby comes?"

"Probably." Casey kissed her belly. "How did you sleep?"

Liz opened her arms and Casey gently lay next to her, resting her head on her breast. "Very plump and soft, Ms. Kennedy."

Liz laughed nervously. "And very sensitive. I slept very well. I loved waking up to find you next to me. It made going to the bathroom at three a.m. almost a pleasure."

"Mama?"

Both women looked at the door to see Skye standing there, rubbing her eyes.

"Hey, Shortround," Casey said. Skye immediately smiled, her eyes still half closed as she jumped up on the bed.

"Shit," Casey said quickly and pulled the sheet over her nakedness. She smiled sheepishly at Liz, who rolled her eyes.

Skye crawled between them and clung to her mother. "Cafey naked," she whispered.

Casey turned bright red and covered her face with her hands.

"I know," Liz whispered back and pulled her daughter close. "She left her PJs at the cabin."

Casey cringed and slipped out of bed, quickly slipping into the boxers and tank top. "I'll go make breakfast."

"You can't cook."

"Oh, well, I'll make the coffee. You make breakfast."

Liz stared at the doorway, listening to Casey whistling in the kitchen. Skye took her thumb out of her mouth. "Cafey funny."

Liz laughed and tickled Skye. "Yes, Casey is very funny."

"Mama, stop."

Liz relented and pulled Skye up to her. "Sweet pea, I want to ask you something."

Skye knelt next to her mother, her blond curly hair all over, her pink cheeks flushed. "You like Casey, don't you?"

"Mmm-hmm."

"Would you like Casey to live with us, sweet pea?" Liz noticed Skye's brow was furrowed in concentration, and for a moment, Liz thought… "What, baby?"

Skye leaned in and whispered, "I have to go potty."

Liz laughed and ran her fingers through her blond curls. "Good girl, Skye. You go ahead."

Chapter 17

"Well, you're a little lighter than I'd like, but everything is in order. Now I see that you don't want to know the sex of the baby." Dr. Haines took off her glasses and smiled.

Casey gave Liz a curious look. "Really? I thought you knew, you keep saying 'she,'" Casey said logically.

"I want to be surprised," she said and shrugged. "Do you want to know?"

Casey thought for a moment, then smiled. "No. Let's be surprised."

Liz reached over and took her hand.

"Is Liz's weight a problem?" Casey asked and held on to her hand.

The doctor shook her head. "No, I've got the results of all the lab tests from your doctor in Wisconsin. You are borderline anemic. Get as much rest as you can. Watch your diet, just as you have been. The baby is due the first week in December. Are you staying in Chicago?"

"Would it be better if we did?" Liz asked seriously.

"It's not imperative. I want to monitor your anemia. As I said, it's not unusual, but if you can, stay in town."

"We live far from the hospital," Casey interjected. She glanced at Liz. "Let's stay here. We can go up north anytime."

Liz nodded and anxiously put her hand on her stomach. The doctor looked at both women and smiled. "Your first I take it?"

They both nodded. "You'll be fine. The only problem I see is your weight. The baby's heart is fine. She's the right size and everything looks good," she said.

Liz smiled nervously and held Casey's hand.

"Stress is another factor to be considered. I don't know your personal life, but I can see you care for each other. That's good. You will need each other. Is there any other stress?"

They looked at each other and Casey shook her head. "Liz?"

She gave Casey a glance but said nothing.

"Why don't I leave you for a few minutes? Your appointment is for Tuesday, three o'clock," she said kindly and walked out.

Casey was watching Liz. "What is it, sweetie?"

"I... Don't be angry. Suzette called the other day. Well, she—"

"She what?"

"She said you and she were together that afternoon when you were late. I know, I know, she was lying. I trust you, Casey."

Casey paced back and forth, her anger rising with each step. Then she looked at Liz, who looked tired and pale, and knelt in front of her. "Okay. From now on, please talk to me. I'm not hiding anything from you. I'm not seeing anyone. You know that."

"I do. Please don't go off now."

Casey put her fingers up to her lips. "No worrying, the baby can hear you. Hey, have you thought of a name? We never talked about it. Wait, let's go home and the three of us will come up with something."

"Skye would never forgive us," Liz assured her.

Casey grinned, but her mind was on Suzette... She wanted to kill the snaky bitch.

They walked into the living room and there stood Niles, giving Skye a piggyback ride around the living room. Brian was sitting on the couch, sipping a glass of wine and laughing hysterically.

"Mama, Nize givin' me ride," she exclaimed as Niles set her down. He blushed horribly as he avoided Casey's smirk.

Skye rushed up to them and reached for her mother.

Casey intercepted and lifted her, kissed her cheek, and handed Skye to her mother.

"No lifting," she said sternly and Liz rolled her eyes. "Niles, thanks. You're a good friend."

Niles grinned. "I like the effect Liz has on you. Thanks."

"Oh, by the way, have you gotten a cellist yet?"

"As a matter of fact, I can have one day after next. He's doing a commercial for soap. Why a cello would make a difference in soap, I don't know." He shrugged.

"Good, I'm telling Suzette tomorrow," Casey said firmly, and Niles patted her back.

"Good, I won't be there," he said; Casey glared at him. "Just kidding."

The four of them exchanged kisses, then Niles pinched Skye's nose. "Good night, you little goddess," he said and kissed her check.

Brian laughed and kissed her forehead. "What a heartbreaker you're gonna be."

After Liz closed the door, she watched Casey as she stood by the fire. The normally green warm eyes now held a dark, cold tiger-like gaze as she looked into the dancing flames of the fire.

Casey paced like a tiger, waiting for Suzette to arrive. Niles watched her as did Jeffrey.

"Case, would you like me to tell her?" Niles offered and Jeffrey stepped up, as well.

Casey looked at them and laughed. "Thanks, guys, but, no, I need to do this. It was my doing, and I have to correct it. Don't worry, I'm a quieter, gentler Casey Bennett," she said and both men laughed along.

It was then that the door opened, and instead of Suzette, Liz walked in, holding Skye. Casey blinked and grinned. "What the hell?" She sighed and walked into the studio.

Niles and Jeffrey watched. "Don't tell me women are not more perceptive than we are, Niles. Liz knows what's coming. Look at her. She looks like a bear protecting her cubs."

Both men laughed. "Casey Bennett in love, with a family no less. Excuse me while I retire to bedlam." Niles laughed and Jeffrey joined him.

Casey walked up to Liz and took Skye as the little blonde reached for her. "Hey, Shortround," she said, giving Skye a kiss. She then looked at Liz. "What are you doing here?" She leaned over and kissed Liz, who sighed as she pulled back.

"Skye and I were out getting Halloween candy, which reminds me, we're going pumpkin shopping tomorrow. So I thought we'd stop by and see where you work," she said lightly.

She looked tired and Casey gave her a worried look. "Dr. Haines told you to stay quiet, not gallivant all over the North Shore," she scolded gently and kissed her again. "But I'm glad you're here. This wouldn't have anything to do with a certain cellist, would it?"

"Don't be a dope."

"You're a lousy liar," Casey said.

"Cafey, pay pinano," Skye said and patted her cheeks.

Casey looked into those blue eyes. "God, you Kennedy women and those blue eyes," she said and set her down. Casey then sat at the piano.

Liz stood by the piano and leaned in, smiling. "Whatever happened to that song you played at the cabin?"

"I gave up on that," Casey said as she played.

"Why? It was beautiful," Liz asked, then closed her eyes and smiled. "My, you play so beautifully."

"That's what I say. She should write her own music and make a CD. I'm telling you, she's written a ton of songs that—"

"Shut up, Niles," Casey said affectionately as she played.

"She plays it like a lover," Niles whispered to Liz, who shivered visibly as she watched the long delicate fingers glide over the black and white keys.

Casey looked at Liz and smiled. Niles looked back and forth between them. "Get a room."

Jeffrey walked up and whispered to Casey, who immediately stopped playing. She nodded and stood. "I'll be right back. Don't go anywhere. I'll take you and Shortround out for lunch."

Liz gave her a supportive smile and wink as she disappeared through the doors.

"Okay, the next sound you hear," Niles warned, and they all heard the bang of a cymbal. Heads turned as Skye was standing by the drums with a stick in her hand.

"I paying, Mama…" she called out and Niles laughed as Liz turned five shades of red.

"You won't be laughing if she put her foot through one of those drums, Niles," Liz said honestly, and Niles made a dash for the curly top…

"Casey, what are you doing here so early?" Suzette asked and slipped off her coat.

"Suzette, we have to talk."

She turned to Casey and gave her a seductive grin. "So had enough family? Come to your senses have you, Ms. Bennett?" she asked coyly and put her hands around Casey's neck.

Casey quickly took her hands away and walked away from her.

"I guess not," Suzette said. "So it's over between us. Is that it? I understand. You and I have had no commitment. It was fun while it lasted," she said and Casey looked at her.

"Suzette, we had to get another second-chair cellist. I'm sorry. You're just not getting it."

Suzette looked like a deer caught in the headlights. "W-what?"

Casey sighed and rubbed her forehead. "You heard me. All three of us agree. I thought it right that I tell you. You're a talented musician," she said, knowing it was a lie; Liz's comment on diplomacy ran through her mind. "This score just isn't for you. Trust me, you'll find—"

"Don't give me that shit!"

"Suzette," Casey said, and the cellist picked up a high-heeled shoe and threw it in Casey's direction. Quick reflexes allowed Casey to sidestep the hurled missile.

"Okay. You're upset, I understand," Casey said as the other shoe flew across the room. Casey ducked too late, and the projectile hit the mark. Right on the nose, it stunned Casey, who staggered back against the doors and stumbled through them and into the studio. She fell backward, blood seeping from the cut on the bridge of her nose. "Goddamn it!"

Suzette flew after her. "You think you can fuck me, then just toss me aside?" she bellowed. "What the shit is this?"

Niles and Jeffrey whirled around when Casey made her entrance. Liz's eyes flew open and Skye pulled at her mother's pants leg. "She say a bad word, Mama."

"You ain't heard the last of it, Goddess..." Niles whispered and put his hands over her ears.

"Suzette, I'm not tossing anyone aside. It's your music..." Casey tried to explain, albeit nasally.

Suzette, breathing heavily, stood there looking like a crazed woman.

"Suzette, for chrissakes," Niles exclaimed.

Skye's eyes widened. She frowned and looked at Casey, who was bent over and holding her nose. "Cafey hurt!" she exclaimed and ran for Casey.

Niles and Jeffrey ran after her. Liz went as quickly as she could.

Skye stood in front of the woman with her hands on her hips. "You hit Cafey. Not nice..." she cried and pushed Suzette's leg.

Suzette stumbled backward and looked down at the blond girl. "What the hell is this? Your fucking daughter, Casey?"

Casey growled, trying to blink the painful tears out of her eyes.

Liz now saw red. She pushed past Niles, grabbed Skye, and pushed her daughter behind her. Niles quickly took the child and held her as she struggled.

"Lemme go. She hurt Cafey."

"Skye..." Liz said firmly.

Skye stopped and looked at her mother. "Mama. Bad lady hurt Cafey."

Liz looked down at her daughter and smiled. "I know, sweet pea..." She motioned to Niles, who gently picked up the feisty three-year-old.

Casey was blinking, trying to focus while holding her nose. Blood was seeping through her fingers. "Suzette..." she said nasally.

173

Liz was looking at Suzette. "Casey, sit down and put your head back, sweetheart." She made sure she emphasized the last word.

Suzette glared at her, breathing like a bull.

Casey heard Liz's calm voice and got extremely nervous.

"Suzette. May I call you Suzette? Now I'm sure you feel Casey has wronged you, and you may be right. However, if you ever attempt to harm her again, I assure you, though I may not look like it, I will make it my life's mission to make your life a living hell. Don't ever think of hurting Casey or our daughter again."

Casey shot a look up at Liz as she said "our" daughter. She blinked and wiped the blood on her sleeve. She walked over to Liz and put her arm around her shoulder.

Niles smiled and set Skye down. She ran to Casey and stood between her and Liz; Skye wrapped her arm around Casey's leg.

Casey looked down and easily lifted Skye into her arms. "I am sorry, Suzette. This is not about what you and I may have been. It's about your music. You've been paid through the end of the month. I think that's more than fair. Goodbye," she said and started to walk away. She then turned back.

"Oh, and don't ever talk to my daughter like that again. You need to watch your language around children."

Liz rolled her eyes and led Casey away, putting a protective arm around her waist.

Niles and Jeffrey quickly intervened and guided the irate cellist through the door. "Suzette, darling, there is an opening at Orchestra Hall. I've made an appointment for you..." His voice trailed off as the doors closed.

Casey set Skye down, standing her on the piano bench. Liz took out a hanky from her pocket and put it against Casey's bleeding nose.

"Cafey hurt?" Skye asked.

"No, Shortround, I'm fine," Casey said.

Liz pinched the bridge of her nose just a little too hard. "I'm sorry. Did I hurt you?" Liz asked sweetly.

Casey winced, then looked down at her. "No, I probably

deserve this."

"Well, you don't have to worry about any more irate women now, do you?" Liz asked and batted her eyes at Casey.

"Only you, my love. Only you..." she said dryly and picked up Skye. "Hey, Shortround, thanks for standing up to that bully for me. You're getting to be a big girl saving me like that."

Skye grinned happily. "Did it by mineself. She hurt Cafey."

"Let's get out of here before you two get into another fight," Liz said and led her two feisty women out of the studio.

Casey was holding Liz close as she stared into the darkness. That afternoon was a telling experience. She was shocked when Skye stood up to Suzette; then she was astonished when Liz called Skye "our daughter." Never had Casey felt so much a part of life. She knew she was forever in love with Liz and loved Skye as her own. However, at that moment, Casey felt loved and needed.

Her life was changing with every passing minute. She could not remember her life before Liz and Skye. It was only a few months earlier. How could that be? How could she love so deeply? She had no clue, nor did she care to delve into it.

She only knew the winds of heaven sent these two... well two and a half and nothing would ever take them away from her.

"How's the nose?" Liz mumbled sleepily.

Casey groaned and felt the Band-Aid on her nose. "Okay. I hope it's not broken."

"Well, my darling, it may be an improvement."

"Very funny. I love you, too," Casey whispered and kissed her forehead. "I am sorry, Liz."

"For what?"

"My past seems to be haunting me."

"Forget the past, Casey," Liz whispered. "Do you have to be at the studio tomorrow?"

"Not really. What do you want to do?"

"Well, it's Halloween soon. I thought, well, if you're not busy, we'd go get a pumpkin."

"Wow, Halloween already. Shortround would love it. Sure," Casey said.

Liz let out an exasperated groan and started to get up.

"The baby sleeping on your bladder again?" Casey yawned and gave her a gentle nudge.

Liz laughed as Casey propelled her out of bed. "You're getting good at that, Ms. Bennett." She groaned as she waddled her way to the bathroom.

Casey laughed and watched her in the darkness. Then she put her hands behind her head and said a prayer of thanks as she sighed happily.

"This is like the Oneida County Fair," Liz said as she looked around the pumpkin patch.

"Help yourself," an older man said as he folded the money. "They're stacked according to price. Pick your own and pay me." He smiled and walked away.

Liz took a deep breath and licked her lips. Casey saw it and shook her head. "Okay, what do you want?"

"A brat with mustard and sauerkraut," Liz replied quickly.

Casey laughed and walked away. Skye was examining the mound of pumpkins when Casey came back with the sausage for Liz and a chocolate-covered pretzel for Skye. She noticed Liz eyeing it. "Don't worry. I got one for you, too."

Liz laughed as she took a big bite. Casey grimaced and looked away. "I can't watch." She turned to Skye, who was still looking over the pumpkins. "See one you like, Shortround?"

"That one," Skye said and pointed.

Casey followed her direction. Of course, she wanted the one on the top of the pile that was completely out of Casey's reach. "How about this one, Shortround? It's the same size."

"No, that one," Skye said. "Peas, Cafey?"

"Okay." Casey looked up at the pumpkin in question. "I guess I'm climbing."

Casey started to maneuver around the mound of pumpkins; she heard Liz's voice, muffled by a mouthful of sauerkraut, say, "Be careful."

"Be careful," Casey said, and as she got a foothold between two pumpkins, she slipped and fell headlong into the pile of them.

She vaguely heard Skye and Liz's screams as the pumpkins came tumbling down, pelting her in the head. She covered her head as they rained down upon her. When it was over, she opened her eyes to see Skye picking up the pumpkin she wanted.

"Thank you, Cafey."

Sitting amongst the pumpkins, Casey winced and pulled one out from under her, stem first. "You're welcome, Shortround."

"Are you all right?" Liz asked.

"I'm just fine, but I've either wet my pants or I'm sitting on a squashed pumpkin."

Liz laughed and offered her hand, which Casey waved off. As she stood and shook her leg, the owner walked up to them and looked at the mess.

"I'll pay for any that were damaged," Casey said. "I know of at least one." She pulled at the seat of her pants.

"No, that's all right. Can I ask you why you didn't use the ladder?" He pointed to the ladder with a big sign on it reading, "Use for the pumpkins out of reach." It was leaning against the vendor's booth.

"Hey, corn on the cob," Liz said eagerly.

Casey tossed the smashed pumpkin down on the pile and pulled out her wallet.

Chapter 18

"Hold still, baby," Liz said as she buckled the belt around Skye's waist. "This old flannel shirt is perfect."

Skye fidgeted while she tried to stand still. "Do I look like hobo, Mama?"

"You sure do, sweetie."

Skye looked at Meredith, who winked and nodded. "Just like Casey did when she was your age."

"I was never that small," Casey said and took the cork from the bottle of wine. "And now, your scruffy beard."

Skye frowned as she watched Casey hold the cork over the flame of the stove. "It too hot, Cafey."

"Nah, it won't be hot." She charred the cork and walked toward Skye, who backed up. "Shortround, I'm tellin' ya, it's not hot."

"You do it," Skye said.

Liz gave Casey a challenging smile. "Yes, Casey, you put some on. Better yet, let me do it."

Skye laughed and Meredith applauded. "Excellent idea, Liz."

Liz took the cork out of Casey's hand and pushed her into the kitchen chair. "Now let's see, we want a beard."

"Paybacks, Ms. Kennedy," Casey said as Skye clapped her hands.

"What a night for trick or treating," Meredith said; she and Liz watched as Casey took Skye by the hand and led her up the walk.

Liz smiled when she heard Skye announce, "Twick or tweet."

Meredith laughed openly. "What an adorable child. Skye's cute, too."

Liz laughed along but said nothing as Meredith stopped and turned to her. "You're in love with my granddaughter, aren't you?"

She saw the crimson color rise in Liz's neck to her cheeks. Even her ears were red. "Yes, Meredith. I believe I could fall hopelessly in love with Casey."

"You sound a little hesitant," Meredith said and was interrupted by Skye as she ran to Liz. She carried her orange pumpkin and presented it to Liz.

"Look, Mama. I got candy," Skye exclaimed breathlessly.

"I see that, sweetie. Did you say thank you?"

Skye nodded and looked at Meredith, "Look, Gamma, I got candy."

"How wonderful, Skye. Are you having fun, darling?" She reached down and chucked Skye under the chin.

Again, Skye nodded, then grabbed Casey by the hand. "C'mon, Cafey."

Casey laughed and allowed her to pull her down the sidewalk to the next house. Liz and Meredith followed behind.

"So I sense a little uncertainty, Liz."

Liz shrugged. "I don't know, Meredith. Casey has been single for so long. And she made her view on commitment and children very obvious."

"That was before she fell in love with you." When Liz did not respond, Meredith continued. "And she is in love with you."

"How can you be so sure?" Liz asked. She smiled as she watched Casey gently prodding Skye up to the front door.

"Well, she hasn't gone trick or treating since she was a child. I haven't heard her curse in a few days."

Liz laughed at that. "I have to agree with you there."

"And I see the way she looks at you," Meredith said. "I know that look. I see it on your face, as well."

Liz bit at her bottom lip while she walked side by side with Meredith. "You need to be patient with her. I can't imagine it's easy for either of you."

"How do you mean?" Liz asked.

Meredith thought before she answered. "Well, given how you met. How both of you loved Julie. And how you have a child and one on the way."

"That's my big concern," Liz said. "I know Casey cares for me and Skye. But to be a permanent part of our lives. It might be too much to ask."

"Possibly," Meredith said in agreement. "But don't give up, sweetie."

Liz smiled and looked at Meredith. "I can't. I'm stuck on your granddaughter."

Meredith laughed and slipped her arm in and held on to Liz's. "I have a good idea the feeling is mutual."

When the streetlights came on, Liz informed Casey it was time to get back. Casey frowned and looked in Skye's pumpkin. "Hmm. Okay, Shortround. You made a good killing here. Let's get back and see what you got."

They sat around Meredith's kitchen table as Meredith prepared the hot chocolate. Casey poured Skye's bucket on the table. Liz laughed at Skye and Casey, who still had the black cork on their faces. Skye knelt on the chair and placed her elbows on the table. She looked at her mother.

"Can I eat some?" Skye asked.

Casey gave Liz a pleading look. "Can we?"

Liz rolled her eyes as Meredith placed the cups in front of each. "One piece..." Liz said. "Each," she added and Casey pulled a face.

"Okay, Shortround. Pick out a good one."

Skye frowned, deep in concentration as she looked over the Halloween booty; Casey did as well. Finally, Skye made her decision.

"Is it okay if I have a piece of your candy?" Casey asked.

"Sure," Skye said absently. She handed the candy to Liz to open it.

Casey picked the peanut butter candy. "This is my favorite."

Liz groaned as she stood. "This child sits right on my bladder, I swear it."

Casey helped her out of the chair and watched as she disappeared down the hall.

Meredith sipped her hot chocolate while Skye placed her candy, piece by piece, back into the pumpkin. Casey watched with a smile.

"I had a nice talk with Liz while you and Skye were begging for candy."

Casey gave Meredith a wary glance. "Oh?"

"Yes." Meredith offered a smug grin. "I told you so."

Casey turned bright red and avoided her look. "What did she say?"

Meredith raised an eyebrow. "About what?"

"You know very well what I'm talking about."

Meredith laughed evilly. "I think she wants to go steady."

Casey laughed along. "Oh, you need to be committed."

"She also has reservations."

Casey stopped laughing then. "She does?"

"Yes. It appears your reputation might be preceding you."

Casey leaned back with a dejected grunt.

"You need to be honest with her, Casey. You have nothing to lose."

"But Liz."

Meredith shrugged. "Well, it's either worth it or it's not." She reached over and took Casey's hand then. "You have to decide, sweetie. It's time, don't you think?"

She watched as Casey drank her hot chocolate; she said nothing.

Casey stood in front of the fireplace, staring at the dancing flames. Liz was sound asleep as was Skye. Trick or treating took its toll on both Kennedys. Her grandmother's words rolled around in her head. So much had happened in the three months since Liz and Skye came into her life; it was amazing just how much.

Never did Casey think she'd be in this position. When Julie broke it off with her five years earlier, Casey was hurt and angry. She had loved Julie, even though in the back of her mind, Casey somehow knew it wasn't going to work between them, not in a forever sense anyway. There was an attraction and love, but not the same way she found with Liz.

"Oh, I don't know," she muttered. Was this all too soon? she thought. Was she jumping in with both feet and not thinking clearly? She was right not to have children with Julie. Now she was on the verge of starting something with Liz, who had a family. Did she want this? This had been gnawing at her in the back of her mind.

Her grandmother said Liz had reservations; Casey's reputation, she had said. Liz was a level-headed, intelligent woman. "Shit," Casey said. Her own indecision now plagued her.

She turned the gas jets off, and as she made her way down the hall, she heard Skye whimpering. Carefully pushing the door open, she looked at Skye as she slept. The nightlight dimly illuminated her bed; Casey gently sat on the edge and lightly ran her fingers through Skye's blond curls, mindful not to wake her. Casey shook her head and smiled, feeling the tears well in her eyes. She adored Skye, probably from the first meeting in the bus depot. She remembered the feisty kid with her hands on her hips. She almost laughed out loud when she remembered Skye yakking all over her shirt. At the time, Casey was completely irritated at the whole situation.

Now? She bent down and lightly kissed Skye's forehead. In her sleep, Skye clung to her fish and rolled over on her side. Casey pulled the quilt over her shoulders, once again running her fingers through her blond hair.

"I love you, Shortround," she whispered and stood. She looked up to see Liz standing in the doorway, tears streaming down her cheeks. She smiled and made no move to wipe them away.

"I heard her whimpering," Liz whispered and stepped back as Casey closed the door, leaving it slightly open.

"I did too. She's okay. Probably dreaming about candy."

Liz smiled and looked into Casey's eyes. "Why are you crying?" Liz asked and wiped the tears away.

"Why are you?" Casey countered, running her hand under her eyes.

"I was touched at your gentleness with Skye," Liz said.

"I love the little dwarf," Casey said and sniffed.

Liz took Casey by the hand and led her across the hall into their bedroom. "And the little dwarf loves you."

Casey stopped and pulled on Liz's hand. "Do you?"

Liz reached up and cupped Casey's cheek. "I believe I do."

Casey grinned and pulled her into her arms. "I love you, too, Liz. I know there's still a lot we need to talk about. I know I'm not the best candidate for this." She kissed her forehead before continuing. "My past sucks."

Liz walked over to the bed and pulled back the covers. Casey helped her as she lay down with a deep sigh. "Your past is over, Casey. Let's concentrate on right now."

Casey nodded as she pulled the covers over Liz and got undressed. She slipped into bed and sidled close to Liz and lay on her side, facing her. Liz turned her head and smiled. "Good night, Casey."

Casey leaned over and lightly kissed her lips. "Good night, Liz." She kissed her again, and this time, Liz returned her kiss and didn't pull back.

Breathing heavily, Casey moved and loomed over Liz, still holding their kiss. When she heard Liz moan, her heart raced. She reached down and cupped her plump breast, letting out a whimper as she ran her thumb over her erect nipple.

Liz easily slipped the tip of her tongue into Casey's mouth, and Casey responded by kneading her breast, reveling in the feel of the silky material. Liz arched her back, then gently pulled Casey's hand away from her breast.

Casey pulled back and looked down into the lustful blue eyes.

"We'd...we better stop," Liz whispered.

Though Casey wanted nothing else but to continue, she

understood. "It's me, isn't it?"

"What?"

"I know what you're thinking, and it's okay. I hope in time, my past won't—"

Liz put her fingertips against Casey's lips. "This is not about you. It's me, Casey. I want you badly, but being pregnant and fat and swollen and—"

It was Casey's turn to quiet Liz with her fingertips. She looked at Liz's lips and lightly ran her finger across them. "I understand how you feel. But you need to know I find you so desirable right now. Just the way you are. I'm not waiting for your body or any part of you to change. So when you feel it's right, it'll be right. Don't worry. I'm not going anywhere."

She then kissed Liz and cuddled her close. "I'll wait."

"Thank you."

"Now go to sleep. Before you know it, it'll be the witching hour and baby will be sleeping on your bladder again."

Liz laughed sleepily and nestled into her shoulder. "You're a good kisser, Ms. Bennett."

Casey tightened her embrace and laughed. "You're not so bad yourself. Go to sleep."

They lay in silence for a few moments until Liz said, "Guess what I'm doing right now."

"I haven't a clue."

"Doing my Kegels."

Casey started chuckling, and soon Liz followed her until both women were laughing uncontrollably.

Chapter 19

With each day that flew by, Casey tried to predict the time of arrival of the new Kennedy.

"Okay. I've got it figured out." She sat at the kitchen table.

Skye was eating a banana and Liz was smiling and obediently listening.

"Now your due date is December 3. That gives us two weeks. Next Thursday is Thanksgiving. Don't worry about dinner, I'll make it."

"Honey, have you ever made a turkey before?" Liz asked.

Casey blinked stupidly. "Well..."

"I can make it."

"No. You're not supposed to. Wait, I've got an idea."

Skye let out a baby groan and put her head down. Casey frowned and gaped at her. "Hey, this will work. Now you tell me what to do and I will make the dinner. Shortround and I will go to the store and get everything."

"I help," Skye said happily.

Casey beamed and pointed to her. "See, this is good!"

Liz groaned. "All right. I'll make a list." She then handed the phone to Casey, who gave her a curious look. "You want to invite Meredith and Niles and Brian, don't you?"

"Of course, but remember, you're not doing a thing," Casey said firmly, and Liz just nodded.

Casey wheeled the cart through the grocery store. "Your mother and her lists," Casey said and looked at Skye, who sat in the seat, her arms folded across her chest in a defiant pose. Casey glanced down at her, trying to avoid the feisty humanoid.

"Cafey, I walk..."

"No. You'll run all over the place and we need to concentrate." Casey looked at the list. "Well, I need to concentrate." She stopped in the produce section and walked away from the cart. "Okay, onions, celery. I can do this," she said and picked up the items. "Potatoes..." She checked off the list.

As she took the items back to the cart, she saw Skye reach over, pick up a tomato, and bite into it.

"Shortround..." she grumbled and Skye pulled the tomato out of Casey's reach. Each time Casey grabbed for it, Skye whisked it out of her way.

"Golldarnit, ya octopus..." Casey mumbled. She was getting better at not swearing.

Skye then dropped the half-eaten tomato on the floor. "Sorry, Cafey," she said with a precocious grin.

Casey glared at her, and to her embarrassment, a woman picked up the tomato and grinned. "Did you lose this?" the redhead asked.

Casey smiled sheepishly. "Th-thanks. I shouldn't have left the little darling alone," she said and glared at Skye, who was still grinning.

"Well, you seem to have your hands full. Is this your daughter? Or are you single?" the redhead asked and looked into Casey's eyes.

She swallowed and grinned helplessly. "Yes to the first question, and no." She smiled and the redhead shrugged.

"Well, have a nice holiday," she said and walked away.

Casey looked down at Skye, who seemed like she knew what the redhead wanted. Is that possible? Casey thought. There was too much she did not know about children.

An hour later, Casey was exhausted and Skye was so cranky her face was flushed.

"Well, that went well," Casey said sarcastically as she wheeled the cart to the car.

Skye folded her arms in a huff. "Cafey, I help," she said and her bottom lip quivered.

Casey stopped the cart by the car and looked down at the sad face. All at once, she felt like a heel. "Skye, I needed to get this done. Did you see how many people there were in that store? Geez, if I'd have let you go, I'd have been chasing you."

"I help," she said in a small voice.

Casey groaned and felt horrible. "Okay. When we get home, you can help me put everything away and help make Thanksgiving dinner. Then we have to send a letter to Santa."

Skye's eyes lit up. "Letter? Mine own letter to Santa?"

"Yep. So whatta ya say, help me?"

Skye patted Casey's hand. "Sure, I help Cafey."

Casey looked down into those blue eyes. "Thanks, Shortround. You saved me again," she said and kissed Skye's nose as she giggled.

"Bottom shelf," Casey instructed and Skye struggled with the bag of flour.

"Cafey, too heavy," Skye said with a groan.

Liz narrowed her eyes at Casey, who tried not to laugh. "What's the point of having a dwarf around...?" She started to joke and Liz continued to glare at her. Casey laughed and picked up the flour and put it away.

"Okay, Shortround, let's try this." Casey handed her the tomatoes.

"Like lady in store," Skye said.

Casey closed her eyes and prayed—no such luck. Women on a whole have radar. Pregnant women seemed wired purposefully.

"What woman, sweet pea?" Liz asked absently.

"Red hair. She like Cafey," Skye said.

Casey shoved Skye into the refrigerator and tried to close the door. Skye screamed and laughed as Casey released her.

"Really? What happened, Skye?" Liz asked as she sat at the table.

"Okay, okay, don't grill the kid," Casey said, holding up her hands in defeat. "Your daughter picked up a tomato and took a healthy bite, then dropped it on the ground. A woman picked it up. Pleasantries exchanged and that was that. Happy holidays, bye-bye."

Skye giggled as she extricated herself from the refrigerator. Casey looked down at the little traitor. "Hold on, you're not frozen yet," she said wickedly and Skye shrieked with laughter and ran to her mother.

On her way to the studio the next morning, Casey had breakfast with her grandmother. Meredith lavishly spread the jam on her toast and took a healthy bite.

"This was a wonderful idea," she said.

Casey drank her coffee and nodded.

"Now tell me how you are going to make a turkey dinner." Meredith sipped her tea.

"I went shopping for everything."

"Another list?"

"Yes," Casey said with a grin. "So Liz will play drill sergeant for me and Skye. She'll boss us around and we'll make dinner."

Meredith sat back and looked at Casey, who munched on a piece of bacon. "You are so in love with this woman."

Casey stopped chewing and looked up. "I-I guess so."

"So have you had sex yet?"

Casey nearly choked on her eggs. "Damn it," she said and wiped her chin. "Gram, what the hell kinda question is that?"

"I think it's a perfectly normal question to ask a woman who is in love."

Casey hid her face in her hands.

"Well?"

"Not yet," Casey said and avoided the curious look.

"I see. In Liz's condition, I'm sure sex is the last thing on her mind. Are you at least sleeping in the same bed?"

"Yes," Casey answered obediently. "Now, you nosy old woman, can we change the topic?"

"One more question. Is Liz practicing her Kegels?"

Casey hung her head but answered obediently. "Yes, Gram."

Thanksgiving morning came with a clang. Casey winced when she dropped the pot on the floor. "Okay. I'm very good with instructions," Casey said and placed the pot back on the stove; she then rubbed her hands together.

For the next three hours, Liz ordered and Casey followed. Only once, when the stuffing needed to be stuffed did Casey grimace, as did Skye, who wore an apron because Casey wore one.

"This is gross," Casey grimaced.

Skye, elbows on the table as she watched, agreed. "Yucky, Cafey." Skye pulled a face and stuck out her tongue.

Other than that, the turkey was in the oven. The local bakery handled the pumpkin and apple pies. Casey was not ready for baking yet.

"Mama, put feet up," Skye said and Liz laughed.

Casey agreed and got the ottoman. Liz eased into the couch and put her feet up; she let out a contented sigh when Casey caressed her calves.

"Don't argue," she said, kissing her deeply.

"Yes, ma'am." Liz closed her eyes.

"Well, I think Santa Claus is about to make an appearance," Casey called out to Skye and turned on the Thanksgiving Day parade.

Skye ran out of her bedroom and sat in front of the television. Casey sat on the couch next to Liz and watched the parade.

"Where Santa?" Skye asked.

"Soon, sweet pea." Liz sighed tiredly and Casey glanced at her.

"You okay, turtle woman?"

Liz grinned and nodded as Casey reached over and caressed her stomach.

Liz laughed. "God, I'm huge! Why does everyone want to touch my stomach? Yesterday, Skye and I were at the store and two people asked to rub my belly. What is that?"

Casey laughed at the mental picture. "I don't know. Maybe

it's because you have a little human growing in there."

Skye turned and looked at them. "They love baby, Mama."

Both women looked at Skye and said nothing for a moment.

"Skye, sweetie. Do you love the baby?"

"Mmm-hmm. I have baby sister to play with growing in Mama's stomach."

"What if Mommy has a baby brother? Would that be okay?" Casey asked as Skye watched the parade intently.

"Sure," she said as she watched.

"What should we name the baby, Skye?" Liz asked.

"Mama, Santa comin'," Skye insisted. Then she shrieked with excitement. "Santa! He comin'," she cried and jumped up and down. She then crawled up onto Casey's lap. "Cafey, Santa comin'."

The baby's name would have to wait.

Thanksgiving dinner was nearly ready. "I love that smell." Casey took a good sniff while she and Skye set the table. Liz entertained Niles and Brian and Meredith.

"Let me do the honors," Brian said and stepped up to the bar. "Martini, Meredith?" He didn't wait for a reply as he mixed the cocktails.

"Liz, I cannot believe the change in Casey..." Niles said. The sound of silverware clanging to the floor stopped him.

All four gracefully ignored it. Niles continued, "You've been a lifesaver for her. You and the goddess."

Liz watched and smiled as she heard Casey instruct Skye where to put the silverware. "She's done the same for us..." She stopped and closed her eyes as another clang rang out. "...I have a great deal to be thankful for."

One more clang and Casey's head popped out into the living room. "We're almost done. Sorry," she said sheepishly.

"I detect that note of hesitation again." Meredith took the stemmed glass from Brian. He handed Liz a glass of ice water. Liz smiled her thanks.

"Make me something exotic," Niles said.

"You're exotic enough," Brian said; Niles kissed him.

Meredith and Liz laughed at their playfulness, then turned her attention back to Liz. "Now tell me."

"I was just thinking of Casey's stance on children. They deserve a mother and father, and I wondered if she truly meant it or maybe she just does not want that with me."

Meredith seemed to understand as she watched her. "Well, all I know is Casey does nothing but talk about you whenever I see her. Niles says the same thing. She talks of you and Skye all day. He said it was becoming quite annoying."

Liz blushed and rested her head against the back of the couch. "I do love that piano player, Meredith."

"I know, dear. And the piano player loves you. Be patient," Meredith said and held on to her hand.

Casey sat at the head of the table, Liz at the other. Skye sat next to Niles and Brian on the other side; Meredith sat next to Liz. They gave their thanks and Casey raised her wine glass. Liz raised her water glass and Skye grinned, raising her sippy-cup like everyone else.

"Nobody knows better than I how much I have to be thankful for. In a couple weeks, we'll have to add another chair at this table," Casey said. The tears welled in her eyes as she looked down at Liz, who mirrored her look. "I am so blessed. Happy Thanksgiving," she said, her voice breaking with emotion.

Glasses gently touched and Skye giggled as Niles touched his glass with hers. Casey winked at Liz.

Liz watched Casey's long slender fingers hold the knife, and with one deft movement, the turkey slid off the platter and onto the table.

Meredith laughed outright along with Niles and Brian. Skye laughed in pure childlike innocence. Casey winced and laughed nervously as she picked up the turkey and gently replaced it on the platter.

Much to Casey's relief, the rest of the meal went without further incident, and the holiday season began.

Chapter 20

Liz was rearranging the cupboards in the kitchen when she heard the doorbell ring. She groaned and quickly waddled up to the door, not wanting to wake Skye from her nap. There stood two men, each grinning. "I got a delivery for Liz Kennedy. Where do ya want it?"

"It goes it the back room, she told ya," the other man grumbled as he held the furniture.

"Well," Liz said and stood back. "The back room is on the right."

He nodded and both men walked the boxes back into the room. Liz was confused as she watched the men open the boxes.

The older man looked up and grinned. "I'm supposed to tell you to go sit down and put your feet up," he said and Liz's eyes widened. "Go, we're getting paid by the hour."

Liz gave them a wary look and walked into the living room. They made several trips as Liz watched them parade back and forth. In an hour, both men had apparently finished.

"Okay, you can look. Merry Christmas," he said and shook her hand.

Liz was completely confused as she walked them out. Then right behind them, the doorman was grinning as he walked up to her, loaded with packages and boxes. "Santa's come early, Ms. Kennedy. Casey told me to tell you to go sit down—"

"And put my feet up, I know, Mike. C'mon in," she said, chuckling. "I think those probably go in the back room." She suddenly sniffed back her tears.

The doorman winked and walked down the hallway. "Merry Christmas, Ms. Kennedy," he said and tipped his hat as he walked out.

Liz cautiously walked into the room and put her hand to her heart.

A crib was set up, a rocking chair next to it and a dresser on the opposite wall; a small changing table sat next to that. The gift-wrapped boxes and packages were set in the crib. A Disney mobile hung over the crib; she then noticed a card dangling from the mobile. She sniffed back her tears once again and opened the card.

My darling Liz,

Motherhood looks so good on you. Our baby cannot come into this world and have nowhere to sleep. Have Skye help you... Tell her it was from Santa Claus!

I love you, only you. Merry Christmas, My Only One.

Always, Casey

PS. I understand you're nesting, but sit down and quit cleaning the cabinets.

"Our baby..." Liz whispered. She held the card to her heart and looked around the room.

"Mama," Skye's sleepy voice called out.

Liz turned to see the flushed face as Skye walked into the room and gazed around.

"Santa came early for the baby," Liz said.

Skye's blue eyes widened in amazement. "He come too soon, Mama."

"I know, but he knew we needed th-this and h-he loves us..." She sat in the rocker and started crying.

Skye ran up to her and put her head on her lap. "Mama happy?"

"Yes, sweet pea, Mommy's very happy," she said and dried her eyes. "Now let's see what Santa brought."

For the next hour, Liz rocked in the comfortable chair as Skye tore into the packages. Liz shook her head in wonderment at all the baby clothes. She laughed when she saw the colors. All white, no preference between boy and girl. Rattles, teething rings. Liz smiled at the idea of Casey Bennett loose in a baby store. God help those poor clerks.

Then Skye opened one and gave it a curious look. "What it say, Mama?" She walked over and handed the shirt to her mother. Liz read it and laughed.

"Casey Bennett, you idiot..." She laughed once more.

It read *Pianists do it Upright* in big red letters across the front of the T-shirt. She read it to Skye, who frowned, apparently not getting the joke and shrugged, then concentrated on the last of the boxes.

"All for the baby?" Skye helped Liz clean up the discarded wrapping.

"Yes, sweetie, wasn't that nice of Santa? Wait until he comes for you," her mother said. Skye grinned and clapped her hands. "We have to send your letter to Santa. How about we do that after dinner?"

Skye was beside herself with excitement.

Casey whistled "Jingle Bells" as she struggled with the huge tree. Mike, the doorman, laughed. "Good grief, Case, will that fit into the elevator?"

Casey stopped and looked at the tree. "Shit, I hope so. Help me with the bags, will ya, Mike?"

He shook his head, picked up the bags, and followed Casey to the elevator. "Was she surprised?" Casey asked.

Mike nodded. "If I wasn't there, she'd have been bawling like a baby."

"I've gotta get this all set up. The baby's due in a week or so," she said as she struggled into the elevator. The smell of pine permeated the elevator.

"You're getting sap all over the place," Mike grumbled as the elevator door opened.

"You have no romance in your soul, Michael," she scolded and kissed his cheek.

She put her key in the door and opened it. "Ho, Ho, Ho!" she said in a low voice and Skye screamed with laughter.

"Cafey... A tree!" Skye jumped up and down.

Liz came out of the kitchen and laughed as she shook her head. "Casey..." she said, chuckling.

Casey was grinning like a kid. She propped the tree against the wall and walked up to Liz and kissed her deeply. "Hi," she whispered. "Were you cleaning again?"

"Yes and yes, I'm nesting. Thank you," Liz whispered against her lips. "You smell like pine."

Casey laughed. "Hey, Shortround," she said and scooped the girl up and swung her in her arms.

Within a half hour, she and Skye had the tree in the stand, right next to the fireplace.

"Wait..." Liz said, sitting on the couch with her feet up. "There's a bare spot. Turn it just a bit."

Casey turned it slightly. "Little more..." Liz encouraged and Casey grunted as she turned the huge tree.

"Lil mo, Cafey..." Skye mimicked her mother and Casey poked her head out from around the back and narrowed her eyes at the little curly top. Liz hid her grin as Casey struggled.

"Perfect!" Liz said quickly. "Right, sweet pea?"

"Wight..." Skye nodded.

Casey flopped down next to them, exhausted. "I need a drink. So anything happen today?"

With that, Skye remembered. "Cafey, Santa come too soon!" she exclaimed and pulled at her hand.

Casey helped Liz up, and Skye ran down the hall ahead of them. Liz stopped Casey and gently cupped her face. "You're a good woman, Casey Bennett," she whispered and kissed her tenderly.

"Mama! Cafey!" Skye called.

Casey grinned as she put an arm around Liz as they walked down the hall.

"Holy cow!" Casey exclaimed as she looked around the room.

Skye was so excited she almost swallowed her tongue. "Can

you be-eve it?" she exclaimed and clapped her hands. "All for baby. Mama loves rocking," Skye said, standing next to the rocker.

"I knew she would, Shortround," Casey said tenderly and winked at Liz.

For the rest of the evening, they decorated the tree as the Christmas music rang out throughout the apartment. Then they all sat back on the couch to admire their work. Between the blazing fire and the soft lights on the tree, a warm comfortable glow bathed the living room. Casey had her arm around Liz, whose head was resting comfortably on her shoulder. Skye was sleeping, laying her head on her mother's lap, her feet sprawled across Casey, who absently caressed the little leg.

"This is life," Casey whispered and looked at Liz.

"Yes, it is," Liz agreed with a sigh. She looked down at Skye, who was sound asleep. "We'd better get her to bed."

Casey eased off the couch and carried Skye into the bedroom. When she got Skye settled in, Skye woke and whimpered.

"Hey, go back to sleep," Casey whispered and kissed her cheek.

"Mine fith," Skye whispered. Though her eyes were closed, she reached out for her stuffed animal, which Casey gently placed in her arms.

"G'night, Shortround."

"Night, Cafey," Skye whispered on the edge of sleep.

Casey walked down the hallway to find Liz nearly asleep on the couch. "C'mon, turtle woman. Time for bed."

"Can we just stay here for a while? My back was killing me, but I'm so comfortable."

"Sure," Casey said. "Lift."

Liz obeyed and lifted her feet; Casey slid under them and sat down, then caressed Liz's tired feet.

"I can't believe what a great massage you give," Liz said. She placed a pillow behind her head and looked down at Casey, who was staring at the fire. "A penny for your thoughts."

Casey grinned and shrugged. "I was just thinking of all that has happened to you and me in these past few months."

"Too much?" Liz asked and absently rubbed her stomach.

"Well, it has been a change for both of us."

"Yes, it has. Look, Casey, if you're having doubts about all this, I totally understand."

Casey stopped caressing her feet and turned slightly to face her. "No, honey. I'm not having doubts about my love for you and Skye. But I will be honest. I doubt myself."

"Why, sweetie?" Liz asked. When Casey was silent, she waited.

"I guess I'm not sure if I'm good enough to be a parent and a partner. I've lived so long alone." She stopped and caressed Liz's foot.

"It's hard for me, as well, Casey."

She heard the sincerity in Liz's voice. "As far as what?"

Now Liz was silent, and Casey waited.

"Sometimes, I feel I was selfish with having this baby. I mean, I wanted to have her. Julie wanted this, as well. But at the time, I was thinking of how to keep Julie home more. It was such a childish and stupid thing." She stopped and took a deep breath.

"Liz. You're a good mother, and you'll be a good mother for this little one."

"It just all happened so fast with Julie."

Casey nodded. "I can imagine it was hard for you."

"She got so sick, so quickly. The last few months were just tragic to watch. When she wasn't having chemo that made her violently ill, she was drained and couldn't do a thing. It just ravaged her body."

Casey said nothing, letting Liz get all this out. She had never spoken about this.

"She was nearly unrecognizable when she died," Liz said in a flat, dull voice. She stared at her feet as Casey continued to massage them. "Skye hardly remembers her. Julie was away constantly. Then when she told me of the bone cancer, she spent most of the time in the hospital or at Joanne's." She saw Casey's inquisitive look. "She's a good friend of ours. Julie wouldn't stay at home when she wasn't in the hospital. Joanne told me that Julie didn't want Skye to see her as ill as she was. The only trouble with that is that I didn't have an opportunity to care for her. We were so happy when I found out I was pregnant. It was almost as if she …" Her voice trailed off.

"As if she didn't want to be reminded of something happy when she knew she couldn't have it."

Liz nodded, her bottom lip quivered. "It was probably better that way. Like I said, Skye hardly remembers her." She took a deep breath and let it out slowly. She did this several times.

"Are you okay?" Casey asked.

Liz nodded and continued breathing.

"Braxton Hicks?" Casey gently slid out from underneath Liz and knelt at her head. "They say if you move, the contractions may stop. They'll be getting stronger now, right?"

Liz smiled and looked at her. "You've been reading again."

"Yes, I have. Now, c'mon. Let's get you up and into bed. How about some chamomile tea?" She helped Liz into a sitting position, then standing.

"No, I've got heartburn," Liz said. Casey heard the irritation in her voice.

Casey nodded. "Higher levels of progesterone."

Liz glared at her.

"It causes that muscle to relax and the stomach acid—" She stopped abruptly when she saw the look she had come to associate with certain death in the blue eyes.

"Yes, I know."

"How about some yogurt?"

"I don't like yogurt."

"Okay, how about a nice warm glass of milk, maybe a little honey in it?"

Liz continued to glare. "Remind me to thank Dr. Martin for giving you those pamphlets." She then grinned reluctantly. "I suppose a big bowl of brownie dough ice cream is out of the question."

"Uh, yeah."

"All right, Doctor. Warm milk it is. I'll meet you in the bedroom. But if you come in there with something chocolaty to eat, I won't be responsible for my actions."

Casey laughed and propelled Liz in the right direction. She then winced at the idea of warm milk. "Good thing she's having the baby."

Chapter 21

It was time. Liz stifled a cry of pain as the second contraction came within three minutes of the last one. She reached for Casey, who was immediately awake.

"Now?" Casey exclaimed as she looked at the clock.

Liz glared at her. "I don't think the baby cares what time it is," she said through clenched teeth.

"How far apart are they?" Casey asked as she quickly dressed. Pulling on her jeans, she tripped on one leg and fell to the floor. "Shit!"

Liz rolled her eyes. "Casey. I don't need a trip to the emergency room." She let out a sigh as the contraction subsided.

Casey stood and zipped the jeans, then flipped on the light. She grabbed the phone and dialed Niles's number. "Niles... It's time... Yes, now... Okay...Call Gram..." She snapped off the phone. "Okay, Niles and Brian will be here in ten minutes. Yesterday, we planned the route they should take."

Liz tried to grin at Casey's preparations but only grimaced as the next contraction came. Casey flew to her side and knelt down. "Okay, I'm calling Dr. Haines."

She dialed the number. "Dr. Haines... Yes... It's time... Three minutes... Yes, yes. Okay," she said and took two deep breaths as instructed. Liz cried out and Casey told the doctor, "We're leaving in five minutes."

"Casey!" Liz cried out and reached for her.

Casey knelt beside her and grabbed her hand. "Okay, let's get you dressed."

"Honey, I'm fine. Just get my slippers."

"Slippers... Where?" Casey said frantically and looked under the bed.

Liz was struggling, and as she sat up, Casey came from under the bed and her head hit Liz in the cheek.

"Damn it, honey, I'm so sorry!" Casey cried out, rubbing her head.

Liz held on to her cheek. "It's all right. Casey, calm down before you faint," Liz said through her contractions. "Casey, oh, God..."

"What is it?" Casey asked frantically. The flood of fluid cascading between Liz's legs had her staring in disbelief. "What in the mother of Christ..."

"I think my water broke, sweetie."

"Your water?" Casey cried out. "Where the fuck is Niles?"

Liz reached for her. Casey knelt in front of her, wild-eyed and worried. "Sweetie, take a deep breath."

Casey took several and nearly hyperventilated. She swayed precariously for a moment as the blood rushed back to her head.

"Now, honey. I love your body, but you might want to put on a shirt."

Casey looked down at her semi-nakedness in disgust and grabbed a sweater and pulled it over her head, then slipped into her shoes.

With that, the doorbell rang. "Don't move," Casey said to Liz. She then flew to the door to greet Niles and Brian.

"Okay, you two stay with Skye..." Casey said and took the keys from him and dashed back to Liz.

"Hi..." Niles called to the frantic figure and Brian laughed as he took off his coat.

"I'll call you when you can bring Skye," Casey called over her shoulder as she led Liz out.

"Did you call Meredith?" Liz asked through her pain as she slipped into her coat.

"Yes. Don't worry. She's coming right over, then we'll meet you at the hospital." Niles kissed her cheek. "Good luck, Liz. Not with the baby, with this one." He motioned to the frantic Casey.

Liz laughed. "Tell Skye we love her. You bring her later, Niles," Liz said as Casey quickly but gently ushered her out the door.

"Casey, please don't get a ticket. I'm fine, we have plenty of time," Liz said wild-eyed as she watched the woman she loved scream down the dark street.

Casey came to a screeching halt at the emergency room. As she dashed out of the car, she forgot her seat belt. The welt across her neck would be evident for several days. She grunted painfully as she fought to unclasp the treacherous belt. "Mother of God!" she exclaimed angrily, nearly ripping the seat belt off the door.

"Casey, sweetheart, please," Liz begged through her contractions.

"I'm all right," Casey said painfully and stretched her neck.

She ran in, got a wheelchair, and stupidly tried to go through the revolving door. After getting wedged between the doors, she looked out to see Liz sitting in the car watching her. Casey heard her muffled yells and pulled the wheelchair back.

"Stupid fucking doors," she yelled and rushed to the automatic door. It slid open and she dashed back to Liz and helped her as she sat with a groan. Casey quickly wheeled her through the sliding doors.

"Casey, honey, slow down," she said as the contractions came again.

Casey maneuvered the wheelchair up to the nurses' station. The older nurse smiled at Liz.

"Having a baby?" she asked and saw the red ugly welt across Casey's neck. "What happened?"

Liz waved her hand in dismissal. "We had a near-death experience getting out of the car."

Casey rolled her eyes as the nurse laughed and took the forms out. "Okay, big picture here!" Casey said helplessly.

"She's worse than a man." The nurse winked at Liz and handed a pen to Casey, who scribbled all the information and quickly set the pen down.

"Dr. Haines called, she's on the way. We will get you all set. C'mon, Mommy," she said.

Casey stood there. Liz looked up and held her hand. "Casey, honey, she's talking to you."

"Oh." Casey blinked. "Oh," she said as if she just figured out the theory of relativity and followed them down the hall.

Two hours later, Liz was sweating profusely and crying with each contraction as she lay in the stirrups. Casey held her hand and mopped her forehead. "It's okay, sweetie."

"How the hell would you know? You're having the next one!"

Casey's eyes flew open in horror and she grimaced as Liz squeezed her hand. Casey had no idea this woman was so strong; she almost dropped to her knees.

Just then, Dr. Haines walked in, smiling. "Well, good morning. How's Mommy?"

"I'm okay…" Casey stopped as Liz glared up at her. "Oh…"

Dr. Haines laughed and examined Liz. "Okay, you're dilated just fine, Liz," she said and checked her blood pressure.

Casey noticed her frown. Liz was too preoccupied with the contractions to notice.

"Okay, Liz. Your blood pressure is a little low, kiddo. We'll need to monitor it as we go," she said and winked.

Casey watched helplessly as Liz cried and tried not to scream with each contraction. "You're doing fine, Liz. Now short breaths and push…"

Liz obeyed and cried out as she pushed. Casey held her hand and gave her encouraging words.

"Push, honey," Casey said, and Liz nodded, then pushed again.

Dr. Haines looked up and checked her blood pressure. All of the sudden, Liz lay back; her complexion dramatically changed from flushed to ashen.

"Okay. Let's get her in the OR."

Casey stood completely confused. "What?"

"Casey, her blood pressure is dropping. I just want to make sure everything goes as planned. Now you wait outside. I'll come get you."

"Is she...?" Casey choked out. Liz was moaning and holding her hand in a vice grip.

"She'll be fine. Now give her a kiss and get out of here," Dr. Haines said.

Casey quickly kissed her while she held on to her hand. "Liz, honey. I love you. I will be right outside. Please..." She stopped and took a deep breath.

Liz reached up and touched her cheek. "It's going to be a girl," she whispered and smiled. Casey grinned and kissed her deeply. "I love you. Tell Skye..." Liz whispered and smiled.

Casey stood there and blinked at the swinging door, her heart pounding in her ears.

Meredith, holding Skye, met Casey in the waiting room. Niles and Brian were right behind them. Meredith released Skye, who rushed to Casey.

"Cafey!" she called and Casey scooped her up and hugged her tight and cried.

Niles put an arm on her shoulder. "You look like hell."

"Mama have baby?" Skye asked.

Casey shook her head. "Not yet, sweetie. Soon, though," she managed to say without crying.

Meredith was quickly at Casey's side. "What is it?"

"Her blood pressure was low. She's in the OR. Dr. Haines doesn't want to take any chances." She looked at her grandmother through the tears that flooded her eyes.

Meredith opened her arms and Casey flew into them and sobbed quietly. "She can't die, Gram. Not now, she just can't."

"She is not going to die. Don't talk like that," Meredith whispered and pushed her back. "Liz has everything to live for, Casey."

Casey sniffed and wiped the tears from her eyes. She looked around to find Niles and Brian playing with Skye.

"Walk with me," Meredith said and slipped her arm in

Casey's.

They walked down the corridor and stopped in front of the chapel doors. Casey stared blankly at the doors, then looked down at her grandmother. "I haven't been to church in ages."

Meredith smiled, the tears welling in her blue eyes. "He doesn't care." She gently pushed her toward the door.

Casey walked in; the deafening quiet hit her like a wall. She sat down in the pew in the back of the chapel and looked at the crucifix above the small altar. She knelt down and whispered, "I hope Gram is right and You don't care. Please, God, don't take her from me. Your winds sent her to me. We haven't even begun to live... I'm begging you," Casey pleaded with folded hands. Then she let out a heart-wrenching sob and buried her face in her hands. "Julie," she whispered. "Please help us if you can. You brought us together. Please..." She sobbed once again and sat back.

After a few minutes, she was emotionally drained. She heard the doors creak open and Skye poked her head in. "Cafey?"

Casey looked back and saw Meredith standing behind Skye. She winked and closed the door.

"Come here, Shortround."

Skye ran up and Casey pulled her up to sit on the pew next to her. "What you doin', Cafey?"

"Praying."

Skye looked up at the altar and frowned. "Like night prayers?"

"Yes, sweetie," Casey said, desperately trying not to cry.

They sat side by side in silence. Though Casey had her eyes closed, she could feel Skye watching her. She opened her eyes to see Skye doing just that. "You praying inside, Cafey?"

Casey's bottom lip quivered as she nodded. "Yes, sweetie."

"Me too," Skye said and closed her eyes.

"We'll pray for Mommy and the baby."

"'Kay, Cafey."

Finally, Skye pulled at Casey's shirt sleeve. "You done? I have to go potty."

Casey looked down at the innocent face and started laughing. She pulled Skye into her arms and hugged her tight until Skye let out a groan. "Cafey, potty."

Casey paced back and forth in the waiting room. Meredith watched television with Skye. Niles and Brian had come back with good coffee; Niles handed a steaming cup to Casey.

"Any news?" Brian asked.

Casey shook her head. She was getting impatient. "It's been over two hours."

"Casey, if Liz can have the baby naturally, it could take even longer."

"I know, I know." Casey continued to pace. She then sat down and took a gulp from the coffee cup.

Right behind her was Dr. Haines. Casey spilled the coffee as she leapt to her feet.

"Is she?"

"She's fine. The baby's fine. Congratulations, Mom. It's a girl."

Casey covered her face and sobbed. Brian and Niles stood on either side of her and Skye clung to her leg. Meredith looked as though she might faint.

"She's very tired. She will need to stay for a day just to monitor the blood pressure. That is one tough woman. She would not let me take the baby Cesarean. It was close. The baby is fine, all ten fingers and toes. We're just monitoring her. But both are fine," she said and winked. "You both can go up."

Casey walked in holding Skye. Liz looked over and grinned. "You look tired, pale, and absolutely gorgeous," Casey said.

Skye reached for her and Casey held her over the bedrail as they kissed. "Hi, Mama. You hurt?"

"No, sweet pea, Mommy's just a little tired. You've got a sister, Skye."

Casey put her down and Skye looked up at both women.

"Hi, Mommy," Liz whispered and saw the faraway, stunned look in the green eyes. "I'm fine, Casey. We have a girl."

Casey could not help it. She lowered her head onto Liz's chest and sobbed. Liz gently ran her fingers through her hair.

"Mama, Cafey cryin'," Skye said in a sad voice.

Liz smiled down at her daughter. "It's okay, sweet pea, Casey's just happy," Liz said and held on to the sobbing woman. "She's just realizing the whole pregnancy thing," she whispered affectionately and kissed her dark hair.

"How about Tara?" Liz offered after Casey stopped bawling.

"Tara? Hmm, okay," Casey agreed with a nod as she sniffed.

"We've got the Skye. Why not the Earth?" Liz asked.

Casey could not help it. She cried openly as Liz pulled her down to her once again.

Just then, the nurse came in. "We've got a little visitor and she's hungry," she said, and Skye jumped up and down.

Casey blinked at the bundle the nurse was holding.

"How lucky can one little girl get to have two mommies...?" the nurse said.

The nurse handed Tara to Liz, who naturally took the infant and held her close.

"Now this is your first. I'll show you how to breast feed..." The nurse stopped and raised an eyebrow.

Little Tara was already nursing against Liz's breast. Liz grinned as Casey just stared and blinked in amazement.

The old nurse laughed. "I guess you don't need me. She may be fussy, just change sides. One side may be better than the other."

Liz looked up at the dumbfounded Casey and grinned. "She's here," she exclaimed and both women giggled.

Casey reached over and smoothed her little head. "She's so teeny," she exclaimed as she watched her nurse the infant. "And I'm so..." She stopped and smiled. "Jealous."

Liz blushed horribly and hid her grin.

Casey looked around to see Skye standing with her arms defiantly folded across her chest. She was frowning up at the new addition.

Casey tapped Liz's arm. Liz looked over to Skye. "Uh-oh," she whispered. "Hey, sweet pea. Come say hi to Tara, your new sister."

"No." Skye pouted and Casey raised an eyebrow.

Now what, she thought. She looked at Liz, who shrugged as if to say, "it's your turn."

Casey walked over and sat down, and tried to pull Skye into her lap. She wiggled away and stood by the door.

"Shortround, what's wrong?" Casey asked. "Tell me, sweetie."

Skye's bottom lip quivered. "Tawa has two mommies. Not fair," she said in tears.

Casey and Liz gaped at each other. Neither saw this coming.

"I want two mommies, too," Skye said very clearly.

Liz was amazed how much older she seemed in just four short months. She raised an eyebrow as Casey blinked. Now what are you going to do, Ms. Bennett? she thought.

"Shortround, come here, please, sweetie." Casey opened her arms. Skye slowly walked up to her, her arms still folded across her chest. "I'm sorry, Shortround."

"Not fair, Cafey," Skye said in a small sad voice.

Liz pretended not to listen as she continued nursing Tara. Casey had to handle this one.

"I know. Do you want me? I mean you already have your mom."

"If Tawa has two mommies, why not me?"

"I have no reason for that. You're right. If your sister can have two mommies, then so can you. I'd love to be your mom, too. I love you very much. I love your mom and little Tara. We're a family, Shortround. I'll never leave and we'll always be together. How's that?" Casey asked, her throat aching as she held back the tears.

Skye jumped into her lap and Casey groaned and held on tight. "You still Cafey?"

"Yes, Shortround, I'll always be Casey and your mom."

After Meredith and the boys visited, Liz was exhausted. Meredith took Skye home with her, which left Casey and Liz alone at last. Casey sat on the edge of the bed and held Liz's hand.

"Well, that went well."

"A little confusing for the poor kid, but yeah, I think I handled that very well," Casey said, pleased with her first contribution to motherhood.

"You did, I'm proud of you, Mommy," she said, grinning.

The nurse came back in with Tara. "Time for another feeding."

Liz took Tara and held her against her breast. Casey was still amazed. "I'm speechless. I love you and I admire you so much for having this baby," Casey said. She reached down and smoothed the little tuft of hair on Tara's head. "You had me worried, Liz."

Liz looked up from nursing Tara. "We're okay."

"I know. I just don't know what I'd do without you now."

"Casey," Liz said. Tara let out a squeak, and Liz pulled her away from her breast and laid her on her chest. "We're going to have a long life ahead of us, honey. You and me and Skye and Tara."

Casey grinned and nodded. Liz gave her a challenging look. "Want to hold her?"

Casey's back stiffened and her eyes were as big as saucers. The color drained from her face. "She's so small."

"It's okay. Just don't drop her." Liz lifted Tara, who was sound asleep.

"Oh, God." Casey ran her fingers through her hair, then wiped them on her jeans. "Palms are sweaty."

She tentatively took the tiny bundle and held her in the crook of her arm.

"Just watch her head."

Casey nodded and laughed. "I can't believe I'm holding your baby."

"Our baby," Liz corrected her.

"Yes, our baby." Casey kissed Tara's forehead. "Maybe she'll play the piano."

Liz grinned as she watched them. "Maybe she will. She'll be whatever she wants to be."

Casey looked up with a tear and nodded. "I love you, Liz."

"I love you, too, Casey."

Tara started to wake and squeak again. "Maybe she's hungry." She gently handed the infant back to Liz, who once again held the baby to her breast.

Casey gave her a curiously seductive look. "Now this nursing thing..." she said as she inched closer and Liz let out a hearty laugh.

Chapter 22

They stood at the crib watching the sleeping infant. It had been almost three weeks and Tara was getting used to the schedule and so was Liz. They moved the crib into their room since the baby woke in the middle of the night. Casey would pick up the bundle and hand her to Liz for the feeding.

"That's my girl," Liz whispered and kissed the little head as she nursed hungrily.

Casey lay on her side watching. "You're such a good woman, Liz. I do love you so," she whispered and kissed her forehead, her lips lingering longer.

"God, Casey," Liz whispered. "It's been a long three weeks."

"I know," Casey said. She reached over and gently stroked Liz's shoulder, then caressed Tara's head, her fingers playing with the tuft of dark hair on the top of her head. "I love playing with her hair."

Liz laughed along as she nursed. She glanced at Casey but said nothing.

"What?" Casey asked.

"I-I was just wondering. We haven't talked much about you and me," Liz said.

"No, we haven't. What's troubling you, sweetie?"

"My body has been on the mend from the delivery and I feel as though I'm getting back…" She stopped as Tara fell asleep. Casey gently took the baby and placed her in the crib. She watched her

211

for a moment before returning to bed.

"Now about your body," Casey said in a low voice.

Liz laughed nervously and pulled the blanket up to her chin. Casey raised an eyebrow but said nothing.

"I need a little time. I want you to find me attractive."

"I think you're beautiful."

Liz's bottom lip started to quiver, so she hid her face in her hands. "I don't feel attractive," she mumbled. "And I'm afraid that this is going to be our relationship. Just sleeping together and nothing else."

Casey smiled slightly and pulled her hands away. Liz's blue eyes sparkled through her tears. Casey gently ran her thumb under each eye. "Now you listen to me," Casey whispered. "We will make love when you're ready. I know these things."

Liz raised an eyebrow. "You do, huh?"

Casey leaned in and kissed her neck. Liz moaned. "Yep. There's a whole chapter devoted to the sex life after giving birth. There are no hard and fast rules and no set time limits." She nibbled at the soft flesh beneath her lips. "The author urged partners to give the mother plenty of time and space and do what we can to reassure the mother that she is desired," Casey whispered against her neck. "I'll be true to my word. I'll wait for however long it takes." She looked up. "How am I doin'?"

Liz let out a nervous laugh. "You're doing just fine. Keep reading."

As Christmas neared, Skye was beside herself with glee waiting for Santa. Meredith laughed as she listened to what was on Skye's Christmas list. When she had finished, Skye ran to play in her room. Meredith watched Liz as she picked up the toys. "Skye, come out here, baby, and clean up your toys."

Skye came running once again and tried to carry all the stuffed animals at once.

"What do you want for Christmas, Liz?" Meredith asked as she watched Skye make several trips to the toy chest.

Liz shrugged. "I'm hard pressed to think of anything I need or want. Look at my life now, Meredith. I have a family and a woman who loves me."

Meredith watched as Liz sat in the rocker, which was now by the fireplace. Since moving in with Casey, Meredith liked the changes Liz made. "This place looks like a home now. That's because of you."

Liz rocked and looked around the apartment. "Thanks. I think Casey likes it, as well. She said it reminds her of the cabin."

"You have that faraway look. What's wrong?"

"God, Meredith. Nothing. I'm very happy and content. Well, except for the two a.m. feedings."

Meredith laughed along but would not let this go. "And what else?"

Liz shook her head. "It's not important. I think I have postpartum depression." She laughed. "Casey should be here. She could tell me what chapter it is."

"Where is that wayward granddaughter of mine?"

"At the studio. She's been there off and on for two weeks. Says she needs to get some composition in order." Meredith noticed she was rocking a little faster. "She has a very good piano right here that she hasn't touched."

Meredith raised an eyebrow. "And you're wondering why she has to go to the studio? And you're worried that Suzette is the reason."

Liz stopped rocking. "Yes, and I hate myself for it."

"Have you talked to Casey about this? And if not, why not? You must know by now that Casey needs a keg of dynamite to talk about anything. She can be quite oblivious." She stopped and grinned. "I mean that in the most affectionate way possible."

Liz laughed then and agreed. "I really don't think Casey is doing anything. I trust her completely. It's just that we, I mean, Casey and I haven't…"

"Had sex?"

Liz cringed. "Why does that sound so bad coming from you?"

"I don't know. Look, my dear. Has Casey talked to you about this?"

"Yes, she's been good to her word."

"Which was?"

"She would wait until I was ready and not pressure me."

"And what's wrong with that?"

"I don't know," Liz said in a small voice. "Nothing, I suppose."

Meredith narrowed her eyes. "I see. You want to be swept off your feet."

Liz shrugged. "Is there anything wrong with that?"

"Not a damn thing. In fact, it's mandatory. But, Liz," Meredith said and leaned forward. "How is she to know? She told you she'd wait until you're ready. You have to give her some sign. Good heavens, you're a woman and you're very attractive. You've bounced back very nicely since you've had my other great-granddaughter." She stopped and grinned. "I love saying that."

Liz stood and placed her hands on her stomach. "I've been pregnant so long I don't know how to act otherwise. Look at me, Meredith, I still look so bloated."

"That will dissipate. You know that." Meredith gave Liz a curious look. "There's something else here. Something other than sex."

Liz turned away from her and shook her head. "You'll think I'm a prude."

"Try me. This I gotta hear."

Liz turned back to her and Meredith was shocked to see the red blotches on her neck and face. "I don't think Casey is the marrying kind."

"Ah, I see. And you need her to be?"

Liz shrugged. "I don't know. There's just so much that has happened. Between Julie dying, Tara being born, Casey and I falling in love against all that's logical. Then she says she would only become a parent if she was married, and she hasn't said one damned word to me about it. How do you think that makes me feel?"

Meredith opened her mouth.

"Well, I'll tell you. I feel like a mistress, and I'm not even getting any sex!" she said loudly. She closed her eyes to calm down. "I know I'm being unreasonable. I thought once I had the baby, my hormones would get back on track." She sat on the rocker once again. "I guess not."

"It's still very soon after Tara was born. Don't be so hard on yourself or Casey."

"I know. You're right." Liz laughed and looked at Meredith. "You look like you could use a drink."

"Now you're cooking," Meredith said. "What are the plans for Christmas?"

"We haven't talked about it. I would love to have you and maybe the boys here."

"Talk to Casey about it. It sounds fine to me. Now," she said and stood. "About that drink."

Casey sat at the piano with the pencil behind her ear as she played. Niles walked over to her and put his hand on her shoulder. "You've been at that for two hours. Go home."

Casey looked at her watch. "Oh, man." She gathered the sheet music and put it in the piano bench. "Do not touch that."

Niles looked offended. "Well, all right. Good grief."

"I'm sorry," she said. "But I'm serious."

Niles rolled his eyes and shooed her away.

She put the key in the door and heard her grandmother's laughter. Looking to the heavens, she opened the door. Liz was in the kitchen and Meredith was holding Tara. She looked up when Casey closed the front door.

"Well, where have you been?"

"At the studio. I'm working on a composition. Where's Liz?"

"I'm in the kitchen, Case."

Casey kissed her grandmother's cheek and kissed Tara on the forehead. "Now go kiss your wife. Oh, wait. She's not your wife."

Casey gave her an incredulous look. "What are you talking about?" she asked over her shoulder as she walked into the kitchen.

Liz grinned as Casey walked up and kissed her. "Yummy, you taste like spaghetti sauce. And speaking of sauce, has my grandmother been drinking? She just said the oddest thing." She kissed Liz again. "I love you. How was your day?"

"I love you, too, and it was fun. Meredith kept me entertained."

Casey sneaked a piece of lettuce; she thought she heard a bitter tone in Liz's voice.

"What's the matter, honey?" She leaned against the counter.

Liz sighed and took the sausage out of the refrigerator. "Nothing really. I'm just tired of still feeling pregnant."

Casey opened her mouth and Liz shoved a carrot stick in and grinned. "I know. There's a whole chapter about postpartum depression." She leaned in and kissed her cheek. "Oh, and we're having Christmas. It's in a week. God, so much has happened I can't believe it's Christmas already. Anyway, I invited Meredith, you can ask Niles. Is that all right?"

"Sure, it's fine with me. I'm looking forward to Christmas. Hey, and remember you said nothing expensive between us."

"Yep. Now go get cleaned up for dinner."

As she turned, Casey playfully slapped her behind. Liz screeched and whirled around. Casey was already gone.

Christmas morning finally came. Skye was beside herself and she patiently waited for Casey to get out of bed.

"Cafey, peas," she begged as she pulled on her arm.

Casey feigned sleeping as she let out a snore. "Mom," Skye said nose to nose.

Casey let out a low chuckle. "Now I'm mom, huh? Okay, you little dwarf..."

"Casey..." Liz insisted at the doorway. She was burping Tara as Casey rolled over and took Skye with her.

"Mama, Cafey naked again," Skye said, and Casey pulled the covers up and covered her breasts.

Liz glared at her as Tara belched.

"Traitor," Casey mumbled and tickled Skye, who shrieked.

"Cafey, Santa come," Skye pleaded.

Casey reached for her robe. "Okay, give me a minute."

Skye jumped down and ran up to Liz.

"C'mon, sweetie. We'll change Tara," Liz said. "That way, Casey can get dressed."

Casey winced when Liz put the emphasis on the last word and slipped into her robe. "I need to get a pair of PJs..." she mumbled. She walked into the nursery and leaned against the door.

Liz was rocking with Tara in her arms. Skye was gently touching the baby's arm. "Teeny hands, Mama."

Liz grinned and put the sleeping infant back in the crib.

It was a modest Christmas. Liz told Casey not to go overboard with the gifts. Casey agreed...

Liz shook her head as Skye sat here amid her stuffed animals. Mostly fish. "So many, Mama. Santa knows I love fith."

Casey grinned and drank her coffee, her new scarf draped across her neck. "I love my present, Mommy."

"And I love mine, as well, darling." Liz touched her new sapphire earrings.

"Maybe Tara would like a few," Casey offered as she looked at all the stuffed animals.

"Can I? I give Tawa some for her bed," Skye said.

"That's a good idea, sweet pea. You're a good big sister."

"Well, that seems to be all," Casey said and looked by the piano. "Hey, what's that over there?" Casey asked as she sat on the arm of the couch next to Liz.

Liz frowned curiously and looked up at Casey. "What did you do?"

"Nothing..." she insisted. Skye noticed the blanket covering something. She looked at her two moms. "Go ahead and take the blanket off, Shortround."

Skye gently lifted the blanket and screeched. It was a miniature grand piano. Skye did not know what to do. "Mine own pinano?" She was almost afraid to ask.

Casey nodded. "All your own, Shortround," she said affectionately, and Liz leaned against her.

"You are amazing," Liz said and rested her arm on her lap and caressed her leg.

Casey swallowed with difficulty. This was the first physical display of affection other than kissing and cuddling that Liz had shown. Slow down, Bennett, Casey thought.

"Now. I've got one more," Casey said.

"We said modest..." Liz whispered and looked back at her.

Casey grinned and pulled her back into her arms, kissing her deeply, her hand wandered up her neck gently to cup Liz's face. She was pleasantly shocked when Liz kissed her with gusto. Casey nearly lost her balance and fell off the arm of the chair. "Wow," she whispered. Casey pulled back breathlessly as she searched Liz's face hopefully.

Liz nodded as she grinned and wriggled her eyebrows. "Merry Christmas, Mom," she whispered in a seductive voice that Casey had yet to hear. It went right to her toes.

Casey closed her eyes and grinned. "Thank you, God!"

She then reluctantly slid out from behind Liz, walked over to the piano, and opened the bench. Skye was unaware. She was happily sitting on the floor, playing the piano like Schroeder from the Peanuts comics.

Casey handed Liz a wrapped box. Liz grinned as Casey sat, facing her. She opened it and pulled back the tissue paper and held up sheet music. Her eyes flew open as she looked at it. "Winds of Heaven," she said as she read the title page. Tears formed in her eyes as she looked at Casey, who was grinning sheepishly. "You told me you gave it up. You finished it."

"That's what I've been working on at the studio these past couple weeks. I didn't want you to find it." Casey then went over to the piano. "Only for you," Casey said and started playing.

"You wrote this for me?"

Casey gave her a lopsided grin. "Well, yeah, you nut."

Liz sighed happily as she listened to the romantic chords her lover was playing for her. She actually shivered as she listened. Liz took a deep contented breath and turned the page. She frowned in confusion as she looked at the bottom of the page. Casey wrote a small note.

My Only One,
The winds of heaven brought you to me. I can't imagine my life without you. This is my gift to you: my love and my life.

I said once there was only one way I would have a family. I meant it then, I mean it even more now. Let's live as the winds of heaven and mix forever. Please, Liz Kennedy, marry me, be my partner, my companion through this life. Don't deny my love. I could not bear going through this world alone, without you and the girls.

I'm making love to you right now...

Liz looked up through teary eyes. Casey was right. She was making love to her right now, through that song. It was haunting and romantic. Liz walked up to the piano as Casey smiled and watched Casey as she played. It was then Liz noticed the small blue box on the corner of the piano. Casey grinned and nodded, then winked.

Liz opened it and put a hand to her mouth. It was a stunning small sapphire with two diamond chips on either side. They matched the earrings perfectly. She looked up at Casey; their eyes met as Casey finished the song with a slow sensual chord.

Without a word, Casey took the ring out and slipped it on her ring finger. On shaking legs, Liz walked around and Casey stood, wrapping her arms around her waist. Liz flung her arms around her neck.

"I love you, Casey Bennett," she whispered against her ear.

"Marry me, Liz. I'm lost without you," Casey pleaded as she kissed her neck.

"I will. I will marry you..." Liz cried and Casey lifted her off the ground and twirled her around.

Skye quickly stood, not wanting to be left out, "Me too. Uppie..." she exclaimed.

Casey lifted her into her arms and the three of them kissed and hugged each other as they danced around the living room.

Chapter 23

It was a glorious Christmas Day. Skye played with her piano and gave her little sister several stuffed animals. Liz made dinner and Casey had a choice. Play the piano or help in the kitchen.

She and Skye sat at their respective pianos…

Niles and Brian came over for dinner and Skye again had a visit from Santa.

Niles and Brian made fools out of themselves with Tara, who grinned and spit up, then grinned again.

But it was Meredith who noticed the ring first. She held on to Liz's hand to examine the ring. "Well, I'll be," she said with a sigh. "It's beautiful, Liz. How romantic."

Liz sniffed back the tears and nodded. "She finished the song, Meredith."

"What?" Meredith was shocked and didn't hide it when Casey walked into the living room. "Casey, all these years. You finished your song."

"Liz's song, Gram." Casey put her arm around her. "Mom said someday I'd find the right one, and I'd be able to finish it. She was right."

Liz kissed her cheek and walked into the kitchen. Casey turned to her grandmother, who smiled and kissed her, as well. "Eleanor would be so proud of you. She is proud of you. I'm proud of you."

"Thanks, Gram."

"You love her always?" Meredith asked.

Casey nodded. "For always. God help the poor woman."

They were both laughing when they heard Niles screeching from the kitchen. He ran out with Liz behind him, shaking her head.

Niles hugged the life out of Casey. "It's wonderful," he said. "It's, well, it's so romantic. And you finished your song for Liz? Oh, my God, that's, well, it's..."

"Romantic," Meredith said.

Casey rolled her eyes and walked into the kitchen. "We need champagne."

Niles looked at Liz. "She's not kidding, is she?"

"Nope. She loves me," Liz said happily and followed her into the kitchen.

Casey was opening the bottle; Liz walked up behind her and put her arms around her waist, kissing the back of her neck. Casey closed her eyes and shivered.

Then Liz's hand wandered up gently to touch her breast. "Oh, God, Liz... Don't do this now..." She moaned and trembled.

Liz was happy to see she had not lost her touch. It had been quite a while. The anticipation of their first time was killing both of them.

"You've been so patient. I won't let you wait any longer, sweetie..." Liz gently cupped her breasts and kneaded them slowly.

Casey closed her eyes. Her breathing was off the charts.

"After we get the girls to bed. Save a bottle of that champagne..." Liz whispered and let her go.

Casey groaned helplessly as she looked at Liz, who picked up a celery stick and munched on it. She walked out of the kitchen leaving Casey aching and unable to move.

Casey ushered Niles and Brian out early. Meredith laughed wickedly as she put on her coat. Liz hid her eyes in embarrassment.

"Okay, okay. We get it," Niles said and grabbed their coats.

"Merry Christmas..." Liz called as both men waved. She

kissed Meredith, who gave her a wiggle of the eyebrow.

"Have fun," she said and kissed Casey, as well. "I expect not to hear from you for a few days."

"I love you, Gram," Casey said. "But can you scram?"

Meredith laughed as she blew them both a kiss and closed the door.

"Casey Bennett..." Liz scolded as they left. Casey ignored her and whisked the tired Skye off the couch.

"Okay, Shortround, beddy-bye time," she announced and carried the sleepy child off to bed.

Liz shook her head. However, she quickly turned off the lights, locked the door, and got the champagne.

She stood in the bathroom and looked at her body in the mirror behind the door. "Not too bad, a little toning. Well, a lot of toning," she said. She brushed her hair and slipped into the nightgown that Casey got her for Christmas. She then put on the silky robe to match and took a deep breath.

In the bedroom, Casey noticed the makeshift ice bucket chilling the bottle of champagne. She smiled and opened the bottle, sending the cork across the room. She then filled two glasses and started unbuttoning her shirt.

"No, you don't," Liz's voice came from the bathroom doorway.

Casey whirled around and her mouth dropped. Liz looked so...

"Absolutely beautiful," Casey said as her mouth went dry.

She quickly took a gulp of champagne. Liz slowly walked up to her, took the glass out of her hand, and took a drink. Casey smiled and closed her eyes. Liz's perfume wafted over her and nearly made her head spin.

Liz set the glass down and unbuttoned Casey's shirt. "I've imagined you doing this for so long, Casey..."

Casey sighed as she reached down and ran her fingers through Liz's auburn hair. Liz gently pushed the shirt off her shoulders and kissed the top of her breast. Casey's sharp intake of breath, followed by a soft moan, continued as she struggled out of her shirt. Liz unhooked the bra and let it fall to the ground.

"My God, Casey, you have a beautiful body," Liz whispered and reached in and cupped both breasts.

Casey was beyond speech. With trembling hands, she reached down to untie the silky robe; Liz offered her assistance as she started to undo the buttons.

Casey pushed her hands away. "I do it by mineself."

"Please, no baby talk. Unless the situation warrants," she said in a low voice. She shivered as she felt the robe fall off and lightly lay in a pool at her ankles.

God, they wanted to go slow, truly they did. However, both women were aching for each other's touch and for their own release.

Casey lay next to Liz, both breathing heavily as Casey frantically kissed her neck. Liz was gasping, running her fingers through Casey's thick hair. "Please, Casey, I need to feel your—"

Casey parted her lover's legs and hesitated. "Are you sure? I mean, I don't—"

Liz put her fingertips against Casey's lips. "I'm fine. You won't hurt me."

Casey smiled and kissed her fingertips; she groaned deeply when her fingers slipped through her folds. "God, Liz..." Casey groaned again and shivered at the initial contact of the woman she loved.

Liz raised her hips, searching for her. "Casey," Liz pleaded as Casey slid her fingers up and down the length of her. The feel of Casey's gentle touch was almost too much for Liz. She cried out and shook uncontrollably. "Casey... Yes, inside, please..." she moaned helplessly.

Casey was barely breathing. Liz looked at the strain on her lover's face and shifted her leg between Casey's. She then lifted and snugly fit her thigh into Casey's crotch, amazed at the warm moist feeling against her thigh.

Casey cried out, "My God, Liz." She then slipped her finger inside Liz's warmth and their moans and gasps filled the quiet room. Casey rode Liz's thigh as she delved as deep as she could, adding another finger, then another.

"Casey, yes!" Liz tried not to scream as she bucked her hips, sending her thigh ramming into Casey.

Casey tried to hold off until she felt Liz was ready. "So close," Casey breathed her warning and delved deeper into Liz, moving her fingers deep within her. She then felt the walls tighten around her fingers. Thank God for Kegels, she thought stupidly.

She knew Liz was right on the edge.

"Come with me, Liz..." Casey pleaded in a low sensual voice, and that did it.

Liz's body tensed as the orgasm rippled through her body. She went right over the edge and took her lover with her.

Their release was fast and furious but amazingly quiet. Gasping and writhing, Liz held onto Casey until she finally stopped shuddering; Casey slowly withdrew her hand. Liz arched her back and let out a low groan as she felt Casey leave her. "Casey," she murmured as Casey slumped over her, trying to regain her breath. Liz clung to her, murmuring her name over and over.

When Casey could move, she rolled over and lay on her back. Liz cuddled close. "Oh, my God," Liz whispered when her voice finally came back.

Casey could only nod. She reached over and picked up the champagne, poured two glasses, and handed one to Liz.

"Wow!" Casey said and touched Liz's glass.

They lay in each other's arms, sipping champagne, not saying much. Then they heard it.

"Mama..." Skye's voice called out.

"That can't be Tara," Casey asked. "Can it?"

"Mama," Skye called out again.

"That's you," Casey said smugly and Liz sat up and looked at her as Casey drank her champagne.

"Why is it not you?" she asked seriously.

"Because. I am Mom. You are Mama."

Liz narrowed her eyes at her but had to admit she was right. Then the little voice called, "Mom..."

Casey scrunched her nose. Liz now sported the smug look, then kissed Casey's neck. "I'll go..." she whispered.

Casey groaned and set her glass on the nightstand. "No, I'll go. If you go, you'll be there for an hour. Cooing and being a mushy mom," Casey said and walked to the door.

"Honey?"

Casey turned back.

"A robe," Liz said dryly.

Casey turned red. "I always forget that," she said and struggled into her robe.

"If it was up to you, we'd be raising two nudists," Liz said and sipped her champagne. "Honey?"

Casey looked at the woman she loved. Lying on her side, she gently ran her hand over her breast. "Hurry back."

Casey actually shivered. "Oh, God." She moaned and dashed out the door.

"Hey, Shortround, what's wrong, sweetie?" Liz heard Casey ask and Skye mumble something.

With that, Liz looked out into the hall and saw Casey hauling Skye under her arm to the bathroom. Skye was giggling. "Hurry up now, kiddo..." Casey was saying.

Liz hid her eyes. "Mother of the year." She sighed and sipped her champagne.

"All done, good girl. You're so grown up," Casey said hastily. Liz heard the toilet flush and was very grateful. She was ecstatic when Casey said, "Wait. Wash your hands before Mama yells at me."

Then Liz watched in horror as Casey ran back with the poor sleepy girl under her arm like a sack of potatoes, arms and legs dangling.

"Cafey! Mom!" Skye complained and Liz hid her face again.

"Good girl. Okay? There you go, honey. Sweet dreams."

Skye mumbled something else. "Here's your fish. Love you, ni-ni, Shortround."

Casey dashed back into the room. "Record pit stop if I do say so myself," she said proudly. Liz glared at her.

"What?" Casey asked in helpless confusion as she laughed and hastily threw off her robe, then slid next to Liz.

"Your daughter is not a sack of potatoes," Liz insisted.

Casey propped herself up on her elbow as Liz handed her

the glass of champagne. "I know, sweetheart. She's, well, she's a dwarf, honey."

Liz tried not to laugh. "Why do you call her that?"

"'Cause I love to see that little vein pop out on your neck," Casey said and gently traced the vein with her fingertips.

Liz sighed at the warm soft touch. "If those piano keys could talk…" Liz whispered.

Casey smiled, letting her fingers wander down to her breasts. She gently rolled Liz onto her back and gazed at her body.

"Let me just look at you," Casey whispered. Her fingers traced the outside of her full breasts.

Liz was self-conscious. Her breasts did not bounce back as well as the rest of her.

Casey watched her face, knowing what she was thinking. "I adore you. I love the fact that you gave your body for our child. I find that extremely sexy," Casey said in a low sensual voice that sent Liz's hips twitching. Casey noticed and grinned, loving how she could arouse this woman so completely. Her featherlike touch encircled her breast, swirling around her taut nipple, turning it rock hard under her caresses. "I love the way your body responds to my touch. No one else will ever know what pleases you but me."

"It's as if I've been loved for the first time. No one has ever made me feel the way you do. Deep in my soul."

Casey smiled as she caressed down the curve of her hip, across her stomach. "To think, only three short weeks ago, little Tara was in there growing." Casey sighed and her hand wandered farther, gently swirling in the soft dark curls. Liz smiled and closed her eyes.

"My God, Ms. Bennett, you do have a way with you…"

Casey leaned in and kissed her cheek, the corner of her mouth, then the full warm lips. Her gently parting those lips, the tip of her tongue teasing them, gently passing across her teeth, then slowly seeking Liz's satiny tongue. Finding it, both women moaned as their tongues darted and lightly danced.

Casey moved over her then, her knee gently urging her legs apart. Liz willingly parted her legs, then sighed as Casey lay between them, lowering her body onto the woman she adored. Casey slowly rocked her hips into Liz. Liz reached around gently to knead her buttocks and Casey groaned as Liz pulled her hips into her. Casey then lowered herself completely, their breasts sensually rubbing together, nipples straining against one another.

"My God." Casey groaned as Liz ran her fingers up and down her smooth spine.

Liz sighed as Casey kissed her again, their lips meeting in a heavenly kiss. She then felt Casey's lips travel down her chin, to her neck, then her breast where she arched her back as Casey took her aching nipple into her mouth, gently suckling. Liz looked down, and as she watched Casey nurse against her breast, she entwined her fingers in Casey's thick hair, holding her head in place. Casey moaned into her breast, sending Liz's body into a quivering state. Casey's hand concentrated on the other breast, gently tweaking her nipple. Liz was in heaven as Casey continued to suckle against her breast.

Then Casey pulled back quickly and stared blindly at Liz. She swallowed and licked her lips.

Liz looked up. "What? Casey, what's wrong?"

"I...your breast. I swallowed... I am so sorry. Your milk... I..." Casey was stupefied.

"I think it's all right," she said, then frowned. "It is, isn't it?" Now she was worried.

"I'll find out," Casey said quickly, jumped out of bed, and grabbed her phone. Pacing naked, Casey waited.

"You're not calling Meredith."

"Good God, no," Casey said.

"Are you calling the doctor?"

Casey stopped pacing and turned bright red. "Oh...I guess that would have been a better idea," she said and smiled weakly.

Liz's eyes flew open. "Who the hell are you calling?" she asked as she pulled the sheets to her breasts.

Casey then winced. "Hi...Roger?" she said into the phone.

"Roger?" Liz groaned loudly and lay back, pulling the sheet over her head.

"Um...Hi, Roger...Hey, is...is Trish there?" Casey asked,

trying to sound casual, placing a hand on her hip. Being naked did not help.

"Casey?" Trish asked sleepily. "What's wrong?"

"I'm sorry I woke you, but well, I have a question. Um," Casey stopped when she heard Liz giggling under the sheet. She laughed, as well. "I have a question about breast feeding."

Liz now snorted with laughter; she pulled the sheet down and gave Casey an incredulous look.

"Breast feeding?" Trish asked.

"Yes, I, um, well, I kinda. Well, you see Liz and I are, and I..."

"Don't say another word. I get the picture. You're fine. Liz's milk is fine. Just leave some for the baby."

Casey sighed with relief. "Thanks, Trish."

"Have fun. This takes breast feeding to a whole new level. I can't wait to explain this to Roger."

Casey happily flipped off the phone and gave Liz a seductive smile.

"What did she say?" Liz asked, grinning as Casey crawled up like a panther waiting to strike.

She lay atop Liz and kissed her deeply. "She said just remember to save some for the baby. If the kids sleep through this, it'll be a miracle," Casey said in a low voice as she lowered herself, kissing between her breast, her tongue slicing down the length of her torso, then darting in and out of her navel all the while her hand caressed and gently kneaded her breast.

"Liz, I want you so badly," Casey mumbled into her stomach, feeling Liz's muscles flutter uncontrollably.

Liz quickly parted her legs as far as she could and gently pushed on Casey's shoulders.

"Was there something you wanted, sweetie?" Casey asked in a coarse voice. "Tell me, Liz. Tell me what you want."

"Casey, please...I..." She stopped. No one ever asked her what she wanted. "I want to feel your tongue all over, honey. Please. Now..." she begged as she felt the throbbing grow.

Casey lowered herself and Liz moaned openly as she felt Casey's kissing the soft dark curls, then her inner thigh. Casey licked and lightly kissed down to her knee and up the other side, purposely passing over her aching clitoris as Liz whimpered.

If the first time was too fast, Casey was going to make sure Liz enjoyed this. She deserved to be loved slowly and passionately by the woman who loved her, always.

Casey kissed the top of her thigh, then reached her hand under her thigh and lifted slightly, running her fingers up and down the back of her thigh. Liz was twitching as she clutched the sheets, biting her bottom lip, trying not to cry out. Casey then figured Liz had endured enough; she leaned in and kissed the soft folds.

"Yes, yes..." Liz pleaded.

Casey lovingly continued to kiss her, then her tongue slipped through the defensive folds, and she tasted her love for the first time.

"Casey, don't stop, sweetie, please don't stop," she begged as she reached down and ran her fingers through Casey's hair.

Casey sighed, loving Liz's touch as she entwined her fingers through her hair. Casey's mouth then engulfed her swollen clit and she gently suckled.

"Oh..." Liz let out a low groan, feeling herself rising. She had forgotten this feeling. Now knowing it was Casey loving her and no one else ever again, it was the most exquisite feeling she had ever experienced.

She arched her back as she felt the flat of Casey's tongue lapping up and down, slipping farther down, then gliding up once again.

Casey felt Liz's body tense. "Now, Liz... Come for me now... Only for me," she mumbled against her.

Liz was overcome with passion at the sound of her erotic command. Wave after glorious wave raked through her body as she gave herself up completely to this woman.

"Yes, Casey," she cried out as her body broke into another orgasm. Yet another welled up and she held onto Casey's hair for dear life, holding her in place, begging her not to stop.

Finally, her pleasure turned into a dull pain and she could take no more. She quickly pulled at Casey, who kissed her way up her body.

Liz then rolled over, pinning Casey under her. Casey groaned as Liz kissed her deeply. Her hand now wandered down to her breast as she roughly kneaded the soft firm breast.

"Casey, I want you, too... I need to be inside you. Deep inside you," she said, and just the sound of her voice sent Casey's heart pounding.

Liz lowered her head and took her aching nipple into her mouth, amazed at how she loved the taste of Casey's body. She was ravenous as she licked and nipped at the hardened nipple.

"Liz, Liz. Please..." Casey was groaning.

Liz was completely intent on satisfying Casey. Her hand wandered down to her stomach, then farther as Casey eagerly parted her legs. Liz was amazed at her state of arousal. The glistening curls throbbed for her touch.

"Liz!" Casey cried out as her hips bucked in anticipation. Liz's fingers swirled around the drenched curls. The scent of Casey was addictive to Liz, who groaned against her breast. Her fingers easily slipped through her folds, stopping when Liz felt her clitoris throbbing against her fingers. Her insistent fingers explored unknown territory, eagerly wanting to know all of Casey, every inch.

She looked up at Casey's helpless look. Her eyes closed, she was completely lost in Liz's touch. "Casey, darling, look at me," she whispered passionately. "You may have known many women, but only I will know your body from now on. You are mine, Casey Bennett, and I am yours. Now and always."

"Yes, Liz. I am yours. I have never felt this much for anyone... ever," Casey groaned in amazement. It was true. Liz was right. It was like the first time. Liz Kennedy touched her soul.

"Now, Casey. Come for me," she repeated Casey's sensual command, and Casey cried out as Liz entered her with one probing finger, then another, and Casey raised her hips to accommodate her.

"More, Liz. Give me all of you, sweetheart, please..." Casey held on to her, her fingers roughly entwining in her thick auburn air. Never had Casey asked nor needed so much from someone. "Now, Liz!"

Liz moved in slow long strokes as the walls within Casey tightened around her fingers.

"God!" Casey cried out as another wave swept through her body. Liz could feel Casey's love cascading over her hand. Finally, Casey's body shook one more time and Liz slowed her rhythm and controlled Casey as she slowly came back to earth.

"I'm completely spent," Casey said in a ragged voice.

Liz reached over to run her fingers across Casey's breasts. "Cut it out, or I'll pass out," Casey said. Liz laughed, but she stopped the caress.

"That was marvelous." Liz kissed her shoulder.

"Yes, it was. And to think we didn't wake up the girls."

"It was touch and go there for a moment or two."

Liz sidled closer, resting her head on Casey's breast. "I'm so happy right now."

"I am too, Liz. It's unbelievable really."

They lay in each other's arms, not saying much. Casey absently ran her fingers through Liz's hair, almost reverently. She felt Liz's eyelashes fluttering against her breast, knowing she was not sleeping. "What are you thinking?" she whispered.

"I was remembering the day you picked us up at the bus depot," Liz said fondly. She absently ran her fingers around Casey's stomach.

Casey laughed and yawned at the same time. "Boy, I was not ready to have anyone in my life. When I saw you for the first time, I—"

Liz looked at her then. "You what?" She propped her head on her hand and waited.

Casey shrugged and laughed nervously. "I didn't come over to you right away. I saw you and Skye, and I just watched you for a couple minutes. I saw you with the porter. I figured you didn't have enough money to give him. I saw the look on your face."

Liz nodded. "Yeah, I was pretty broke, Ms. Bennett."

They were silent for a moment or two. "It was totally illogical, but I resented Julie for putting us in this position," Casey said and looked at Liz, who nodded.

"I understand. I felt a little resentment, as well." Liz took a deep breath and let it out slowly. "Do you mind if we talk about Julie? I know we just made wonderful love, and we should be talking about the future…"

"Sometimes, the past is part of the future. Of course I don't mind. We've never really talked about any of it." She meant it, but suddenly a wave of insecurity rippled through her. She put it in the back of her mind as Liz spoke.

"When Julie told me she had bone cancer, as I said, I was devastated. I felt so bad for her. I wanted to comfort her somehow, but she pulled away from me. She became sullen and detached, and I honestly couldn't blame her. I have no idea what I would have done in her situation." She stopped and took another deep breath and Casey waited. "My thoughts then turned to Skye and my pregnancy. It was just so surreal that we found out the insemination worked, and I was pregnant a few short weeks after Julie found out she had cancer. It was…"

"The best thing in your life and the worst."

Liz nodded and stared straight ahead. "It happened so fast," she whispered and wiped away the tear from her cheek. "We had barely time to adjust to it when she got so sick, so weak, so fast. Within six months, she was gone. She spent most of the time away from us."

"I know, when you told me that, I couldn't believe it. Why do you think?"

"She said she didn't want Skye to see her that way. Actually, Julie was a very solitary woman, very private. She had told me she wanted to die alone with no one grieving or crying over her. So in the last few months, she stayed away until she had no choice but to go to the hospital. As I said, she stayed with Joanne."

"Don't you think that was odd?"

Liz agreed. "There was nothing I could do. I tried to understand, and part of me does. It was her life, her decision how she wanted to spend her last months. I went over every day, well, every day Julie would allow. There were days she didn't want to see me. For a time, I thought she and Joanne were having an affair."

"Do you still think that?"

"No, and at this point, it doesn't matter. When Julie collapsed and they rushed her to the hospital, Joanne called. She graciously watched Skye while I stayed most of the time at the hospital. But it was only a matter of days. Julie was so drugged on morphine she barely knew I was there. It was just too sad, Casey."

Casey swallowed her tears and merely nodded. Liz reached up and caressed her cheek. "I'm sorry to bring this up."

"Don't be. Julie was a part of our lives."

"Where did you meet Julie?" Liz asked.

"I met her in Chicago. We shared a cab at the airport. It was raining. She had a layover and we had dinner," Casey explained. "It was the uniform, I think."

Liz smiled affectionately. "It got me, too."

They both laughed for a moment until Casey said, "Our relationship started quickly. It was fast and furious with Julie. Never sitting still for too long, and that was fine with me. It was a time in my life where I was constantly on the move, as well. Between Chicago and LA, I tried to get the same flight she was piloting…" Her voice trailed off as she smiled.

"You had a good time with her," Liz said. It was more of a statement than a question.

Casey nodded. "Yes, we did, Liz. We lived a very…" She stopped and laughed when she remembered the appropriate word. "A very Bohemian lifestyle. Never really settling down. So when she started the talk about having kids—"

"You panicked," Liz said with a smirk.

"I'm not sure panicked is the right word, but I was floored. Children were the last thing on my mind, even though we discussed it. I knew she wasn't thinking about the future. She wanted a playmate, I think. And I'm not oversimplifying. Julie loved the idea of having a child, but she was not responsible. Hell, I wasn't, either. So it caused a huge rift between us."

"And that's what ended it."

"Yes. She pushed it so much I was tired of arguing, tired of explaining and trying to understand this. It was about five years ago when she had a layover in Denver. I flew out there to meet her—"

Liz sat up fully now. "Denver?"

Casey raised an eyebrow. "Yeah. Why?"

"When was this?"

"I said about five years ago, in the winter right before—"

"Valentine's Day," Liz finished for her.

Casey raised an eyebrow, then it dawned on her. "Don't tell me."

"Yes. I lived in Denver. I met Julie and we started dating a few days before Valentine's Day five years ago."

They both sat in silence for a moment. Casey's mind was reeling, trying to remember that time—the last time she saw Julie. "We had a horrible argument. I was at my wit's end with her. I went to Denver in hopes of us getting back. We calmed down and talked nearly all day and night before we both just realized it was over. We grew apart in the last year and the love just faded," Casey said and sighed deeply. "She kissed me and said, 'See ya, Case,' and walked out of the hotel room. That was the last time I saw her."

"I can't believe it," Liz said in amazement. "What are the odds of this?"

"I have no idea. I heard from her about a year later, she called out of the blue and told me about this woman she fell head over heels for."

"Julie told me about you at one point. She went on and on, and I'll be honest. I was tired of hearing Casey Bennett this, Casey Bennett that," Liz said with a laugh. "When Julie's lawyer mentioned your name, I wanted to reach across the desk and staple his tongue to his forehead."

Casey raised her eyebrows in surprise. "That's a tiny bit extreme, baby."

Liz laughed out loud, then winced as she looked back at Tara's crib. "I was pregnant and I believe I was craving ice cream at the time."

Casey laughed and pulled Liz back down beside her. "As well I know."

They lay once again in comfortable silence. "Liz?"

"Hmm?" Liz replied in a sleepy voice.

"Do you think Julie knew we would fall in love?"

Liz looked up into Casey's eyes. "I don't know. We'll never know, Casey. But one thing is for certain."

"What's that?"

"I have never loved anyone as much as I love you. You make me feel well loved, Casey Bennett. You're a good woman and a good friend." She laid her head back on Casey's breast.

"I feel the same way, Liz. And I love Skye and Tara, as well. We're a family. For always."

"Forever, always," Liz whispered on the edge of sleep.

Casey clung to Liz, holding her in a tight embrace until both women at last drifted off into a peaceful sleep.

Epilogue

Casey nervously stood by the fireplace in the log cabin as the fire warmed the cold February night. They had rearranged the living room to accommodate the few guests.

Niles reached over and straightened her collar. "You look beautiful," he whispered.

Casey wore an ivory-colored silk blouse tucked into a pair of brown wool slacks accentuating her tall frame. One red rose stood alone on the lapel of her tweed blazer that hung open.

"Got the ring?" she asked quickly and Niles nodded patiently.

Then the old priest walked over and took his place.

"You look as nervous as a cat, Casey..." he said; Casey gave him a sick smile.

She saw her grandmother holding Tara, who thankfully was sleeping.

Meredith winked at Casey. "I love you," she whispered.

"I love you, too, Gram."

"Well, it's not St. Patrick's," Meredith said. "But as I said all those years ago, you try keeping me away."

Casey smiled and kissed her. "Thanks, Gram."

Meredith sat in the front row of chairs. The guests may have been few, but they were Liz and Casey's closest friends. Marge's children were sitting patiently. Jeffrey gave her the thumbs-up as he sat next to his wife. Roger and Trish smiled happily; Roger gave Casey a look of pure admiration. All the people who meant the most to her and Liz were here.

Then Casey heard the bedroom door open; she grinned as she saw Skye walking out first. She wore a tweed jumper and blouse underneath because "I dress like Cafey," she had told both of them. Liz was relieved. "At least she wants to wear something," she had said.

With her blond curls pulled back, her blue eyes smiled and she waved to Casey as she slowly walked up to her. Casey gave her a short wave and a wink.

What Casey saw next transformed her, and her heart would never be the same. On Brian's arm was the most beautiful woman Casey had ever seen.

Liz wore a tweed skirt and matching blazer, complementing her companion's coloring with her thick auburn hair worn down and flowing. In her hands, she held a small bouquet of red roses.

As Brian led Liz to her life, Casey's breath caught in her throat. Around Liz's neck was the gold necklace with the dream catcher charm. Casey's eyes filled with tears as Liz smiled and put a hand up to fondly caress the charm.

Brian and Niles stood as witnesses; Casey and Liz turned to the priest.

"Well, these are the marriages I find most appealing. This union between these two women is special. Special because we live in a very precarious world where unfortunately love is not measured by what is in one's heart but by gender.

"Casey Bennett and Liz Kennedy have proven that love transcends gender. That love is quite simply... Love. Nothing more and nothing less. When two hearts find each other, nothing else really matters. It truly is what Christ preached: to love one another as he has loved each of us. This is why I applaud and rejoice in their union.

"In a world of racism, hatred, and the unwillingness to accept others as they are, these two women stand as an example of all that is good in this world. Of what we strive for and we hope someday will be. It is therefore my honor to join them in matrimony. Join hands..." he said and smiled.

Casey took Liz's hand in her own and held on tight.

"Do you, Casey Eleanor Bennett, take Liz Kennedy? To love, honor, and cherish always? To forsake all others and know only this woman for the rest of your time on this earth?"

"I do," Casey said in confident voice. Liz squeezed her hand tightly.

"And do you, Elizabeth Therese Kennedy, take Casey Bennett? To love, honor, and cherish always? To forsake all others and know only this woman for the rest of your time on this earth?"

Liz nodded, trying desperately not to cry. "I do," Liz said finally as she fought back the tears. Casey rolled her eyes affectionately and held on tight.

"Rings?" he asked and Niles handed Casey the ring. "Place it on her finger, and tell this woman of your love and commitment."

Casey slipped the ring on her finger and grinned happily. "All my life, I've been running, and all the time, I was running to you. Thank you, Liz Kennedy, for saving me…"

Liz blinked back the tears, then Brian handed her the wedding band.

"Place it on her finger, and tell this woman of your love and commitment."

Liz held Casey's warm hand and slipped the ring on her long, slender finger.

"I've found myself in you, Casey Bennett. You are my heart and deep in my soul. I thank God for your goodness and kindness. I'll love you forever and always."

Casey grinned and leaned in for the kiss. The priest coughed gently and Casey turned bright red.

"Impetuous…" Liz whispered out of the side of her mouth.

Casey playfully pinched her beloved as she held her arm.

"In the sight of God and these witnesses and friends, I now pronounce you partners in this life. To live and love in the eyes of God," he said and grinned. "Now, Casey, you may kiss your bride…"

Casey grinned and pulled Liz into her arms. She looked down into those blue eyes and kissed her deeply. Liz returned her kiss, completely breathless as Casey let her go.

Skye pulled at Casey's blazer. As always, she scooped her up and held her tight and gave her a big kiss. Meredith handed Tara to Liz. The baby woke and started crying as Liz held her close and rocked her.

"Tara cryin' again..." Skye said sadly and Casey laughed.

"That's because she's just a baby, not a big girl like you, Shortround," Casey said and tickled her stomach. The four of them held on to each other as the party started.

Through all the kissing and hugging, their eyes met in a loving gaze; both found heaven and happiness there. Casey winked and raised her wedding ring finger. Liz smiled and raised hers, as well. "Always..." they both said.

The winds of heaven brought them together. Casey and Liz would ride those winds however fair or stormy for the rest of their lives. They would grow old together, watch their daughters start families of their own, and spoil their grandchildren.

In the end, they would find comfort in each other's arms, as they would sit in front of the fire in the log cabin they loved.

Even death would not separate them. The winds of heaven would gather them and they would mix forever with the sweet emotion—forever, for always.

About the author

Kate Sweeney was the 2007 recipient of the GCLS award for Debut Author for *She Waits*, the first in the *Kate Ryan Mystery* series. The series also includes *A Nice Clean Murder, The Trouble with Murder,* which won the 2009 GCLS award for Mystery, and *Who'll Be Dead for Christmas?*

Other novels include *Away from the Dawn, Survive the Dawn, Residual Moon,* recipient of the 2009 GCLS award for Speculative Fiction, and *The O'Malley Legacy.* She is also a contributing author for the anthology *Wild Nights: (Mostly) True Stories of Women Loving Women,* published by Bella Books.

Born in Chicago, Kate resides in Villa Park, Illinois, where she works as an office manager—no glamour here, folks; it pays the bills. Humor is deeply embedded in Kate's DNA. She sincerely hopes you will see this when you read her novels, short stories, and other works by visiting her Web site at www.katesweeneyonline. com. E-mail Kate at ksweeney22@aol.com.

Survive the Dawn
By Kate Sweeney
Release: July 2009

With the serum now in her bloodstream, Dr. Alex Taylor must find a suitable laboratory to continue her work to help the woman—well, vampire—she loves, Sebastian. Together they travel to Devon, England, where Sebastian hopes her old, old, friend, the flamboyant vamp Gaylen Prescott will assist them. All the while, they try to keep one step ahead of Nicholae, the elder in the hierarchy, who wants Sebastian destroyed.

They find themselves deep in the catacombs of Guys Hospital in London and to Kendra, a sultry vamp who knew Sebastian quite well a century before, too well for Alex. Kendra is conducting similar experiments of her own.

Alex becomes a reluctant comrade to this sexy vampire, and together they find a way for Sebastian and her world to survive the dawn.